PROLOGUE

'Don't look down. It's the golden rule if you've never done an abseil before.'

But I've already seen over the ledge. I've seen the sheer side of the crag and the dizzying distance to the bottom. I hesitate as a swell of terror immobilises me.

'Come ON! This is an emergency. We've all got to get away!'

I feel the others closing in around me, urging me to hurry. Oh God, why did I volunteer to go first?

Do it or die, I tell myself as adrenaline suddenly pumps through my veins.

'OK. Ready.' I've got no choice. There's no other way out.

I drop backwards.

Scrambling, bouncing, with my teeth clenched and a gritty scream at the back of my throat, I cling on to my makeshift rope because my life depends on it. My knee scrapes on something abrasive; I unbalance and rebound, my shoulder slamming into the savage rock.

For a moment I let go, and suddenly I'm swinging, spinning, my cheek grazing a patch of something thorny.

Then I'm falling, as if the knot has snapped, and I yell and flail, grasping wildly at the branches and tufts as I slide down the cliff.

Someone shouts my name before I hit the bottom.

I pass out momentarily, before realising that I am still alive, still breathing. I'm not injured; I'm just shocked. The ground is cold. Squidgy. Something squelches as I move my feet. I wriggle onto my side and open my eyes.

I'm in some kind of marshy, mossy bog. The wet, spongy surface has probably saved my life. My arms are scuffed and my face stings, but it doesn't feel like I have broken any bones.

Shaky and stunned, I push myself into a sitting position and look around.

There's another shout from the top of the cliff. 'Are you all right?'

I can't answer. I can't breathe.

There is something beside me, butted up against my hip.

I can't speak. All I can do is scream. This is the nightmare that keeps on giving.

'Are you all right? What is it?' The call comes down to me again.

It's a man, in black trousers and a white shirt with the sleeves rolled up to the elbows and the top two buttons undone – the same attire he wore during dinner last night. One of his shoes is missing. His chestnut hair is stringy with blood that has baked dry in the sun, and his brown decaying eyes stare lifelessly up at the smoky sky. There is a sharp piece of twig wedged underneath his wedding ring.

I can't look. I don't want to remember what might have happened.

There is a clamorous humming: a busy sheet of flies hovers over the surface. The unbearable heat shimmers around him, and maybe it's my imagination, but it seems like there's already a putrid stench in the air. Repulsed, I scramble, crab-like, away.

I WANT
WHAT
YOU
HAVE

BOOKS BY HAYLEY SMITH

The Perfect Girlfriend
Such A Loving Couple
The Childminder

I WANT
WHAT
YOU
HAVE

HAYLEY SMITH

bookouture

Published by Bookouture in 2025

An imprint of Storyfire Ltd.
Carmelite House
50 Victoria Embankment
London EC4Y 0DZ

www.bookouture.com

The authorised representative in the EEA is Hachette Ireland
8 Castlecourt Centre
Dublin 15 D15 XTP3
Ireland
(email: info@hbgi.ie)

ISBN: 978-1-83525-547-6
eBook ISBN: 978-1-83525-546-9

And then I realise: the others. They're going to come down here and see him too, aren't they?

Then they'll question everything about him and about us, peeling back the layers of my life until there's simply the truth, bare and exposed, and I can't keep it hidden any longer.

'Gong baths?' Sophy has a twinkle in her eye. 'I wouldn't want to go if there weren't any gong baths.'

I pick up my phone and stab madly at the website menu. Even though Sophy's only teasing me, I have to reassure her on every aspect of the place.

'There.' I turn my phone to show her the picture of three women lying barefoot on a lush patch of grass with a semicircle of gongs around them. 'Gong baths. You've got to go now.'

Sophy sighs, a wry smile on her face. I wait for her to say something but she's staring, looking at me as if I'm mad.

'I really want to go,' I say. 'I think it will be good for me. In fact, I think it's the perfect thing that has come at the perfect time. You know how desperate I am to be a mother.'

She lifts her cup to her lips again.

'Please?' I use my whiniest voice for effect. 'You're my best friend. I wouldn't want to go with anyone else but you.'

'It just seems too good to be true. There has to be a catch.'

I shake my head. 'No catch. It was a valid giveaway on an account that I follow. I had to tag a friend that I would take, and obviously I tagged you. There's no way I'd want to take anyone else.' I'm grateful that Sophy doesn't remind me that I don't actually have any other friends.

'A giveaway though? I mean, I've put myself forward for stuff before – books, lipsticks, restaurant vouchers – and never won a thing. And then you supposedly get an all-inclusive week away for four of us that must be worth a fortune.'

'I know, it's unbelievable, isn't it?' I still can't stop smiling about it. I've read the message about fifty times already in order to keep convincing myself that it's true. 'It looks gorgeous...'

'Surely it must be a scam?'

'No. No, I've had a proper confirmation email from the retreat itself. And the giveaway was from an Instagram account I've been following for a while now.'

'Oh, you mean... yes, I know, you're going to say Addie's Five-a-Day, aren't you? That influencer you're addicted to?'

'Well, it's hardly an addiction. You follow it as well, don't you? I'm sure I've seen you commenting on her stuff.'

'Yes, but I'm not such a superfan. I don't copy her look the way you do.' She nods at my hairstyle, at the new puff-sleeved top I'm wearing.

'Well, anyway. It's Addie who's done the giveaway. And she was the one who actually sent me the message to say that I'd won.'

Sophy lifts her left eyebrow flippantly. 'Yeah?'

'She's already put out a few reels about this retreat. You must have seen them?'

Sophy smiles and relaxes. I can tell that I'm starting to win her over. 'Ahh, yes I did see something a couple of weeks ago. A place in the mountains. Wales, wasn't it?'

'Yes! That's the one. She's been endorsing it. They've got pictures of her on the official website and everything.'

'But what's with the *fertility* element?'

'Well, it's for couples. I've read things about how it's good to take a break and get away from your normal circumstances. Your body – your reproductive system – reacts positively to being in nature and hearing birdsong, and eating the right food and—'

'So it's a holiday where you go and get pregnant? I'm not sure if I'm ready for another just yet. Although, weirdly, Tom was only suggesting yesterday that we might want to think about a sibling for Olivia soon so that they can be playmates.'

'There you go, then. Maybe I should be speaking to Tom about this. He could be easier to convince.'

Sophy laughs before putting a serious face on. 'No, Gemma. Maybe you should be speaking to Matt about this. I'd love to know what *he* thinks.'

Hmm. Matt.

I purse my lips as I look down and nervously stir my tea.

I brace myself later as we're sitting with our evening meal.

'You're probably going to freak out when you hear what I'm about to say.' I'm gripping my glass of water, to prevent my hand from shaking, as I prepare to introduce the subject to Matt.

He stops eating and looks at me with raised eyebrows, an unchewed piece of steak nestling in his left cheek.

'I know that it's only been a few weeks since we got married, and some people probably think that we shouldn't have rushed into things after such a short relationship...'

'What?' His face is crestfallen. Oh God, he must think I'm having second thoughts.

'Don't look so stressed. It's nothing bad.' I reach across and grasp his wrist because his fork is clenched firmly in his hand. 'I *love* being with you.' It's true, even though there are still times when my ex, Reuben, roams into my dreams while I'm asleep.

'What then?'

I take a deep breath. 'How about we go away somewhere? Because...'

'Where d'you fancy? I could book a holiday for us. We never had much of a honeymoon, did we? I know it was a nice couple of nights in the Cotswolds, but I sort of regret that we didn't do something bigger and better. I should have insisted—'

'Well, let me finish what I'm trying to tell you. You see, I've actually *won* a week at a retreat. An all-inclusive spa-type thing that looks fantastic.' I pick up my phone and flash him a picture of the glorious bedroom that I've copied from the website. 'They've sent me some dates, and Sophy and Tom will be going too as part of the prize, all four of us together, so it should be a lot of fun...'

'Why did you think I'd freak out? Oh hang on, it's not somewhere like Outer Mongolia, is it?' He guffaws as if he's cracked the funniest joke ever.

I snigger along with him for a few seconds. 'No, it's in Wales. So, not difficult to get to. A really beautiful, remote area actually, right up in the mountains. The views look fantastic and there's loads of wildlife.'

'Awesome.' Matt chews his piece of steak and swallows it, not taking his eyes off me. He's waiting.

'What?' I sip my water.

'What's the catch?'

'There isn't a catch. Like I said, it's free, for all of us. It's a prize in a giveaway from someone I follow on Instagram.'

'Ah.' He shakes his head.

'No, it's not a scam. It's real. I've been in touch with the retreat by email since finding out. How can it be a scam? No one is asking me for money.'

'Why were you worried about discussing it, then?'

I have to make it clear. Well, when I say clear, I mean partially clear, which will be enough for now.

'Well, it's sort of a special thing for couples.'

'So... oh God it's not a swingers' event, is it?'

I laugh far too loudly until my eyes are streaming. 'It's not swingers, I can guarantee it. Do you really think Sophy would want to go to something like that?'

Matt winks. 'Maybe Tom though?'

'No, let's be serious. Look, it's like a health retreat. So there's vegetarian food and massage treatments, and no actual alcohol at the bar because—'

'No alcohol? Well, there's no wonder you thought I might freak out. A week on holiday *alcohol-free?*'

'Would it be a problem?' I hadn't considered that this might be an obstacle. Matt isn't a massive drinker, but he likes wine with his evening meals sometimes and a couple of pints of craft ale at the pub on a Friday night or a Sunday lunchtime.

He wrinkles his nose before picking up his wine glass for a hefty slurp of Shiraz. 'It wouldn't be my normal choice of holiday, but if you're keen on the idea...'

'The bedrooms and everything look amazing – just look at that jacuzzi bath – and we could really spend some time getting closer, if you know what I mean?'

'Well, that bit sounds attractive.' He stabs at a chip.

'Some couples go there to get pregnant.'

He sets his cutlery down and gapes at me. 'You're suggesting that we...'

'Well, I did wonder about having a sort of gamble with things. Stop taking my contraception while we're there and see what happens?' Little does he know that I haven't used contraception for almost two years. From the first time we had sex it was easier to let him think that I was taking care of everything. 'Don't worry about that sort of thing,' I told him, as he dug around in his wallet for a condom, and I suppose he simply made the assumption that I was on the pill. We never discussed it further.

'Well.' He blinks and shrugs. Then he smiles. 'Well, that *would* be a gamble, wouldn't it?'

I nod and return his smile, resuming my meal with a level of satisfaction about how the conversation has gone. There will be time to subtly do some extra work on him before we go. I will email the retreat and request the option of the later date that is on the list, because the weather is likely to be better then, and our marriage will have progressed beyond the three-month stage.

And, according to my secret ovulation calendar, that particular week will be the prime time for conception.

'He's OK with it, then?' Sophy's voice is loaded with disbelief.

'Yeah. We chatted last night and I've emailed the place to

ask for the week at the end of June. That's still fine with you and Tom, isn't it?'

'Yes, Tom's delighted about it, hoping that we can make a little brother for Olivia. He's even convinced *me* that it's a good idea.' She winks playfully.

Sophy has been with Tom for ages, fifteen years or more. Childhood sweethearts. She'd got pregnant with Oliva eighteen months ago, immediately as soon as they began trying. The first actual time. Maybe it was because they were so connected, so in touch with each other.

'So, just to go back to Matt... does he actually *know* how desperate you are for a baby? Does he know how long you've been trying? And is he happy to potentially become a father even though you haven't known each other for long?'

Why does she have to drill down on all the little specifics? I hate having to lie to her. Since our school days, we've trusted each other implicitly and nothing will ever break the bond that we've had for over twenty years.

'Look, Soph, I've explained quite a bit of what the weekend is about, and we've decided that we're going to have a try.' I give a hearty laugh, attempting to sound genuine. I don't need to tell her that he's unaware of the level of my desperation.

'So, Matt is cool with the baby element?'

'Everything's good,' I say breezily, although I'm barely convincing myself. 'You don't need to worry about me. Pack your bags and get your own fallopian tubes ready for those gong baths.'

TWO

ADDIE

I've done giveaways before. Make-up, books, vouchers for bars and restaurants, family trips to a zoo or theme park. Sending out that congratulatory private message to the winner always gives me a huge sense of satisfaction. It's like benevolence but power at the same time. A weird combination.

This is the biggest giveaway that I've done. Nothing else prior to this has ever come close. When Carys, the owner of the retreat, suggested it, I thought there had to be some catch, but there wasn't. It was all part of our collaboration, and she just wanted to grab the attention of my Instagram followers because they seemed like the ideal audience to appeal to in terms of age, gender and aspirations.

But still...

A full week at a luxury retreat for two couples was a mega prize. Although I'd suggested picking two separate couples, Carys seemed to think that it would be better for dynamics if they already knew each other. So if a follower tagged a friend then they would both get to go with their respective partners.

I sit at my laptop. Gosh, my heart is pounding as I consider how to word the message.

Hi Gemma, I am pleased to let you know…

No. That doesn't convey anywhere near enough zest.

Dear Gemma. You may remember the giveaway you applied
for recently in which you tagged your friend, Sophy…

Oh goodness. That is way too formal. I don't want her to be
wary and think that it's some kind of scam. Some of the giveaways I've done have resulted in people changing their minds
and leaving their vouchers unclaimed, or even ignoring my
message and blocking me. Yes, really!

So this time I can't get it wrong. The message needs to hit
the right spot without any confusion or ambiguity; it needs to
genuinely resound with the winner.

Gemma, you've won my giveaway!!!

Hmm, that's a positive start. I want to make her scream with
excitement so that she gets on board with it immediately, ready
to spread the news to her husband and friends.

Imagine yourself at LunaBliss, the luxury retreat in the hills,
with an all-expenses paid week of pampering and fabulous
food…

I get into the swing of the language then as I paint a picture
for Gemma of the retreat's beauty and charm, inviting her to
check out the website.

To book dates that are suitable for you and your party, please
contact LunaBliss directly, using the reference 'Addie's
Winner'.

My hands are shaking a little. I wish I could be a fly on the wall when she opens the message. Inhaling deeply, I recheck the wording and adjust the punctuation slightly.

Send.

There, I've clicked it.

All I need now is for her to accept.

I have no doubt that she will though: all her comments on my reels show how much she admires and trusts me. Leaning back in my chair, a smile of satisfaction creeps onto my face. She's completely unaware of my identity, isn't she? She thinks I'm simply an internet influencer, sharing advice and life skills, a total stranger in cyberspace, someone who's got what *she* wants.

She doesn't remember the connections we had.

Maybe I was the type of person then who was easily forgettable. Or maybe she's just blocked out that period in her life.

Well, whatever. It will be thrilling to see *her* in the flesh again.

THREE

GEMMA

Matt was a rebound relationship, a Tinder discovery when I was drunk and sad and needing someone to hold my skin against. He's only been in my life for a short while: fifteen weeks in total, from that first swipe right. A whirlwind of dates, then he moved into my little rented terrace less than two months later, with his stuff in holdalls and plastic boxes, a *thank you* bouquet of flowers for me tucked into his armpit. I let him have half the wardrobe and two of my dressing table drawers, the ones that Reuben had vacated just after Christmas.

We clicked. Our interests were similar and he made me laugh at a time when I really needed to laugh. In bed he was passionate and considerate and even left me love notes under the pillow, something that Reuben had never done before. I felt special with Matt.

'He's smitten with you,' Sophy told me. 'Anyone can see with the way that he looks at you.'

I glowed inside with the thought that someone was obsessed with *me*, instead of it being the other way round. And although my heart was probably still trying to heal from the break-up with Reuben, I said *yes* immediately when Matt asked me, during a tipsy walk home from a bar one night, if I would marry him. It was impulsive on both our parts, and although I wasn't completely sure if I was in love with him then, I was certain that I had to keep him on my hook. He could be the perfect husband and I couldn't risk letting him go at that point. I know, I know, everyone thought it was crazy because our relationship was so new and unfledged, and everyone told us we should at least wait a while and have a decent period of engagement blah blah blah...

It was a cold, sparkling day at the end of March when we skipped up the steps of the registry office to exchange rings and vows, with Sophy and Tom as our only witnesses. I wore a sixties-style lace wedding dress, high-necked and knee-length, and Matt hired a tweed suit. Afterwards, the four of us ate at a hideously overpriced restaurant on the outskirts of the city before Matt and I travelled to spend a few days at a country house hotel in Oxfordshire. It wasn't the wedding I'd envisaged, but the lavish ceremony and reception had been the dream that I'd had with Reuben, so it felt appropriate to do something completely different with Matt.

We're still getting to know each other, really, but there's a thrill about being in that early discovery stage of a relationship. He's reasonably good-looking, with dark hair mottling grey around the temples, and he has kind, chocolatey eyes and a firm, stocky body that I'm getting used to. His cooking skills are decent – although he only uses a limited range of ingredients – and he's tidy around the house, having already got to grips with the programmes on the washing machine. On the whole, he's coming across as a decent catch.

Yeah. He's a lovely guy. Sophy and Tom think so, too.

I'm pretty much over Reuben now. I've stopped tearing up at random moments: when certain songs come on the radio, or when I see the back of someone with the same hair, or when I'm walking down the street and catch a whiff of a bloke wearing the same cologne he used to wear. He means nothing much to me any more.

Until six months ago we'd been an item, together for over five years. Our futures were mapped out: we were settled, stable, our relationship a permanent fixture. We had that special language of real, solid couples, where we could finish each other's sentences, where we could telepathically know what each other was thinking, where we could send out secret signals during social events to communicate a wish to leave.

We'd been engaged, with a date set for our wedding, a shared Pinterest board and a deposit on a divine venue for the reception. We'd been planning to have children. Not just planning, but actually *trying*. We'd picked baby names; we'd checked out local nurseries; we'd bought a flat-pack cot from Ikea that is still in its box in the attic. At the back of my bedside drawer a multipack of Ultra Early Pregnancy Tests contains four unused ones.

Reuben had broken my heart. That was the gist of it. I had put my faith completely in him, devoted my life to him, loving him totally and unconditionally.

I thought later that maybe it shouldn't have been unconditional. It should have been on the condition that he wouldn't shag around with someone else.

During the time of all the wedding planning and dreams of parenthood I thought he would love me forever. But I was wrong. Because at some point in our relationship he'd been seduced by a temptress whose name began with 'D'.

I never got to the bottom of how long he'd been seeing her, and he would have likely got away with it for longer if he hadn't made the mistake of sending a text to me that was intended for *her*.

Hey, D, I've managed to escape for the evening – told G I'm

out with the football guys. Can you spare a couple of hours for a
meet up? Missing you like crazy. xxx

That was the message. It pinged through and, puzzled, I read it over and over before realising what it was, at which point I went and threw up in the kitchen sink, and when I'd finished and returned to look at the text for the millionth time, there had been five missed calls and a voicemail from a fraught Reuben, telling me that his phone had been hacked. As if I'm an idiot.

He was such a poor liar. He was back home within thirty minutes and struggling to look me in the eyes.

'Phones don't get hacked like that,' I told him. Even though I desperately wanted to believe that they did.

'Well, when I said hacked, I meant that one of the football guys—'

'Which one?'

'—well, Steve, he's a bit of a joker. He must have got hold of my phone and sent it as... just... like a prank.'

'But why would he do that?'

'It's just the sort of thing he does. He messes about with all the guys like that. He did it to Connor, too, a couple of weeks ago.'

'Give me his number,' I said. 'I want to talk to him. To ask him why.'

'Come on.' Reuben gave a hollow laugh. He looked at the floor and shook his head.

'Give it to me.'

'It was a joke. That's all.'

'Give me his number.'

'It was nothing. There's no point making a fuss and he's my mate...'

'Who's D? Danielle? Diana? Daisy? *Daisy*! It's that fucking cow from behind the bar at the White Swan, isn't it? The one with the fake eyelashes and virtually all her flesh on show.' I pressed my hands over my eyes to hide my raw, ugly face, swollen from sobbing.

'No! No, it isn't. There's no one. Oh God, Gem, why are you making such a thing of this? We trust each other, don't we?'

He took my phone out of my hands and deleted the offending text.

'Tell me who she is.' I wept. 'Tell me how long you've been seeing her; tell me what you've *done* with her.'

Initially, he denied there was a *her*; he denied all my accusations.

'Babe, how can you accuse me of deceiving you?' he said as he held me tightly. 'Haven't I given you everything?'

Well, yes, he *had* given me plenty – he'd propped us up financially all the time that I'd dawdled in my dead-end job, and pampered me with some nice gifts and holidays, and then the promise of our fairytale wedding was a backdrop to all this – but did that really entitle him to seek extra pleasure elsewhere?

Maybe I should have been more of a career girl instead of relying on Reuben; maybe he would have had more respect for me if I had contributed on an equal footing. The thing is, I haven't done much with my life; I didn't make much of an effort at school, always keeping my expectations low.

If people ever ask what I do, I tell them I am a receptionist for a logistics company, but in all honesty, I am just a general dogsbody for a local haulage firm. It is a dull and mindless job where I am paid minimum wage and get no perks and no Christmas bonus. I answer the phone, forward emails, file pieces of paper, make tea and clean the toilets. My office is a cold, scruffy portacabin at the end of a lorry park; I can't even wear nice clothes or shoes to work, because I have to walk through an expanse of mud and puddles of engine oil to get to it. The truck drivers, although friendly and warm-hearted, are all men who often tell sexist jokes and leave the spartan lavatories in a mess.

Obviously, I've yearned for years to have a different job, a position in a plush office and colleagues to lunch with, somewhere to dress up for, a vocation that I wouldn't be embarrassed about. But nothing presented itself, and I lacked the motivation to go out and get it. Despite having been one of the popular girls, alongside Sophy, for a big part of my school life, I ended up as a nobody, a quiet, normal person keeping her head down and getting by. Ultimately, I have accepted my fate, thinking that my job will be adequate enough to tide me over until I am able to devote myself to motherhood.

Pulling Reuben was my biggest achievement. Having him by my side while I planned our swanky wedding and tried to get pregnant had been enough for me then.

All I'd done was dream. But dreaming had failed me.

Reuben had failed me.

The confession of his unfaithfulness came out gradually, like a bruise, and we wrangled through the text that didn't physically exist any more, as I unpicked each phrase and we argued and debated those thirty-two words and three gut-wrenching kisses that I'd committed to memory like it was some kind of court case.

Eventually, Reuben got weary of our fighting and told me that, on a whim, he'd had sex with someone after a work conference. It wasn't his fault, though. He'd been drunk and she'd been pushy. He'd told her all about me, and made it clear about our plans to get married and have kids so that she would understand he wasn't available. She'd listened to him as he unloaded his work stress onto her. Like, *really* listened, as if she was actually interested. He'd been flattered; he'd been grateful that someone would take notice of him.

He wasn't in love with her, he'd said. But him and this 'D' woman had clicked somehow, just for a brief period – there had been a meeting of minds – and that was the attraction. Not what she looked like. Not at all.

What did she look like? I asked him, but he refused to say. Just… he flicked a hand out. Just normal. Nothing special. He'd just enjoyed talking to her.

But you had sex with her, I reminded him.

It wasn't as if it was in *our bed*, he protested, as if that made it all right. I pressed him but he was vague about the location of their misdemeanour.

I wanted to know her name, where she lived, what she did. My jealousy was an outpouring that waited for him every evening when he came home from work.

'Babe, it's over. It won't help you to know all this. Let's draw a line under it and move on.' Reuben pleaded with me and looked sad. 'I don't want to lose you. We've got this far together; we've got a deposit on the wedding venue, haven't we? And, you could even be pregnant right now.'

I didn't tell him that I wasn't, that I'd done five tests over the last two days and all of them were negative. I let him think that there was still a possibility from that month's efforts.

In the end it all came to some kind of conclusion and we agreed not to talk about it any more. I tried to believe him when he told me that it was over. I tried to go back to trusting him.

But something had been lost during this episode. The essence of our relationship had been diluted too thin. My heart was splintering; my mind was eating itself. The space between us became brittle and everything had to be done and said so carefully. I couldn't voice my fears to Reuben any more, and all I could think about in my spare moments was him with *her*.

Sophy was the only one I felt able to pour my heart out to.

'I know it's irrational,' I told her. 'He had a short fling with someone, basically a one-night stand, and now it's over and I honestly do believe him, but I'm struggling to get over it.'

'You've had your heart broken,' she said to me. 'A partner's betrayal is a difficult thing to accept.'

I'd met up with her on a bleak January day, during that

period of time when the suicide rates were high and everyone was analysing their lives, where I would usually be considering leaving my job and getting a better one before doing nothing further about it. That day, though, Reuben had been a more important subject for me to worry about.

I'd sat with Sophy in our regular coffee shop, and she'd had pity on her face as we talked about forgiveness. She'd advised that we make time for extra date nights. She'd said that we needed to find more common ground. Eventually she'd checked her watch and told me that her breasts were leaking which meant that Olivia would be needing a feed, and she got up and went, leaving me to forlornly scroll through my wedding Pinterest pictures on my own.

And when I got home, when I stepped into the hall and noticed the empty coat hooks, and then the strange gaps on the shelves in the living room, and the blank wall above the fireplace... that was when I'd realised that Reuben had packed up all his stuff and left me.

FOUR

ADDIE

A social media career is ideal for someone like me. What is the saying... 'hiding in plain sight'?

I was removed from society years ago, shunned by my peers, a reclusive outcast with the words *killer* and *murderer* ringing in my ears that I thought would stick around for ever... Gosh, it doesn't bear thinking about, does it? There is no way I could have had a normal life and a normal job, and so I changed my look and bravely put the past behind me, venturing onto Instagram to become an online success story.

I blindly switch off the camera at the end of my huge, impressive kitchen – polished granite worktops, six-ring range cooker, bespoke oak cabinets with colour-changing lighting and integrated wine fridge – before taking a piece of kitchen roll to blot my black tears.

'Isn't this supposed to be waterproof?' I squint at the tube. 'God, that stings!'

The Instagram reels aren't always a breeze. Some things are a one-shot success, then other times I'll be at it for over an hour trying to get it right. All the people who think that being an influencer is simply a matter of posting selfies and chatting about products have probably never tried it themselves.

I am proud of what I've achieved. Why wouldn't I be? I remember the background that I came from; the caustic accusations; the bountiful hatred. But I waited it out and kept a low profile, then single-handedly, over the last few years, I built up Addie's Five-a-Day, gaining a following that grows daily and earns me an enviable salary.

Understandably, though, not everyone is a fan of what I do. I sometimes get messages from weirdos; I get random dick pics, and stupid things delivered to me, like cannabis cookies, and the cremated remains of a fan's pet poodle. Once I was sent a small plastic bag of what looked like pubic hair trimmings.

I bin a lot of the products that are sent my way. If it has any value over twenty pounds then I often list it on eBay. The rest of the stuff is donated to my local charity shop; it makes me feel good that I am doing something for the community.

'You're basically on the verge of being a celebrity,' someone said to me once. 'You could be on television; you could have your own show.'

I laughed off their suggestions. 'Don't be silly. That's not how TV works.'

Could it really happen, though? To *me*? Their suggestion set me off thinking, and a crumb of ambition lodged itself into my head. A magazine-type show would be just my sort of thing, and obviously there would be an accompanying story in the newspapers all about my history. I imagined rags to riches articles and blurry old school photographs of me from twenty years ago turning up – *can you believe that someone like THIS, after all that happened, could make such a success of herself?* – and wondered what all my old classmates would make of the most detested girl in the school being on television.

* * *

Babies? *Really?* My mind had diverted onto a subject that didn't usually enter my head or my inbox.

It was around a year ago that the seed got planted. I was sitting at my laptop with a quizzical look furrowing my forehead. Someone – a potential sponsor of my account – had emailed from a retreat called LunaBliss.

Instantly, I was intrigued, because it sounded so... different.

A *fertility* retreat?

Research was required, and I hopped onto their website to see what it was all about. The photographs looked amazing, displaying a mountain paradise with a natural pool, starry skies, and panoramic views. Couples linked fingers and gazed longingly at each other; a beautiful woman with long hair in a floaty dress clutched a manicured hand to her petitely pregnant belly. Vibrantly coloured smoothies garnished with petals and berries sat in tall glasses on a bar attended by a gorgeously tanned man in a white shirt and bow tie. A full moon created a glorious backdrop for a hammock beside a flame-filled firepit. Smiling people in loose clothing effortlessly posed in the lotus position beside a waterfall.

The supporting text described how an experience at the retreat would offer a fertility-boosting menu, an environment that helped to revitalise the perfect balance of emotions between couples planning parenthood, and holistic treatments including alignment with the lunar cycle that could physically optimise the reproductive system.

No way! A droll smile crept onto my lips.

Yet each sentence and each picture on the website tapped unconsciously into my sentiments, and before I realised what was happening, I visualised myself with a swollen stomach, feeling phantom kicks, imagining the miracle of an unborn child growing in my body.

Oh gosh!

I exhaled and snapped my gaze away from my laptop screen.

A baby? *Really?*

Back then, I'd never properly considered having children because I'd become too embroiled in my career. I'd become too satisfied with the single woman's lifestyle. Maybe after I'd found Mr. Right and had my dream wedding it would be a possibility.

I shook the thought out of my head and checked the message again.

Dear Addie, the email read.

Here at LunaBliss we've been fans of your account for a while. We're looking to team up with a reputable and influential source that can reach out to our market, and we think that you could be the perfect fit. How would you feel about coming along to have a look at our beautiful site in the mountains?

This could be a lucrative deal, I told myself, clicking through the pictures again. And even if it wasn't, it could be a fascinating weekend away.

I hadn't been on holiday for a while. I deserved a break, didn't I? And I wouldn't even need to leave the country or catch a plane.

It was a great idea, wasn't it?

Normally, I wouldn't have been that impulsive, but it only took seconds to convince myself, and before I realised what I'd done, I'd hit the *reply* button to let them know that I was interested.

FIVE

GEMMA

This fertility retreat is going to be the place where my dreams will come true. I am sure of it. At a time when my head has only just recovered from my break-up with Reuben, and my body feels like a shell from thirteen months of trying for a baby with him, I need it more than anything. It will be the perfect starting point for me to be cleansed from my past and to embrace the early joys of my relationship with Matt. And then, surely, I will be able to get pregnant.

The giveaway on Addie's Instagram account was huge. She put up a reel of herself at the retreat with her arms spread wide and a breeze rippling her sleeves and hair. There was a link and a quote of endorsement:

> This is the most gorgeous, heavenly place on earth. It's THE place to come and prepare yourself for parenthood. If, like me, you're thinking about conception and wanting absolutely the best experience for that significant moment in your life, then I can't recommend it highly enough!

It went viral, and I was proud to be in the first hundred

people who applied. Addie's follower numbers grew as the applications poured in. No way would I win this giveaway. Not when literally tens of thousands of people were applying and sharing and tagging their friends. No way, I thought, resignedly, bookmarking the page so that I could later organise a paid break.

But then...

Oh my God, the way my heart pounded when I got the message direct from Addie!

Things are definitely looking up for me now. Meeting Matt. Getting married. Winning a holiday at a fertility retreat. Everything is going in the right direction.

I watch Addie's video again. Six times. I see myself there, standing on that same mound of moss, admiring that vista, inhaling that crisp, clean air. Wearing the same turquoise sweater and batik-print harem pants, because I bought them a couple of days after the Instagram was released.

Oh God, I can't wait!

'Tell me about *you*,' I say to Matt, one night when we're out at the pub. 'You hardly mention your background. We're married but there's still so much I don't know about you.'

He shrugs and holds his palms out. 'What do you want to know? I'm not hiding anything.'

'Well... Like, have you had loads of girlfriends? Was there anyone special that you'd like to have settled down with? What do you think about fatherhood? I know you don't have kids from previous relationships, but have you ever tried for a baby? You've never mentioned...'

'Hey!' He rubs a foot up my leg, lifting my skirt. 'What is this, twenty questions?'

'Sorry. Sometimes it feels like we launched into a whirlwind relationship without knowing anything about each other.'

He laughs. 'Well, no, I've never tried to have a baby. I

haven't had *loads* of girlfriends. A couple of years ago I was with someone and we moved in together and considered buying a house, but that didn't work out and I lost my job at the time and had some mental health problems. For a quite a long time I went back to live with my parents and didn't socialise much.'

'Oh, OK. I just wondered.'

He swigs his drink. An elderly couple squeeze past our table, dragging a golden cockapoo behind them. Matt reaches down to coddle its soft fur with an admiring *ahh*, before it is led away to a place by the fire.

I smile at his display of affection for the dog. 'Have you ever had a pet?'

'Only a guinea pig, when I was six. But I'd love to have a dog at some point. And I would love to have kids, too. Sooner rather than later. I think I'd make a good father.'

Oh. My. God.

My whole body buzzes as this piece of information soaks in like a drug. Maybe this is all meant to be. Reuben leaving. The fertility retreat. Getting together with Matt who would *love to have kids sooner rather than later.*

I gaze in awe at him and grin the widest smile, imagining myself with Matt, swinging a toddler between us and being the perfect little family.

'Anyway... tell me about you. Tell me about when you were younger.' He leans back in his seat, folding his arms.

'How much younger?' Understandably, Matt is a bit prickly when I talk about Reuben, so my recent past needs to be avoided.

'I don't know. Like, when you were a teenager. What are your memories of school?'

My stomach flips. I'm unable to keep out the series of visions that slam into my mind. The sports changing rooms. A hand grabbing my hair to smash my head into a desk. Our teacher crying at the front of the class.

I reach for my wine glass, a tremor in my hand. 'I'd rather forget about my school days.'

'Oh, not a good time?' His eyebrows knit together sympathetically. 'Did you get bullied?'

'Just don't go there.' I break away from the gaze that he fixes on me, to seek out the golden cockapoo as a distraction. Obviously, our marriage is young and there are still lots of things to find out about each other, but...

You don't have to tell each other *everything*, do you?

THE RETREAT

SIX

GEMMA

I'm nauseous with anticipation as we pick up Tom and Sophy to go to the retreat. All my stuff is packed into a rucksack in the boot of the car. Flouncy kaftans. Sequinned sandals. Dresses for our evening meals. Another pair of the batik-print trousers that Addie recommended, this time in red. There's also new under-wear for the occasion, virgin white, and it feels symbolic.

'It nearly broke my heart to say goodbye to Olivia,' Sophy laments. 'We've never left her for this long before.'

'We went to London in February,' Tom reminds her.

'But that was just a weekend.'

'Er, three nights, remember?'

Sophy cups her breasts as she stands by the car. 'Look, this is going to be for a whole week and I've literally only just stopped feeding her. It's an emotional time for me.'

'But she loves going to your mum's house.' Tom winks at us and leans into the open car window. 'We *all* love it when she goes to Grandma's house.'

'I'm sure she'll be fine. She's pretty good at sleeping through the night now, isn't she?' I smile reassuringly at Sophy as she plonks herself in the back seat.

We travel through the dusk, leaving the dual carriageways and trunk roads behind. Sophy hands out sausage rolls and crisps and the radio is a buzz of white noise in the background.

The traffic thins out. Two hours after setting off we are meandering through villages, past cottages and farms, then onto skinny, winding lanes that spider away from civilisation and take us up into the hills where the signs are in Welsh.

Our ears pop. Our headlights catch the wary eyes of sheep; an owl launches silently across the path; brawny clouds hold back the moon. We haven't seen another vehicle for at least fifteen miles.

'Wow, this is a bit spooky,' I remark. 'It's like we're the only people out here.'

Matt exhales as he brakes and gears down ready for more hairpin bends in the road.

'Christ.' I hold onto the sides of the passenger seat as we jolt through a pothole. A yelp of surprise spills out of me as something hits the windscreen before flittering away. 'You could come out here and die and no one would know.'

Matt doesn't say anything. He fixes his stare on the narrowing track and ignores my remarks.

I turn and look out of the window, craving a speck of light that might indicate a house or another car but there is nothing.

We are utterly alone.

* * *

With a bluster of gravel, we pull up in the car park of a barn that has been converted into some kind of office building. A welcoming light glows cheerily above the front door. An open-backed farm buggy waits under a porch.

I let my body relax a little. 'Well, this doesn't look too bad, does it?'

Matt gets our rucksacks out of the boot of the car. The office door opens before we approach it.

'Hi, you must be Gemma? The giveaway party?' A woman in jeans and a green cashmere sweater greets us with a confident smile. 'I'm Carys. Come on in. We've been waiting for you. I expect your trip was a bit of a nail-biter?' She gives a knowing laugh.

'That last part...' says Matt, shaking his head.

We step into the office as Carys explains what will happen at the retreat.

'All right, so here's the plan. You need to leave your car here because the site is only accessible to off-road vehicles. We'll head out in the buggy and get you settled in. There's some glorious weather forecast for the week, so making use of the natural pool is highly recommended. Addie, the Instagram star, will be arriving for the evening meal tomorrow and then spending the rest of the week with you.'

'Addie? Wait, she's doing like a meet and greet? She's coming here?' This is a surprise I didn't know about. Will it spoil the mystique of her online presence? Already, this feels a little niggling, an added pressure.

Carys nods. 'Yes, she's going to be leading the yoga sessions, and on Tuesday she will be doing a workshop on healthy relationships. Her partner will also be joining her from Sunday onwards, so please do give them some space.'

'Yeah, no. That's fine. That's understandable,' I reply.

Carys suddenly slaps her hands onto her thighs. 'OK. Time to go. Erik is going to take you in the buggy – sorry, we'll need two trips to get everyone and the luggage there – and then I can show you around.'

Erik appears in the room, jingling a set of keys from his index finger.

'Oh, I nearly forgot,' says Carys. 'Mobile phones. You'll need to hand them over and I will lock them in the safe until you go home. I'm sure you've read the retreat rules and understand that we don't want negative distractions on site. They'll be completely secure here. And, as we made clear in the email, it's not as if the retreat is completely out of touch with the rest of the world. We do have a radio system on site that the staff have access to, so that guests can be contacted in the event of an outside emergency, with your child, for example.'

'Yes, we've left details with my mum,' says Sophy with a slight wobble in her voice. 'I'm sure everything will be OK, even though it will be weird not being in touch with her for all this time.' Tom presses a reassuring hand to her back and kisses her hair.

'What about other emergencies?' I ask meekly. 'Like if there's one at the retreat?'

Carys briefly looks at me as if I'm stupid, before informing me that the radio system is obviously able to work both ways, in and out.

'All eventualities have been covered,' she says. 'Risk assessments, health and safety. You've really nothing to worry about.'

We reluctantly hand over our phones to Carys and go outside to take our seats in the buggy.

A shiver runs through me.

'OK?' Matt asks.

'Oh, I don't know. It suddenly seems a bit daunting. Being in such a remote location with no phones.'

Matt puts his arm around me. 'We don't have to do this if you don't want to. Babies can be made anywhere. We could go home. It's up to you.'

'I don't know.'

'It's only a week, though. Like, what could possibly go wrong in a week?'

I smile. 'Let's take a gamble.'

Matt winks suggestively in reply.

Erik gets into the driver's seat and starts up the buggy. 'Keep your arms in and hold onto the bar.'

We rumble through the car park and onto a rough track up to the mountains.

Matt exhales, and we tip our heads back to look at the stars, marvelling at the clarity of the Milky Way against Snowdonia's blackness, gasping as a bright light shoots suddenly across the sky.

'Wow, look at that!'

'It might be a meteor,' I say.

An omen.

SEVEN

GEMMA

The journey is worse than the most terrifying rollercoaster I have ever been on. We're jolted and bounced, hanging on with gleaming white knuckles, as the buggy takes us through a ravine before making its way up a steep mountain path that is challenging even for goats. Our bodies are rigid with tension, not knowing which direction the vehicle is going to veer in next. At one point Matt slips and almost falls out as we lurch over a rock, and I grab at his sleeve, screaming.

'Not long now.' Erik casts his eyes back to us rather than keeping watch on the path that is hardly visible in the buggy's pathetic headlights, and I'm petrified that he might accidentally drive us over the edge.

It's about fifteen minutes later when we emerge, thankfully unharmed, high up on a ledge that has a spectacular panoramic view of the magnificent night sky. I can imagine that in the morning we will see nothing but miles of hills and mountains.

'Wow,' I say, gazing around. 'This is pretty amazing.' I've seen the website photographs but even they haven't prepared me for this astounding experience. My heart engorges with adulation and I feel instinctively tearful for a moment.

There is an aesthetic glass-fronted building, strikingly lit and set into the mountain, with pretty pathways snaking away from it, through pergolas and archways of rock all dripping with fairy lights.

Carys shows us through huge glass doors into the central point of the retreat, housing the bar and restaurant, and treatment rooms.

We wander around, admiring the exposed stone and subtle downlighting, running our hands over the shiny marble bar and reading out the labels on the optic bottles. Lime. Passionfruit. Rose. Ginger. Sour cherry.

On the walls are canvases all with one obvious subject. Close-ups of tiny baby feet. A pregnant belly showing through the flimsy fabric of a flowing white dress. The stubble on a man's cheek as he kisses a fist of chubby infant fingers.

Matt squints quizzically at me. 'So it really is a place to come and make a baby?'

'Look, if you're not one hundred per cent... There's no penalty if we change our minds...' I snort out a laugh to reassure him.

He wraps his arms around me. 'Hey, hey I'm cool. I want what you want. Having a child with you would be the best thing ever.'

'Really?' My eyes shine with adoration.

'Really.'

Carys breaks the spell. 'Come on, lovebirds, I'll show you to your pods.'

We follow her along the paths through the pergolas that are strung with fairy lights, and she unlocks the accommodation that is earmarked for me and Matt.

'They're all exactly the same,' she tells us. 'Apart from the colour of the chaise longue.'

We have a sunflower yellow one at the bottom of our bed.

She shows us how to operate the lighting and air conditioning – everything is run by solar power – and points out the file of useful information regarding mealtimes, menus and treatments. Above us is a skylight through which we can see the stars and the round, buttery moon. Everything feels calm; everything smells pure and new. There is a shelf that holds a geranium scented candle and a stack of books whose titles include *The Goddess's Guide to Ovary Pampering* and *Awaken Your Fertility*.

Carys opens a cupboard door to point out a wicker basket. 'This is your welcome pack. All top-quality complementary products for you to use as you wish. There are also free toiletries in the bathroom, along with slippers and silk robes.'

'Ooh, lovely.' My body gives out an involuntary shimmer of gratitude, and I beam excitedly.

We move around the room, touching the bewitching furnishings.

'What's this control panel for?' asks Matt, and Carys tells him that it's for piped manifestation music that plays at a particular frequency – 528Hz – which will enhance hormones for virility and conception.

He grimaces comically at the information. 'I'm more of a Foo Fighters guy myself.'

Tom cackles, and I give a sympathetic eye roll to Carys so that she doesn't think we're taking the mickey on our free holiday. But she nods in good humour and says that she's going to leave us to it as she leads Sophy and Tom away to check in at their own luxurious accommodation.

* * *

Matt closes the door behind them and plonks his rucksack in the corner before kicking his shoes off. He fiddles with the controls to dim the lighting and switch on the soundtrack, which fills the room with a low, pulsating chord progression. I remove my coat and put a flame to the candle.

'Well. Here we are.' I thread my arms lasciviously around Matt's neck, combing my fingers into his hair.

We embrace and he nuzzles my throat, and the new, more fertile version of me notices how firm his muscles feel through his shirt, and how gratifying it is to be pressed up next to him, to really grind myself against him and imbibe his savoury smell – how have I never noticed *that*? – and then suddenly, we are tearing at each other's zips and buttons, and kissing, devouring each other with inflamed appetites that have us collapsing onto the bed.

We scramble out of our clothes, flopping around like breath-less fish as we struggle to remove sleeves and trousers.

Eventually, we're naked, and I pull him on top of me, and into me, digging my nails into his skin, and biting into his shoul-der. The posts of the bed tap rhythmically into the wall and the frame squeaks under our thrashing. Some animal instinct has inhabited us both and we writhe and pant recklessly, forgetting that Carys or other retreat staff might be outside and in earshot.

Afterwards, we switch off the lights and lie bleary and debilitated on top of the duvet, looking at the expanse of the galaxy through the skylight. A worm of sweat skates from my temple, down my neck and onto the pillow. The manifestation music is still thrumming its trippy tones, and I let it soak into me, feeling an utter serenity that has been a rare thing since Reuben ran away.

The air is warm and humid; the aroma of newness mixes with some hint of lavender that flavours the bedding; my emotions are swollen with expectation.

'I love you,' says Matt, in the darkness, as he rolls on his side to trace a finger onto my shoulder. 'I really *do* want us to have a baby.'

I smile, imagining his sperm reaching my egg, and the cells dividing and dividing and dividing over and over again until there is a miniscule foetus with limbs in the pit of my womb, a tiny miracle that will be my child.

Could it really be? Could it really have happened this time? I don't want to jinx it, but maybe, just maybe it has.

EIGHT

GEMMA

We meet up with Sophy and Tom for breakfast. On the menu are blueberries with yogurt followed by scrambled eggs, spinach and avocado, accompanied by orange juice and green tea.

'No full English?' Matt remarks, which annoys me a little because we've already discussed the healthy menus on offer at the retreat, so it shouldn't come as a shock that he hasn't got bacon and sausage on his plate.

'This is actually quite nice,' says Sophy.

Tom has already finished and is sitting with his arms folded. 'So, the meditation thing. Is it optional? Is it only for you two girls?'

'I got the impression that we were all supposed to go. In the leaflet, it says that it's only thirty minutes so it's not as if it's going to take up too much of our day.' I sip my green tea, which has the flavour of grass cuttings. I can only think that it must be doing me good.

'And then we're supposed to meet someone at dinner tonight? What's all that about? Will we need to be on our best behaviour?'

'Well, it's the person who chose us for the retreat. Her name is Addie and she's on Instagram, a sort of influencer...'

Tom groans. 'Not some pretentious twenty-something demonstrating Botox and eyebrow stencils? I can't stand all that sort of thing.'

'No, she's not like that. She's probably a similar age to us and she does things like recipes and household hacks and fitness. She's quite normal and even sounds like she has a Yorkshire accent too. I think that's why I like her, because she's just like us.'

'Is this the Five-a-Day thing you keep telling me about?' Matt pushes away his herbal tea, untouched.

'Yes, I must admit that I've been a bit addicted to her account since finding it. I'm probably one of her top followers.'

'Do you follow her, too?' Tom asks Sophy.

She shrugs. 'Yeah, but not to the same extent. You buy *all* the stuff Addie recommends, don't you, Gemma? I mean, you've even copied her look and hairstyle and everything, haven't you? You're a *super follower*, aren't you?'

'I'm not *that* bad.' Heat has sprung into my cheeks as I realise how irritatingly true Sophy's words are. Everything I'm currently wearing has been purchased due to Addie's reels. Even my earrings.

'You must be excited to know that she's going to be here?' says Matt. 'It'll be like getting access to the VIP area at a concert.'

Am I excited? There's a scurry of nervous butterflies in my stomach to think that I will be face-to-face with someone I've been trying to emulate for over a year. What will she think of *me*?

Tom wags a finger in my face. '*Never meet your heroes.* Have you ever heard that saying?'

'No. Why shouldn't you meet your heroes?'

'Because they'll let you down and you'll be disappointed.'

'Don't be silly,' I say, trying to sound flippant.

A woman in a yellow dress appears at our table. 'Meditation time in twenty minutes. I'm going to set the room up. See you soon.'

The four of us creep into the therapy room, and squat to remove our shoes. There is a circle of yoga mats waiting for us, and a chubby white candle flickers in the middle of the floor.

The yellow-frocked woman is standing in the corner with a sedate expression and her hands clasped, and instead of speaking she indicates with some mystical eye contact that we should sit on the mats and stare into the dancing yellow flame.

I take my place and force myself into a cross-legged position. Soft, almost inaudible music that is gentle and breathy, begins to play from hidden speakers in the room.

My mind wanders and I can't concentrate on the candle. I see a fleck of dried mud on the floor and revisit last night's white-knuckle journey, wondering if there is a way that I could do the return route at the end of the week on foot instead.

'Dispel all thoughts from your mind.' The woman, who hasn't changed her position in the corner, instructs us in a purring tone. 'Clear your head. Just focus on the flame.'

I cast a look towards her, and it's then that I notice the glass vase sitting on the windowsill. Six black lilies, half open, stand out of the water. A sudden sensation of dread washes over me. The muscle under my left eye tics for a few seconds and I cough as I choke on my breath. There's something I can't retrieve in my mind and I don't know why, but it has triggered an involuntary churning in my stomach. I try to catch the attention of Sophy, but she's busy concentrating on the flame.

Black lilies. What a weird choice.

Focus, I tell myself. Clear out the thoughts. The thing is, my head will only stay empty for a matter of seconds.

A cramp creeps into my right thigh so that I have to change position. Matt closes his eyes and lets out a long, audible breath. Tom surreptitiously pushes back the sleeve of his sweater to check the time on his watch. How long have we been here? Minutes? Half an hour? It is impossible to tell.

The candle dips and hisses for a few seconds, threatening to go out, but then it recovers and I'm taunted by the flowers again, taking another look to see if they really are black or maybe just dark blue or purple.

No, they are black. I shiver briefly and close my eyes.

Oh God. I've remembered now.

Chill out. Chill out, it's OK, I tell myself, controlling my breaths so that my racing heart will slow down.

Sophy disrupts the serenity by clambering onto all fours where she does a few cat and cow yoga stretches, before reclining on her side and watching the candle once more.

I exhale. I won't look at the lilies again. The session feels interminable, when I really want Matt to be enjoying himself. I want him to have a positive experience; I want him to be mentally and physically primed so that by the end of the week there will be three of us going home instead of two, and our marriage will be sealed with the promise of a child.

I return my vision to the candle and try to breathe mindfully while I think about things like blue skies and lush grass. My stomach whines as it begins to digest my breakfast, and Sophy casts a look of amusement my way.

Then, without warning, everything is over.

The woman presses her hands together in a prayer formation. 'Thank you, everyone. I hope you have been cleansed with this session. You're now free to go, but if you wish you can stay for further contemplation.'

We look around at each other, somewhat bemused. Tom is the first to stand up and put his shoes back on. I'm the only one that bothers to say thank you to the woman before we go.

* * *

Outside, it's bright and scorching in the cup of the mountains.

'Did you see those flowers?' I say to Sophy. 'In a vase on the windowsill?'

'No. What about them?'

'Black lilies. Six black lilies.'

She raises an eyebrow but says nothing. The tic in my cheekbone jumps again.

'Does anyone fancy a swim?' she asks. 'We could have a walk to the waterfall. I'm assuming you all brought swimming costumes?'

'I'll sit this one out,' says Tom. 'It's gonna be freezing.'

'Isn't cold water supposed to be good for depression?' I say.

'Yeah, well I'm not depressed, so I'd rather just relax here and read.'

Matt is quick to agree with him. 'Me too. I'll give the water a try another day. I think for now I'd rather sit in the sun and keep Tom company.'

We change into our costumes and bring the thick, fluffy towels out of the pods. Leaving the men behind, we tramp up a mountain path, following the sound of trickling water. The sky is vast, and I can't remember ever seeing such natural beauty. No roads, no houses, no industrial buildings. Over another ridge, the track drops down and we turn the corner as the watery sound becomes a crescendo.

'Just look at it.' Sophy spreads out her arms, and there it is in front of us. A lake, turquoise and translucent, largely still, apart from one end that ripples where it is fed by a sumptuous waterfall. 'It's gorgeous, isn't it?'

It is stunning. There is a small, stony shore, and we walk down to the water's edge and take off our flip-flops to dip our feet into the icy shallow. I feel myself smiling – properly wide-mouthed grinning – with the raw experience of being somewhere different and doing something that I've never done before.

I dump my towel on the shore and venture in further. 'Come on,' I shout to Sophy. 'It's really refreshing.'

She hesitates for a moment, then trawls suddenly towards me, stumbling on the gravelly floor.

'Whoa!' she squeals, and I reach out to try and save her from falling, but it's too late. She splashes into the water, gasping, stunned by the cold and unable to speak.

I laugh at her reaction, at her flailing arms and legs, and then suddenly she is swimming, propelling herself through the clear water towards the cascade at the other side of the lake. I watch enviously as she holds her head under the rush of water, flattening her hair onto her face, letting it run into her open mouth as she yells with ecstasy.

Jealousy challenges me, and before I can stop myself, I plunge in and flip onto my back, shrieking high-pitched up to the brash blue sky as I kick my way through the water towards Sophy.

'How mad is this?' she roars.

I reach her and we clamber onto the rocks to sit under the centre of the waterfall, letting it pelt down on us as we look out beyond the curtain of water.

'What is it?' I say as a puzzled look spreads across her face.

She moves away from the rushing water's route and flops back into the pool with a clumsy front crawl, casting her eyes up to the side of the mountain.

I dip into the water to swim after her. 'What? What are you looking at?'

'Nothing. I thought I saw someone, that's all.' There is a deep ridge between her eyebrows. The mood has changed.

'Who? Tom and Matt?'

'No, not them.' She scans the mountainside again. 'Just something...'

My heart has started pounding. There *is* something. A sense of weirdness that I can't quite put my finger on. 'I've got a strange feeling, too. D'you think we're being watched?'

Sophy frowns. 'I don't think we're on our own.'

NINE

GEMMA

The guys are horizontal on sun loungers when we return to the pods.

'Good swim?' Matt opens one eye and gives a leery smile at the sight of me in a wet bikini.

'It was amazing.'

'But cold?' asks Tom.

'Once you get in and start moving it's great. You just have to get over that first hurdle. The water is beautifully clear.' Sophy is now a convert to wild-water swimming.

We go to our pods to shower and make the most of the expensive complementary toiletries. When I step out of the bathroom, Matt is reclining on the bed, his head propped on an elbow.

'What?' I laugh as he reaches out and pulls my towel away.

'We've got almost an hour before lunch,' he says. 'Plenty of time for some fun.'

Maybe it's the novelty of the four-poster bed, or the invigorating swim, or the sight of the dazzling sun and blue skies through the skylight, or the fresh air and different surroundings, but my body is burning with lust. I'd flicked through the pages of one of the books on the shelf this morning, to find a mantra that has now lodged itself in my mind: 'my ovaries are full of potential'. I'm silently repeating it to myself now, over and over again, believing it to be true.

Matt gets up to lock the door and switch the glass to privacy setting, before removing his clothes. I spread my damp hair on the pillow. Outside, there is the mewing sound of buzzards, circling high above the mountains.

'Maybe we should have the mood music on again.' Matt adjusts the control panel until there's an oscillating swell of sound filling the room.

I watch as he removes his shorts and T-shirt, unable to stop myself from comparing his body with the memories of lithe Reuben.

But it didn't work with Reuben, did it? I tell myself. We tried for so long and a baby didn't happen despite our best efforts. Maybe I wasn't destined to have a child with him; maybe Matt will be the one instead. Or maybe keeping me childless is karma's way of punishing me for what I did before.

Stop it. Stop thinking like that, I tell myself. Don't go there.

'You're looking pensive,' Matt remarks. 'What's in that gorgeous head of yours?'

'Well, I was wondering if you find it sexy and intriguing that we don't yet know everything about each other?' I say as he snuggles beside me and nibbles at my neck. I let myself become inflamed by his touch; I close my eyes and welcome him in, the softness of his limbs surprising me every time.

'Hmm... yeah, maybe. Perhaps it adds to the excitement that I'm a man of mystery,' he murmurs. 'And you're my femme fatale.'

Femme fatale?

I try to push the other thing out of my mind again. He doesn't need to know everything, does he?

* * *

Afterwards we lie together, naked, on top of the crisp white duvet.

'So, how would you feel if we ended up making a baby this week?' I ask.

'You don't think we should have got to know each other better first?'

'Some people click straight away and don't need to know every single thing about each other. So stop worrying. You don't need to look for skeletons in my cupboard.'

Matt laughs. 'No, I'm not. It's just... I don't know. People keep secrets, don't they? They have things in their past.'

'Well, I'm all good.' I'm aware that my tone is a little prickly. 'And you said earlier that it was fun to be a man of mystery, didn't you?'

'Hey, it's OK. And there aren't any mysteries with me. There's nothing in my past that won't make me a decent father.' He gently slides his warm hand over the base of my belly. 'The little fella could already be here, listening to us. And I'd be delighted, I really would.'

I try to relax, to let my body return to a soft and welcoming state as he touches me.

He kisses me. 'I want us to be open. To always be truthful with each other.'

Oh God. How could I possibly begin to tell him?

The spasm is back again under my left eye as his warm lips smother mine.

Lunch is quinoa salad on baby rainbow chard leaves, drizzled with some kind of minty dressing. I pick out the pomegranate seeds that have been sprinkled on top and scrape them to the side of my dish.

'I know it all looks incredibly worthy, but this food actually tastes quite nice.' Tom is tucking into his meal with relish. 'I wish there was more of it. Or at least some apple pie and custard afterwards.'

'We'll probably go home much fitter with this kind of diet all week. Hiking around the mountains, swimming in the pool: my skin is going to be glowing with goodness.' Sophy has her amber hair piled on top of her head; her face is fresh with vivacity.

I wonder where she is in her ovulation cycle. Does she have the same app as me? She was so quick to get caught with Olivia. Maybe we could both conceive at the same time, then we'd have our children together and they would be in the same class at school.

Matt has finished eating. 'Do you want me to get you something from the bar?'

'If they have anything mango based I wouldn't mind. With plenty of ice, please.' I cast a look towards the bar, where a smart waiter in a white shirt and bow tie is arranging a row of glasses.

Matt gets up and I watch as he goes to put in my request. As he waits for my drink to be prepared, he sidles to the end of the bar where there's a vase – oh God, another one – and he leans over to sniff one of the flowers...

'Are you OK?' Sophy is shaking my arm as I hold my breath.

'What?' I snap out of my brief trance.

'You just went really strange.'

I inhale deeply and look again. Matt is walking back with a tall glass of fizzing orange liquid decorated with a cherry and a cocktail umbrella. He's nowhere near the flowers.

Sophy turns to see what I'm staring at.

'Black lilies,' I say. 'More of them.'

TEN

GEMMA

I select one of the books from the pile on the shelf. Its subject matter is about achieving a conception-ready womb, about getting the right balance of hormones, about optimising inner health. Apparently, high levels of cortisol can interfere with menstruation and reduce the chances of getting pregnant. And cortisol can be elevated during times of stress.

This is bad news. I have been jittery since lunchtime, with my heart rate raised and even skipping beats at times. It's because of the black lilies. Stupid little things like that can frequently trigger me, and although I consciously try to control my anxieties – I have even done online cognitive behaviour therapy sessions in the past – this thing with the flowers has really set me on a path of apprehension.

I realise that it's probably nothing. It's a coincidence. The choice of colour must be something to do with the décor, the branding of the retreat.

But black lilies are quite unusual, aren't they? I mean, it's the first time I've actually seen any since...

Stop it, Gemma. I put a hand over my heart and take more

deep breaths. You're being absurd. How can you be worried about something so stupid? Stop it.

I return my attention to the book just as Sophy peeks around my door.

'Hiya, I wondered if you fancy coming with me for a head massage? The guys have finished, so the room is available now.'

Matt and Tom went for a hot stone treatment after lunch, eager to make the most of all the freebies.

'Er, yeah, whatever.' If I go, it might help me to relax, although there were those flowers in the room earlier and if I see them...

'Are you OK?'

I wave a hand. 'It's nothing. Just my stupid overthinking brain.'

She raises an eyebrow at me.

'No. It's nothing.' I take a breath. 'Actually, it's the flowers. There were more black lilies on the bar, did you see?'

Sophy laughs. 'I knew that's what you were going to say. But, listen, anyone can buy whatever colour flowers they want. And black lilies do look classy.'

'But have you seen them anywhere else? Because they're funeral flowers, aren't they? Why would they be here?'

'Look, I don't know.' Sophy holds up her hands. 'Honestly though, I think this isn't really an issue. We're here to have a nice time, to do all the chilled-out stuff and make babies. Are you going to come for a massage with me or not?'

I sense that Sophy is somewhat irritated by my agitation. 'OK, let's go.' I put the book back on the shelf and follow her to the treatment room.

It's the same woman in the yellow frock from the meditation session who is doing the massages. Apparently, she doubles up as the retreat chef with assistance from Jozef, the barman. She tells us that her name is Eloise as she works on us in relay, using a floral oil that calms my nerves. I keep my eyes closed so that I don't see the lilies on the windowsill.

There's more of the fertility music playing, oozing like syrup from the hidden speakers, and I nestle into the atmosphere to soak up the positive vibes.

It must be around twenty minutes after Eloise began the massage, when I jump with a start, realising that I have dozed off.

'Gemma?' Sophy's voice cuts into the tranquillity. 'I was just asking Eloise about the black lilies. Didn't you hear me? Were you actually asleep?'

'Sorry. I couldn't help it. I feel so... woo. You know? It's better than wine.'

Eloise presses her fingers into my temples again. 'The black lilies are symbolic,' she says. 'Isis, the Egyptian goddess of fertility and motherhood, was often portrayed with this particular flower in her hand. And here, around the Welsh hills, we love magic and symbolism, so it seems fitting that we display them at the retreat.'

'But I thought people had them at funerals?'

'Yes, there are other links with death and mourning, too. But *we* like to think that death and birth come in cycles, and our part of that cycle is the birth element. Plus, they look stunning, too, and last for ages if you change the water regularly.'

So that is the explanation. I don't need to worry at all. The flowers have been selected for their practicality as well as their connection to an Egyptian goddess.

Sophy sits up slowly beside me. Eloise dabs the excess oil from my hairline and steps back from the bench.

'Maybe she's changed her mind. Maybe she's not coming after all.' Sophy cuts a dainty piece of salmon fillet and pops it into her mouth.

I turn my head again to watch the door behind me, but there's still no sign of Addie. Even so, there is a single place set at the table beside us. How long will we have to wait? Should I eat my meal more slowly?

There is a murmuration of wild creatures in my stomach. I don't know if I have got the right balance with my look, despite my efforts.

My face shines radiantly with Foxyface foundation (one of Addie's recommendations), and I spent at least an hour earlier in the bathroom preening and styling my hair in readiness for her presence. The full-sleeved maxi dress in burnt orange chiffon hangs flawlessly off my body, much to the admiration of Matt. 'Is this something that she's advertised, too?' he'd asked, running his hands over the soft fabric, and I had to admit that yes, it was, although the one that she had modelled on her Instagram account had been in a dark teal.

I am the last one of us to finish our main courses, and we wait for the plates to be cleared so that the dessert trolley can be brought out.

'I've got a rash on my arm,' Sophy says, proffering the inside of her wrist across the table. 'I don't know if I got bit or something when we were swimming. Or maybe it's a reaction to the free toiletries.'

I check my own skin for something similar, but there are no obvious blemishes. Then Tom is examining his, too, and we're all engaged in this apelike behaviour when the huge glass door clunks behind me.

Suddenly, I feel a hand on my shoulder.

I swivel my body around, to come face-to-face with the person who has been my virtual life coach for the past year.

'Snap!' Addie laughs and tweaks the sleeve of my dress.

I stare up at her, horrified, as heat rises into my cheeks. The Foxyface foundation has got no chance of holding back this level of redness.

She's wearing the exact same frock as me. Not the dark teal one, but the burnt orange version, just like mine.

'Woah,' says Matt, leaning back and folding his arms. 'You two look like twins.'

ELEVEN

GEMMA

There is a gnarled rock of indignity in the pit of my stomach. I am caught off guard. Hastily, I push back my chair so that I can stand up to greet Addie.

There's a clatter of cutlery and condiments, and I grab at the wobbling pepper grinder.

'Shit!' I hiss to myself as I knock over my full glass of green juice, and the liquid runs down the edge of the table, onto the skirt of my dress.

Sophy, in mother mode, fusses with a napkin, moving the crockery around, and I dab at the horrendous stain which has now ruined my outfit.

'Oops,' says Addie, stepping away from me as if I'm somehow contagious. 'What a mess.'

Matt is out of his seat and shaking hands with her, introducing himself. I'm grateful that he's taking the lead, even though I have run through this scenario in my head so many times with me being the one in charge. Now, though, I just look like a loser.

'So, which one is Gemma?' Addie points and smiles at Sophy.

'I am,' I say, miserably holding the saturated fabric of my dress.

'The winner of the star prize!' She looks back to me with a pitying smile.

'Yes, thank you.' I try to behave normally instead of the shamefaced failure that I have become in the last few minutes. 'It's been lovely so far.'

Addie looks across to the barman and clicks her fingers. 'Hi, Jozef, sorry to put you to extra trouble, but would you be able to clear this up for us, please? And bring me the menu too, because I'm starving.'

Her whole demeanour shouts *superstar celebrity*, unlike me and my group that stand pathetically by our wrecked table. Matt gives a sympathetic look and moves next to me to rub a consoling hand over my back.

'Did you have a good journey?' Tom asks Addie, because the silence is excruciating. Although it's not totally quiet as there's still the drip drip drip of my spilled green juice dropping from the table onto the floor.

Addie doesn't reply. She's checking her phone.

'*Phone?*' Sophy mouths to me, her eyes fiery with resentment.

I'm also annoyed that Addie hasn't had her mobile confiscated and placed into the safe with ours, but I put a finger over my lips, concerned that Sophy will voice her irritation and upset Addie and then our holiday will be spoilt. Maybe she's allowed to have her phone here because of her superior status.

The barman arrives with a cloth, and we shuffle out of his way as he works on our table, stacking the empty plates and cutlery.

'Did you bring a menu?' Addie asks, and the barman apologises and disappears again.

'We didn't get a menu. Or a choice,' Sophy whispers, and I give her a hefty nudge.

'What are we doing now?' Matt says in a low voice, nodding towards the door in suggestion that we make our exit and leave Addie alone.

'What about dessert?' Tom picks up his unused spoon.

The barman returns and passes a menu to Addie before continuing to clear our table. He gives us a look that says he's surprised to see us still here.

'We didn't get dessert,' Tom explains.

'Ah, I see. Well, would it be possible for you to come back in about half an hour? It will give me time to get this sorted out so that I can attend to our other guest.'

Addie has seated herself at her own clean table and is ignoring us while she scans the menu that we weren't offered. We traipse outside discreetly, into the evening's warmth.

'Christ, she's not very sociable, is she? If that's supposed to be a meet and greet, I wouldn't give her five stars for the greet aspect of it.' The door hasn't fully closed before Sophy is voicing her disgruntlement. 'Arrogant cow.'

'It was my fault. If I hadn't caused all that chaos, I'm sure she would have been friendly. I feel so bad for making a mess.' I run a hand over my sweaty forehead, smearing my foundation. 'Look at the state of me. I need to go and change.'

We return to our separate pods and I put on a different outfit and reapply my make-up.

'Well, this dress is ruined now. That stain isn't going to come out.' I rub the fabric under the cold tap but the large greeny brown patch won't fade. 'And I can't believe we were wearing the same thing. God, I felt so humiliated.'

'She was probably as embarrassed as you were,' says Matt. 'I could tell that she felt sorry for you.'

'Could you?'

'Yes. It was weird though, seeing you both together like that, in the same clothes. I mean, I've never seen her Instagram account so I didn't know what to expect, but your hair and everything, same colour, same style, same length. Even the same shade of lipstick. Anyone could have mistaken you both for sisters.'

I shrug. 'The thing is, she advertises stuff that I like, and I buy it and use it.'

'But it just seems like you've copied her.'

I shrug again. Matt is right. I had been copying everything for the past year. Not only how Addie looked, but her recipes, home décor, lifestyle hacks. There was some inexplicable magnetism about her that made me want what she had.

Sleep doesn't come easily. My mood is all wrong, and I curl up, clinging stiffly to the pillow while Matt spoons me for a while until he falls asleep and I push his heavy arm off me.

I replay the mortifying incident with the green juice over and over in my mind until it has never happened. I visually select each outfit that I've brought with me to choose a different one from the orange dress, and imagine myself gracefully meeting Addie: we air kiss and laugh at each other's jokes, chatting effortlessly, until me and Matt squeeze up on our table so that Addie can bring her food over to sit with us, and we share tasters from each other's plates and then she tells us funny anecdotes about her life as an influencer.

The bed is too warm.

I throw off the duvet and flop around, trying to get comfortable, trying to stop my brain from overthinking everything.

Something at this place feels unnerving. Conflicting. It's not simply the mortification of the evening meal; it's more than that. Perhaps the expectation of conceiving is too much of a burden. But it's like my dark secret is trying to rise to the surface like cream, and I don't know why.

Maybe my reproductive hormones are clashing with my conscience. Oh God, I don't know, but it all feels off.

Should I tell Matt? Should I come clean about my past? Would that help?

No.

Oh God, no way. Don't go back there at all.

TWELVE

ADDIE

Erik drove me to the site yesterday afternoon. I was awash with a see-saw of excitement and apprehension almost to the point of nausea. All the secrets that I was holding inside me – one of them quite literally! – simmered with expectation.

There was no sign of anyone when I arrived. Maybe they were all having lunch or an afternoon siesta. I discreetly took my luggage into the pod that was allocated to me and unpacked everything. I swallowed my folic acid supplement with my vitamin-fortified juice drink and did my breathing exercises, and I could have lounged around on the bed and read a book, but the weather was so nice and I knew that I wouldn't be able to concentrate.

The sun was blazing, so I decided to walk towards the waterfall. I followed the path around the curved incline until the lake came into view, shining like a sapphire-crusted mirror.

A squeal pierced the tranquillity. A peal of laughter. I shielded my eyes from the sun and scanned the scene. There, at the other end of the pool, bobbing under the rush of water, were two people. I couldn't make out their features because they were too far away, but I sat for a while on the side of the hill and watched as they splashed around.

Well. Well. Well.

A shrewd smile tweaked the right side of my lips. Here were the women who had won my giveaway, my star prize of a week here at this luxury retreat.

Gemma and Sophy.

They lapped up and down the length of the lake a couple of times, towards the waterfall then back again. There was more whooping, more laughing.

I hugged my arms around my knees, my eyes pinned to the figures in the water.

Their noise stopped suddenly. I followed their gaze, up into the sky, then to the side of the mountain where I sat. Despite the sun burning the top of my head and my shoulders, a shiver ran across the back of my neck. I stood and continued on the path which threaded upwards, behind the source of the water-fall. Then the sun bolted behind a cloud for a second, and a precarious stillness charged the air. I froze in my steps and looked down again at the women, overwhelmed by a feeling.

The feeling that *I* was being watched by *them*.

The evening meal was an opportunity for me to see them close up. To see how their bodies had aged and plumped; to see how time and regret had put lines around their eyes.

They were still recognisable. The tone of their voices hadn't changed at all. Continuing to live in the place where you were brought up ensured that you held onto an accent. Mine had softened now, probably from being away in those intervening years.

I didn't give anything away at that point; I just wanted to observe and get a handle on how they were. Anyway, there was no need to surprise them or create a scene, because Gemma accidentally did that herself. Gosh, everyone's expressions – even Jozef, the barman – when we ended up face-to-face with each other wearing the same outfit! And then the drama when Gemma knocked over the green juice. It couldn't have gone better if I'd planned it.

Afterwards, when they had all gone, I spent some time chatting to Eloise, the other member of staff. She'd been with the group yesterday in the treatment room.

'How did they seem?' I asked. 'Comfortable with everything?'

'Yeah.' She waggled a hand and laughed. 'There's one of the women who's obviously a fan of yours. She's copied your hair. And your make-up style.'

'And my frock.'

Eloise grimaced. 'Oh dear. Not the stalker type, I hope?'

'Not as far as I know, but she's quite an avid follower of my Insta.'

'Well, in the sessions she seemed a bit jumpy and not as relaxed as the others.'

'Hmm. Did you remember about my recommendations, you know, the little extra things?'

'Of course. The poetry book is in her room, and the fresh flowers around the place look lovely. I put them in the treatment room and on the bar.'

'Lilies?'

'Of course. Black ones, just like you asked for.'

A memory whacked me then, like a mis-thrown football. Black lilies, woven into a heart-shaped wreath, sitting on the polished wood of a coffin lid.

THIRTEEN

GEMMA

'Apparently, Addie's partner arrived about ten minutes ago, literally melting with sweat. The buggy wasn't able to get all the way through the ravine because of a fallen tree, so he had to walk the last mile and a half carrying all his stuff.' Tom presents this information while we eat our Sunday lunch, which turns out to be a salad bowl, largely consisting of alfalfa, shredded peppers, some kind of mustardy celeriac slaw and a hefty sprinkling of pumpkin seeds.

'Did you see him? What's he like?' I ask.

'No, it was Jozef who told me. They've got to get someone to remove the tree, and apparently its trunk's massive, the size of a bus.'

'So, we're all technically stuck here?'

'Well, I don't know. He didn't say when it would be removed.'

Matt pushes the celeriac thing to one side of his dish. 'I'm not really a fan of this. It's got a funny taste to it.' He actually looks like he's going to throw up. 'Why couldn't we just get a Sunday roast? Every meal seems to be leaves and raw vegetables.'

I'm disappointed with Matt's negativity about the menu. At least Addie isn't here in the dining room to hear him. Maybe she's taking her meals in the privacy of her own accommodation, as we haven't seen her yet today.

'I love the flavour of all the meals,' I say in defence of the food. It might be my imagination, but even my skin feels better since being here. Everything is so fresh, so wholesome. Surely, it has to be improving my inner workings.

'Do you think Olivia's OK?' Sophy puts on a sad face and takes hold of Tom's hand. 'I feel so guilty about leaving her. What if she's having abandonment issues and hates us when we return? I mean, I know there's the emergency radio thing and all that, but would it really have been so bad to have had my phone and been able to contact her on FaceTime, because this total separation thing just feels wrong.'

'I know. I'm missing her like crazy, despite getting the best sleep in the last few nights than I've had since she was born. She'll be all right, though. You know how much she loves being with your mum and she's stayed there before...'

'Only three nights max.'

'Well, this is a good trial for if we need a break when the baby arrives.' There's a twinkle in Tom's eye as he looks across the table at us, doing a dramatic double-take for effect.

I see Sophy give his foot a tactical kick.

'What? Wait, you mean...?' I drop my fork. Jealousy jolts through my belly like a flame.

Sophy's smile is a shining, gleaming celebration of her success. 'Yes, we suspected that we'd hit the jackpot before we got here, although we hadn't confirmed it, and then we found a welcome pack in our room that contained some pregnancy tests...'

'She did one about half an hour ago,' Tom butts in. 'And there were two definite blue lines on it.'

'Yep, pregnant again.' They gaze lovingly at each other, and

I bite down on my bottom lip. Matt hasn't said anything and I daren't look at him.

'Well, congratulations,' I say, trying to control the wobble in my voice and the welling in my eyes. 'That's such lovely news.'

I get a true sense of my own womb then. Empty. Ineffectual. A fallow organ in the pit of my abdomen. Will it *ever* happen for me? Those two blue lines on the test that I have yearned for with all my being? I keep hoping and hoping, thinking that surely it must happen next month, then the month after and then... Still nothing.

Is it my fault? Would some kind of medical intervention mend me? How far would I go to have my own child? Obviously IVF would be the first option. Egg donor? A surrogate? Oh God, it doesn't bear thinking about. I just want my own body to surprise me. That's all.

My chin trembles without warning. I poke at the tears in the corners of my eyes before they have chance to slip visibly down my face and reveal my torture.

Suddenly, Matt scrapes back his chair and comes to me, to wrap his arms around me and kiss my forehead. 'Us next,' he tells me. 'Don't you worry, it will soon be our turn.'

FOURTEEN

ADDIE

I'm scheduled to lead the yoga class this afternoon. Dressed in my favourite supersoft sports leggings and vest, I'm waiting with the mats lined up in front of me, performing some limbering stretches as the group arrives in the cleared dining room.

'Don't kill us,' says Matt, taking a place at the end of the row and doing a few lunges.

Tom slots in next to him and runs on the spot for a moment. It's almost nauseating to see how both of the guys are trying to be teacher's pet. Sophy rocks gently from side to side, her hands cupped over her soft belly. Gemma stands rigid, arms folded, her attention focused towards the bar. Maybe she's in a petulant mood because she's wearing the same trousers as me, although hers are a slightly lighter green. Ironically, too, she's even got her hair tied up in the same scrunchie. From the back, someone could quite easily mistake one of us for the other.

'OK, let's loosen up a bit,' I say, beaming my best Instagram smile. On the periphery of my vision, I feel Gemma's glare.

We warm up and do a few sun salutations. How tough should I be on them? A little playfulness wouldn't hurt. So I attempt to get them doing headstands before abandoning their disastrous efforts in favour of some core-work on the mats. At this point I notice that Gemma has taken out her scrunchie and put it on her wrist.

By the end, as I stand over them to do a final guided relaxation, it seems like the session has gone well. Their eyes are closed; their breathing is heavy. I walk between their static bodies feeling satisfied and powerful.

'Namaste.' Everyone murmurs in unison before they begin to open their eyes and bring their limbs back to life.

Sophy scrambles into a sitting position and gives me a sly squint. 'Addie? I hope you don't mind if I ask you a question.'

'OK.' Something feels a little ominous. 'What?'

Sophy and Gemma share a look that I can't decipher.

'Like, is there something you've been hiding from us? A secret?' Sophy winks and adopts a devilish tone.

My heartbeat jolts; my stomach flips. Gemma freezes and looks towards me.

'What?' I ask as I feel the smile drop off my face. 'I don't know what you mean.'

Sophy points her finger at me and wiggles it in a circle. 'I've got you sussed out. Nothing gets past me.'

Gemma's eyes are bulging with expectancy. She has a hand to her chest as if she's holding her breath. Maybe she doesn't know what Sophy is talking about.

I squat down and start to roll up my mat, ignoring both of their questioning faces.

'I take it your followers don't know? You've kept it quiet from them, haven't you?' Sophy has a mocking expression. 'So come on. Tell us about it.'

'What?'

'Tell us your *name*.'

A flush has risen into my cheeks and my heart is hammering. Goosebumps lift the downy hair on the back of my neck. I have seriously underestimated Sophy, thinking that she would simply come here and meekly tag along with Gemma. Has she found out who I actually am?

'What's all this?' Tom chips into the conversation. 'Come on, let *me* into the secret, too. What's the mystery with her name?'

Sophy turns to her friends. 'Have none of you noticed? Am I the only one? Addie's wearing a wedding ring.'

My body slumps with relief. My lungs release a grateful laugh. I splay out the fingers of my left hand to display the thick, gold band.

'I don't remember seeing you wearing it on any of your Instagram reels,' says Sophy. 'So, is it a recent development, or have you always preferred to let your followers think you're single?'

I laugh again, maybe a little crazily. 'Gosh, you *have* sussed me out, haven't you? You should be a detective. Me and my partner tied the knot three weeks ago, so yeah, I'm a bit of a newlywed. We thought it would be the right thing to do.'

'You never said anything about it on your Instagram.' Gemma sounds as if she's accusing me of something.

'We didn't want the publicity. In fact, we went off – eloped, sort of – and did it privately at Gretna Green, you know, the old blacksmith shop, so there was no need for a big event.'

'No need for a big event? Addie, you thrive on publicity. It should have been a mega celebration with everything videoed for Instagram!' Everyone laughs as Sophy berates me.

I put on an apologetic face. 'Sorry. But we wanted to keep it low key, you know. We don't have big families and...'

'Hey, you don't need to explain,' says Tom. 'I wish we'd done something like that instead of the whole expensive palaver we had. We've only just managed to pay it off the credit card.'

'Yeah, we had a quick and simple do, didn't we?' says Matt, looking over at Gemma. 'It was wonderful.'

Suddenly, I feel brave, I feel like I really want to stir things up. They're going to find out anyway.

'Actually, the main reason we got married was that we're having a baby.' I link my fingers over the place where my little one is residing.

Sophy jumps up. 'Oh wow, congratulations.' She swoops in for a hug, to press her cheek against mine, and we embrace awkwardly for a few seconds.

'That's brilliant news,' says Tom, squeezing an arm around my shoulders as soon as Sophy has let me go. 'How many weeks are you?'

'Eleven,' I reply. 'It's as big as a decent-sized strawberry.'

'Will this be your first child?' Matt asks with a nervous glance towards Gemma, who has turned away to stare out of the big glass doors.

'Yes. It's a bit scary, but I knew that my biological clock was ticking so I just thought, well, girl, it's now or never. And I couldn't bear the thought of growing old childless.'

Sophy gives a squeal, flapping her hands and jiggling her feet like a toddler. 'So, are we going to meet the lucky guy, then?' Blimey, she won't leave me alone.

'Yes, of course.' I nod enthusiastically. 'He's here now and will be joining us for evening meal.'

Sophy claps. 'Awesome. Well, congratulations, Mrs... what are we calling you now?'

'Just keep calling me Addie.' I wink.

The door slams. I look up and through the glass I see Gemma, flouncing off down the path. She hasn't even packed her yoga mat away.

FIFTEEN

GEMMA

Maybe I shouldn't have stormed away like that. Perhaps it looked a little petulant. I don't want everyone – and particularly Addie – to think that I'm a moody cow, because I'm not like that usually. It's just... oh, to get a second baby announcement in the same day is mental torture for me. I'm jealous of them. That's the bare bones of it. I want what they have.

I know I should have stayed to offer my congratulations, but I wouldn't physically have been able to get the words out of my mouth without blubbering at the realisation of my increasing failure to be like them. So I had to remove myself from their revelry. I had to return to our pod to relieve my anguish with a burst of profanities and burning tears, before dousing my face in cold water so that my upset wouldn't be too obvious to everyone.

The air is too hot. Stifling, humid, threatening. Blades of grass and clusters of heather shrivel under the sun's fiery beams.

'There's nowhere shady to sit,' says Matt, dragging the lounger into a different position. 'That's what this place is lacking.'

'Just leave it,' I snap at him, for no reason other than everyone else seems to be having babies apart from me.

'Hey.' Matt crouches beside me and kisses my arm. 'Come on, don't be grumpy. Let's look forward to the meal later.'

'Oh, let's all celebrate tonight, shall we? I'll probably knock over a beetroot smoothie, and Sophy and Tom will be sharing information with Addie and her husband about their foetuses and it's going to be like "mine's the size of a grape and mine's the size of a tomato" and all the baby talk about birthing plans...'

'Hey, it won't be long before we're doing the same. And I'm sure that Sophy will be discreet. I mean, she didn't mention anything about her pregnancy to Addie at yoga, did she? Perhaps she wants to wait a while before she goes public.' Matt stretches over me to plant his lips on my forehead.

'Yeah. Yeah, you're right.' I take a breath. The evening meal doesn't need to be an ordeal. There won't be any more pregnancy announcements. I should chill out and look forward to it as if it's nothing special. It's only food, isn't it? As long as I don't spill anything this time, then surely nothing can upset me.

I wear a dress that wasn't a Five-a-Day recommendation and was actually my own choice instead, to ensure that I won't be embarrassed yet again by a duplicate fashion choice. It's a rich burgundy colour, fitted, sleeveless and knee-length, in a shimmering silky fabric. My hair is woven into a neat French plait, courtesy of half an hour's worth of arm-aching persistence, and I've gone for dark and dramatic make-up in order to steer away from the bright and fresh colours that Addie normally favours.

Matt thinks that I look sensational.

'Wow, *you've* made an effort,' says Sophy, when she comes with Tom to knock on our door to call for us. 'I've gone with more of a beachwear vibe.' A sandy-coloured dress in a light, crinkly cheesecloth looks as if it's been thrown over a bikini.

Her marmalade hair hangs loose and her face is clean and bare. She's got flip-flops on her feet.

'Oh no, d'you think I look overdressed?' A flutter of concern that I will appear ridiculous rears up in me.

'You look gorgeous,' Matt assures me, pulling on my hand so that we start to make our way to the dining area rather than go back inside to deliberate over my outfit.

Addie will be dressing up, surely she will, I tell myself as we enter through the glass doors and see that the tables are pushed together.

We take our seats – me and Sophy on one side with our backs to the doors, with Tom and Matt opposite us – leaving the places beside me and Matt for Addie and her husband. Jozef brings us glasses of mocktails, and we chat and make small talk as we wait for the others to arrive.

Tom pats his stomach. 'I hope they're not going to be too much longer. I'm starving.'

Matt looks across at me and I offer him a nervous smile. I won't be properly settled until I've seen what Addie is wearing.

Fifteen minutes later and the couple still haven't shown up. Jozef brings out some bowls of olives and sundried tomatoes with an apology that Addie and her husband are possibly running a little behind schedule.

'Behind schedule?' Sophy looks bemused. 'She's only in the pod over there. The husband arrived earlier apparently. It's not as if they've been to work and the rush-hour traffic is a nightmare, is it?'

'Maybe she can't decide what to wear in case it clashes with Gemma.' Tom laughs. So does Matt. I bob my tongue out at them both.

Everyone tucks into the olives and tomatoes apart from me, because I'm concerned about dribbling oil onto my dress. My stomach rumbles. The waiting is excruciating on so many levels.

'Ah, I think they're here now,' says Tom, looking towards the glass doors as two shadows slope past.

'Finally,' says Matt with a sigh.

I want to play it cool and casual, so I don't immediately scramble to my feet like Sophy and Tom do. I pick up my drink and take a languid sip as Matt stands and steps forward ready to hold out a welcoming hand.

Suddenly, the atmosphere changes.

I hear Sophy whisper – 'oh my God' – as she grabs my shoulder, forcing me to stay in my seat.

'Hi everyone, good evening and sorry for the delay.' Addie's smug tone draws me to turn my head towards the couple as they enter the room, leaving the glass doors swinging behind them. 'I'd like to introduce you all to my new husband and father of my child, and the love of my life...'

My head reels. I'm too stunned to breathe, and my legs quiver as if they'd be incapable of holding me up.

Addie's new husband and father of her child.

He looks almost as shocked as I am as he stands there with a horrified smile fixed to his face.

Reuben.

I remember when he was the love of *my* life.

BEFORE THE RETREAT

SIXTEEN

GEMMA

I retrace the timeline where it tangled with us all. It must have been a year ago. Probably longer. Me and Reuben were together, settled, in love.

Cosy on the sofa with our feet up on the coffee table, he'd been watching television while I'd been scrolling the internet until I was seduced by a link to Instagram.

'What a gorgeous dress. Do you think that sort of thing would look good on me?' I'd nudged Reuben, and he'd turned away from the football game to look at the video on my phone, of a twirling woman in an emerald dress with a plunging neckline and voluminous sleeves.

'Hmm, yeah. You're thinking for Ed's wedding?'

'Yes. It would look good next to your new suit, wouldn't it? We'd be a pretty eye-catching couple.'

Reuben had laughed. 'Although I think what makes that dress stand out is the colour of the model's hair.'

I'd looked at him with a raised eyebrow. I could tell in his eyes that what really made her stand out was the size of her breasts rather than her hair colour. 'She's not really a model.

She's an influencer and she puts out five reels every day. It's an account called Addie's Five-a-Day.'

'That's novel.' His attention had already returned to the football.

'Hmm.' I'd clicked on the heart and rewatched the video three times as I considered dyeing my hair the same shade of red and moving my parting from the centre to the side.

'Would you ever want to get your boobs done? Like, enhanced?' Reuben had said without taking his eyes off the screen.

'Do you think I need to?'

'No, no. Of course not. I just wondered.' He'd taken a handful of Pringles and cracked a new can of beer. 'Anyway, we need the money to go towards the wedding.'

Slightly offended by Reuben's unprompted discussion – which fortunately never went any further – I'd browsed through Addie's other reels on her grid. I could have got jealous of her at that point for having a better figure than me, but I didn't. The thing was, she came across as a lovely, genuine person and not some show-off floozy seeking attention by putting her flesh on show. In most of her videos she was wearing casual clothing – not too tight, not too revealing – just the sort that I would wear. And her account wasn't all about clothes. The next reel had showed her recommending a book: a delicious and compelling read that combined eroticism and food with a surprise ending that had made her cry. It had a beautiful gold cover and she'd suggested putting it on a shelf with the design facing outwards.

What a great idea, I'd thought. I'd hearted the reel, made a mental note of the book title and decided to look out for it next time I went into town.

Addie's Five-a-Day account was full of intriguing content and I'd worked my way through it. There she was, in a trendy bar sipping Sav Blanc and wearing a Joe Brown embroidered jacket, delivering a short amusing monologue called 'Making the most of your Me-Time'. Next, a reel demonstrating a powder-based foundation that claimed to last twelve hours (it apparently didn't, as the follow-up clip showed). Then she was on a blustery mountain with her hair dancing around her face as she venerated the benefits of being in the open air, even if it was spitting with rain. 'Get away from your technology,' she'd advised, which I found a bit ironic, as I was watching her on mine. Then she was demonstrating a hack with some kind of headband thing that enabled you to quickly and easily get your hair into a formal knot.

I'd gone through most of her content, impressed with her style and honesty, feeling an affinity with her subtle northern accent, and imagining that if I were an influencer then I would be just like this woman. Admiration poured out of me like syrup.

'Yeah!! What a kick.' Reuben had jumped up from the sofa and cheered as his team scored. He'd turned to me and flicked his finger at my phone. 'You missed a great goal. Why don't you put your phone down and watch this with me instead of all that Instagram crap? It's much more entertaining.'

Perhaps I should have listened to him. But I didn't.

I'd clicked on Addie's Five-a-Day *follow* button instead.

SEVENTEEN

ADDIE

I can't forget the evening that triggered everything. Springtime, possibly May, last year, and some months before the email arrived from LunaBliss asking me to endorse their retreat.

It was at a point when I had only around twenty thousand followers on my account and notifications of new ones were more of a novelty – and I also remember I'd had a couple of notable 'celebrities' as new followers around that time, too – so I took more interest as they came in.

The sun had just set and I'd closed my curtains. I'd been sitting at the kitchen table and there had been a glitch while I'd been trying to upload a new reel. I think it was a recipe for baked goats cheese with chilli jam. And while I was sitting there getting frustrated with my laptop and my lack of skills and trying to google why I couldn't get it to work, a notification pinged.

I clicked to see who the new follower was.

Gemma Morgan.

When I saw the name and tapped the profile to confirm that it really was the same Gemma Morgan that I'd known, I wasn't immediately hit with a rush of adrenaline, suffocating vertigo or anything like that.

Instead, a slow realisation built up inside me.

Memories came flowing back, little by little, as if they were squeezing through a gap that I'd accidentally left open.

I went to make a cup of tea and while I waited for the kettle to boil, more images popped into my mind, more snippets that induced feelings of fear and disquiet and contrition.

I paced around as my brain took me back into the past, playing reel after reel of images that had been involuntarily blocked by my sanity for twenty years.

Then, in response to my retrospection, I sat down for a while to create a music playlist that boomed out track after mournful track from The Cure, Joy Division, Sisters of Mercy, and The Mission. I turned the volume up full, opening the patio doors to let the sound fly away.

Although it was dark, I went outside into the back garden and, inexplicably, spent time swapping some of the pots of forget-me-nots with the pansies and herb planters. With only the dim glow from some ineffectual solar lights, I rearranged the chairs for the bistro set, pulling a few weeds from between the greening slabs. I stood with my back to the wall for a while and scrutinised the scene before getting the secateurs and attacking an unwieldy clematis that stubbornly clung to the fence.

My elderly neighbour came out and confronted me. 'What are you doing? It's late at night. You're breaking all the trellis. Look at that gap: the fence is damaged now.'

I stared at him and could feel the manic look in my eyes.

'It's not the best time for gardening,' he said, stepping back from his side of the border. 'Not in the dark. And what's with all the horrible music blasting out?'

I couldn't reply, but I abandoned the wrecked clematis, to be possessed by a frantic bout of lopping at the branches of a corkscrew hazel.

'Have you taken drugs?' my neighbour shouted over the broken boundary. 'I could call the police.'

'No!' I screamed back at him so loudly that he retreated to the sanctuary of his kitchen door, where he checked that the key was in the lock.

'Look, love.' There was a tremble in his voice now. 'Please stop it, you're scaring me. My wife's indoors and she's not well; she's trying to sleep. There's no need for all the racket.'

I stopped. I threw the secateurs onto the table and put my hands on my hips. Laughed hysterically for a long time. At one point it seemed like my laughing might turn into crying, but I pulled it back and controlled the wobble in my face.

'Shall I call someone?'

I could see the shadow of the old man who was still there by his kitchen door, peering through the new gaps in our boundary.

'No. No, I'm OK now.' My heart palpitated; my breaths caught in my throat and I felt faint. I edged back indoors, wondering whether to go and lock myself in the bathroom for my own safety.

The patio doors slammed with the wind, and I stumbled into a stool at the breakfast bar. Despondent, my face caved in. My shoulders sagged and I sank back against the wall. The music played on, and the baked goats cheese and chilli jam video uploaded magically at that point without my intervention.

Gemma Morgan.

My new follower. Surely, she wouldn't realise who I really was? Even so, I couldn't possibly follow her back. I wouldn't want to risk *that*.

I washed the soil and sap from my hands, and then my soul started to change, to evolve, as I took myself back twenty years to when Christopher Bray had been my only friend. He had been my everything. I'd loved him.

I'd loved him too much.

EIGHTEEN

GEMMA

The more I watched, the more I wanted to be like Addie. I couldn't get enough. Within five days of following her content, I had the book with the gold cover displayed prominently on my shelf and the headband on order from Amazon.

I loved that her accent was so similar to mine – there was definitely more than a touch of Yorkshire in there – and the reels she made in her own house gave me the chance to glimpse the kind of lifestyle she lived. Stylish, with bold colours on the walls but softened with cosy throws and cushions, not too sleek and showy but almost *achievable*, even in a small, rented terrace like the one where I lived with Reuben. Although the camera angles captured an enviably vast Shaker-style kitchen, Addie made it seem unpretentious with the light-hearted way she delivered her fun, and sometimes even a little chaotic, recipe hacks: she splattered passata on the floor; burnt the toast; and once sliced the end of her finger with a vegetable knife that she was trying to recommend. She was normal, and the type of existence that she put out to the world was within the reach of someone like me.

And, more importantly, her account was such a positive

distraction from the point in every month when my pregnancy test stick would fail to show the coveted two blue lines.

'You've never got that phone out of your hand nowadays,' Reuben said, only a few weeks later, as we ate baked goats cheese with chilli jam, recipe courtesy of Addie's Five-a-Day.

'She's such a nice personality and puts out some great posts every day,' I explained. 'But it's not only clothes and make-up. She does crafting. Fitness advice. And then there's all the lifestyle stuff. Mindfulness and mental health. She's currently involved in helping to develop some kind of secret wild retreat in the mountains. And look at this new one, she's in a vegan café here, sampling their kebabs that are supposed to taste just like real lamb and going crazy about how great they are.'

Reuben took the phone out of my hand and zoomed in. His eyebrows fused together. 'Hang on... I'm sure I know that place. It's called No Bones. Down that little cobbled lane near West Market, remember where I mean?'

'Is it?' I leaned over to watch the video with him.

'You can see behind her through that window... you know, the statue on the corner, next to the Four Feathers pub? That's it, right there.'

I reclaimed my phone to rewind the reel and watch it again, a buzz of excitement starting to tingle in my veins as I recognised the location.

'Oh yes, you're right! Yes, it is. Well, she *must* be local then. I got the feeling that she lived around here. So, that would explain the way she talks and some of the phrases she uses.' I was stirred up even more. 'We could go and try the café out if you like. What if I book us a table for Friday night?'

Reuben grimaced in alarm. 'Vegan?'

'Let's try it. It could be really nice.'

So I reserved a table – the one in the window so that I could sit in the seat where Addie had been – and we turned up and ordered the same doner kebabs that she had eaten, and even Reuben had to admit that the food was surprisingly good.

'Are you hoping that the Instagram woman is going to turn up?' He winked. 'So that you can fangirl all over her and get a selfie?'

My heart skipped suddenly and I looked around at the other tables. She was definitely not there, though.

'No. I don't know.' Somewhat embarrassed, I set my cutlery down on my plate and thought about Reuben's question. Did I want to meet her? Would I get starstruck and tongue-tied in her actual presence? I shook my head and laughed. 'No, don't be silly. It's just a social media thing; it's not like she's a celebrity.'

'Well, I don't know,' said Reuben. 'She is a sort of local celebrity. She's got more followers than most of the bands that play around here.'

He was right, I suppose, but I was dubious about meeting her in the flesh. Maybe I was afraid of being disappointed. Her Instagram account was all I needed; she was an online friend giving out advice and guidance, and I didn't need to worry about whether *she* liked *me*. I trusted her judgement implicitly, knowing that she would never let me down. It was an easy relationship to maintain. Even my best friend, Sophy, could be a bit arsy at times. But Addie...

Reuben flashed me a little knowing smile and said nothing further on the subject. I finished my food and left a large tip.

A couple of weeks later, and with even more of Addie's Five-a-Day endorsements in my possession – an album by a band called Nick Parker and the False Alarms, an ultimate-grip yoga mat, and a new brand of harissa mayo – Reuben came home from work one evening with a surprise for me.

'Wait till you see this.' His face was a picture of exuberant delight and he couldn't keep still. He tapped at his phone.

I watched as the video started to play. Was it one of Addie's Instagrams that I hadn't yet seen? There she was, in a park wearing the quirky designer sports gear she always favoured – this time leopard-print leggings and a stretchy top with the huge face of a tabby cat on it – the slight sheen of perspiration on her face and shoulders as if she'd just finished a run.

'Hiya! Addie here! It's fab to know that you're enjoying my recommendations. Please keep watching my Instagram and invite all your friends to follow me too, and, as I heard that you're going to a wedding soon, you really should treat yourself to that amazing emerald dress.' She looked up then and winked at someone. 'Or get your boyfriend to buy it for you.'

The video went fuzzy for a second and the back of someone's head appeared in the shot as the words *'are we done now?'* could be heard.

'What was that?' I asked him. 'It's not... it can't be on her account...'

'No, it's not on Instagram.' Reuben beamed at me. 'It's a video, just for you. I got you a personalised message from your superhero.'

I did a little dance on the spot and squealed with pleasure. 'What? How? Did you have to email her? Did you pay for it?' I couldn't really accept that it was for *me*.

'No. You're not going to believe this, but I was heading through Graves Park after work and I saw her. Looked like she'd just finished a run and was doing some stretching. I loitered for a bit – obviously I didn't want to look like a stalker – and then went to tell her that you've been enjoying her reels. And I thought, why not ask if she'd do a message for you. Look... proof.' Reuben clicked on a photo and showed me the selfie he'd taken with her afterwards. She had her thumb up to the camera and he had his arm around her.

'Wow. That's awesome.'

'She was so cool about it. And the funny thing is... it turns out that I sort of know her. She's the sister of this guy called Will who used to be in the pub football team. We ended up chatting and she gave me his number so that I can look him up again.'

'So she *is* local, then?'

'Yes. That's why she ends up recommending a load of Sheffield businesses: bars and shops and cafés. I told her that we'd been to No Bones on her say-so and she seemed really pleased.'

'Amazing.' I laughed and shook my head. 'And you're going to get in touch with her brother again?'

'Yeah, why not? Meet up for a drink and a catch-up. See what he's been up to.'

All this degrees of separation thing.

Me and Addie weren't that far apart; I felt closer to her then. She wasn't just an influencer on an Instagram account. She lived nearby. She had personal links to *us*. It even started to seem like we were properly connected.

And I didn't know just how connected we were about to get.

Things moved up a gear on the evening when I arrived home with a new look. Reuben did a double-take and it was a complete mouth-falling-open-in-shock moment.

'What?' he said, his eyes almost popping out on stalks. 'What is going on here?'

It had been an impulsive decision and quite out of character for me. A late period had given me false hope for a pregnancy for a few days even though the tests weren't showing two lines, but then when the dreaded bloodstain had maliciously appeared, I'd dealt with the disappointment by making an appointment at a classy hairdresser's, blowing a chunk of my meagre monthly wages on a decent colour and cut. Then onto the beauty salon for brow reshaping and to get my nails done with lovely French tips (God knows how long they would last in the grotty confines of my portacabin office!) And as if that wasn't enough, I caught a tram up to Twisted Moon studios and got my right helix pierced with a subtle silver ring.

I gave a twirl and a wink, tucking my swinging, glossy hair behind my ear to display the new jewellery. 'Do you like it?'

'Yes, but... Why? You looked fine before.'

'Well, I needed to perk myself up. I was feeling really crap after another negative pregnancy test and I haven't had my hair done for ages. And then I went a bit mad afterwards with the other stuff. You're OK with it, aren't you? Don't you think it suits me?'

Reuben blinked and rubbed his neck. 'Yeah. Yeah, it looks great. It's just that, you know, that Instagram thing you're always watching?'

Oh, here we go, I thought. He's going to do the fangirl rant again.

'Well, it literally looks like you're trying to turn yourself into *her*.' He shrugged his shoulders and then reached out to touch the ends of my newly cropped hair.

'I've turned into *me*, that's all.' I swept a handful of my hair over the top of my head, enjoying the power and silkiness and weight that the new side-parting seemed to give. My fresh confidence took me back to my schooldays, to the time when me and Sophy strutted around school, knowing how we were the fashionable girls that everyone wanted to follow. I hadn't felt like that in years, but my afternoon of rash self-indulgence had boosted my spirits to a new level. 'This is me. The *new* me that is at some point soon going to be your wife and mother of your child. So, get used to it.'

'Hey, it's fine.' He pulled me into his arms. 'It's all good. I love it.'

NINETEEN

ADDIE

After Carys's invitation, I went to see the retreat for myself. All my stresses were left behind as I found myself in the mountains, away from the rush and grime of city life. I went wild-water swimming twice. It was freezing but there was an addictive adrenalin rush that I would never have got from a pool in the Costa del Sol. Around me, there was a continual panorama of something to feast my eyes upon: the array of wildlife; the whorls of crows that appeared without warning above me; the blazing sunsets and the breathtakingly starry skies.

It was a heavenly time, and I returned home feeling truly renewed.

My skin looked fresher; I had a new vitality in my bones; there was a bounce in my step. It was as if I had brought back something of the wild. But there was an odd feeling deep in my belly, too, a feeling like something was missing from my life. I hadn't realised before, but... oh gosh, what had happened to me?

A baby. I wanted a baby.

The retreat visit had got under my skin somehow. I had returned and continued with all my Instagram reels, interacting with my followers and dealing with the day-to-day admin and goods that continued to be sent through the post, but... something was off.

It was like I was a different version of myself.

I downloaded a period tracker app on my phone. I shunned my usual lunchtime ham sandwiches for things like avocado salad with watercress and wild rice. I limited my alcohol units to no more than three per week. I caught myself browsing through the Mothercare website before I was even aware of what I was doing.

Stop it, I told myself. You haven't even got a boyfriend. Stop getting obsessed.

But I was thirty-five, and time was running out.

There was a flurry of deliveries. Handmade chocolate. A range of lip glosses in six colours. Funky-shaped Post-it notes and glitter pens, with the stationery company offering decent money for me to advertise. An invitation for a free meal at The Cider Barn, a new bar in town.

I sighed, wondering whether it was really worth continuing with my Instagram career. Where would it all end? Might there actually be more to life in the real world rather than all this internet stuff?

The money was good, though. Incredibly good.

This deal with the upcoming retreat endorsement was a boost, I thought, giving myself a moment to remember the simplicity of the vast Welsh landscape, the clarity of the icy waterfall. I felt suddenly tearful. Something inside me yearned for open space, endless sky.

I exhaled and clapped my hands together positively, turning back into my normal motivated self. I needed to get on top of the reels. Setting up the tripod, I decided to do a few clips in the kitchen. There were some recipes I was excited about, including one with courgettes and feta cheese, and a cleaning hack that would be suitable.

Later, I sat at the kitchen table to draw up a plan for the week, making a few notes about the products. Then I rang The Cider Barn and booked a table for eight o'clock on a Friday evening before the end of the month, to go and do a video review.

After showering, I tried on some of the products that had been sent to me for possible inclusion, putting all the unusable stuff into a box in the spare room ready to be taken to the charity shop.

I got the camera rolling and, in full influencer mode, began to chop courgettes for my recipe with a smile on my face and a tone of enthusiasm in my voice.

Finally, an hour later, when the casserole dish was out of the oven and I'd served a portion onto a plate, I switched off the camera and wiped down the worktop. It was almost five o'clock and I'd had enough. I needed some me-time, some fresh air before getting back to my laptop to edit and upload the five reels that would be required on my Instagram the next day.

I changed into my favourite running outfit: a quirky T-shirt with the face of a tabby cat on it, and leopard-print leggings, and I headed off out to the park to do some yoga stretches and then my usual three-mile route through the woods.

The day was fine and warm. A smattering of fluffy clouds enhanced the pastel sky. My feet pounded the path, and I reached the point where the path split into two, taking the left fork. It brought me round in a circle to the grassy opening, where people on their way home from work were cutting through to the car park. My Fitbit told me that it had taken thirty-four minutes. A bit slower than last time, I thought.

I did a couple of quad stretches and a downward dog to flex out my muscles. No one usually bothered me, but I noticed someone loitering on the periphery of my vision. A guy with a phone in his hand and a half-smile on his face.

He caught my eye and moved over; some magnetic quality made my insides prickle. A hot spot burned on the back of my neck.

'Hi, sorry to interrupt,' he said. 'You're Addie, aren't you?'

TWENTY

ADDIE

The Cider Barn was, as expected, a cider-themed gastro pub, serving a range of overpriced scrumpy and cider-based cocktails. I was allocated a table in the best corner of the house – my 'fame' always ensured this type of treatment – where I selected the cider braised pork belly from the limited menu.

A paddle of three sample glasses of the most popular ciders was brought over to my table, and I got out my phone to record a clip of me tasting the drinks, before swinging the view around the room to show the other diners and the Friday night vibe. Surprisingly, it was a bit muted. I would have expected more of a buzz at the end of the week.

My food arrived. I cast my eyes over the main course: a small portion in the centre of a sizeable white plate, the edge of which was decorated with snippings of what looked like apple peel and sage. I filmed a talk-through of the food before chewing the first forkful ponderously for my followers.

'Mmm. It's good. Succulent. And that maple mustard flavour pairs really well with the' – I picked up one of the glasses and took a swig – 'I think it might be the perry. Mmm, gorgeous.' Beaming a smile into the lens, I stabbed my fork into the meat. 'Going in again.'

I switched off my phone. A forty-second reel would suffice. The meal was fine but I didn't eat it all; I'd always found pork too heavy to digest easily. Give me seafood any day.

'Was everything all right for you?' the waitress asked as she collected my plate.

'Yes, thank you.'

'Would you like to order dessert?'

'Actually, I'm fine, thanks. I'll pass.'

I checked the time: it was ten minutes to nine. Another waitress was manoeuvring around a large party of young men that had just arrived to see if they could get a table without a prior booking. I considered whether to phone for a taxi, or whether to walk further into the city centre and get a bus.

Give it ten minutes, I decided, then get an Uber. There were two glasses of the taster ciders remaining, and I thought that it would look churlish if I got up and left without drinking them.

I watched as the group of men were led to the other side of the room, where additional staff shuffled three tables together, rearranging the candles and cutlery.

Stag do, I initially thought, but then I noticed that the usual element of bawdiness was missing, and two of the blokes were actually carrying briefcases. Leisurely, I sipped as I slipped into people-watching mode, which was one of my favourite pastimes.

A work event, I concluded, surmising that the guy on the end of the table was the new kid in the company, and the one in the middle with the loudest voice, ordering the drinks, was a manager of some sort. They moved chairs and hung their jackets on the backs and swapped places, and one of them dragged off his tie and undid the top buttons on his shirt so that he could run a hand inside the collar and around the back of his neck, and I found myself focusing on the tanned skin of his throat and the dip of his clavicle...

He seemed familiar. Where had I seen him before?

Suddenly, he looked up. He stared straight at me, and our eyes fused.

Oh gosh. I remembered.

I pulled my gaze away first, and took a long swig of the rhubarb cider as I turned to the window with a flush over the bridge of my nose, watching through the window at girls in stilettos tottering along the pavement.

'Hey, you might not remember me but...' The throaty guy was now standing in front of my table, extending a hand.

'Erm?' I smiled playfully and reached out to shake his hand. I wasn't usually this friendly with fans but I did recall that this bloke rang a different bell altogether.

'Sorry. I'm Reuben. We met in the park a few weeks ago. You'd been running, and I got you to do a video and selfie. And then it turned out that I knew your brother. Remember? We chatted about Will and then I did actually contact him after all those years. We've had a couple of get-togethers since as part of a snooker team...'

'Ahh, yes. He mentioned that he'd joined some snooker thing. Yes. Nice one.'

Reuben. I did indeed remember this guy from the park a few weeks ago. I remembered his smile and the dimple it made at the base of his cheek. I remembered his easy laughter, the trace of his alluring musky scent, the way his blond hair quiffed naturally at the right side of his temple. I remembered how I'd caught the fleeting outline of his biceps as the sun had flashed through the fabric of his shirt, and I remembered how the sight of it had caused me to shift my weight onto the other foot so that I could hook my hand onto my hip and thrust my breasts towards him in the clingy cat-face sports top. I remembered how I'd driven home, startled by the arousal that he'd caused in me, and I also remembered how, when I'd got home, I'd stripped off and stepped into the shower and touched myself under the blameless flow of water as I imagined him pressed up naked behind me.

'Ahh... Reuben. Yes, I do recall the selfie. It's great to see you again.' I pushed out a chair with my foot and indicated for him to join me, but he stood awkwardly, looking back towards his group who were shuffling through paperwork, as the waitress arrived at their table with a tray of drinks.

'Are you alone?' he asked me, and I took it as a sign that he was flirting a little; he was testing me.

'Absolutely. I've been doing some filming. Checking out The Cider Barn offerings. But I'm off-duty now.'

'And will you be staying around for long? It's just that I've got a work debrief that will take about an hour, but if you're still here later I could buy you a drink to say thanks for doing the video?'

He seemed genuinely nice and not someone who would relentlessly pester me online over the next few weeks: I'd had plenty of experience of those types over the years.

And anyway, he was hot.

I checked the time: it was almost nine o'clock. I hadn't booked an Uber yet. 'Sure, that would be great. I'm going nowhere for a while.'

He beamed and rubbed his hand inside the neck of his shirt again. 'Well. See you in a bit.'

The waitress was on her way back to the kitchen. I caught her eye and summoned her over.

'Hi,' I said. 'I've changed my mind and would actually *love* to get a dessert. Could you bring me the menu back, please?'

'Certainly.' She issued a languid smile.

I settled back into my seat and waited.

TWENTY-ONE

ADDIE

'Your girlfriend, then. Did she enjoy the video I recorded for her?' *And are you still with her?* was the question I really wanted to ask, but obviously we needed to build up a rapport before I got onto the more personal questions. At that point I didn't even know his girlfriend's name.

Reuben laughed. 'Yeah. It took her by surprise. She's a massive fan of your Instagram stuff. Clothes. Books. Trying out all the recipes and everything. She goes running now, and she never used to do anything like that, so you're obviously a good influence on her. And she's even had her hair done the same as yours.'

An icy finger scooted its way down my back. 'Really? That's a bit...' I shivered. 'You know. Weird.'

Reuben waved away the oddness as if it was nothing to be alarmed about. 'Sorry. I made it sound a bit crazy but it's not. She just went and got a makeover and... well I suppose you should be flattered. Imitation is the highest form of praise and all that.'

'I suppose,' I conceded. In fairness, I'd had crazier fans than her, like the ones who sent me rants typed in capital letters for using tinned tuna that wasn't assured to be dolphin friendly. 'Well, just let me know if she plans to start stalking me. Perhaps I should give you my number so that you could send me a warning?' I delivered a subtle wink and thought I saw him writhe in his seat.

'I don't think she's a stalker.' He spread his legs wider and scratched his neck. 'But it might be useful to get your number. I mean... I hang out with your brother a lot so...'

'So?' I peered teasingly at him through lowered eyelids, knowing that I did a decent seductive look.

Reuben ran a hand around his throat as he used his other one to open up the contacts on his phone. He paused for a moment, the *name* box empty.

'Not sure whether to type my name in?' Another sultry smile hung itself on my face.

'It's not that...'

'Let me do it.' I reached over and took his phone out of his hand.

I typed the letter 'D' into the *name* box and then put in my mobile number before returning it to him.

'"D"?' he asked, puzzled.

'Yeah, why not.' I giggled. 'You'll remember it's me. Delectable. Dynamic. Delicious.'

He looked at me intensely, his dark and mysterious eyes gleaming.

'What are you drinking?' I took my bank card out of my purse and waved it at the barman who was watching us as he wiped the counter.

'Oh, I'm driving. So just a soft drink, please. Anyway, I offered to buy *you* a drink.'

'No, don't worry, I'll get them. And then maybe I could cadge a lift home from you?' Another coy peek ensured the flow of electricity between us.

We chatted for over an hour, using my brother Will as an

invisible pillar to prop up the conversation. Pub nights, family anecdotes, funny stories about things they'd got up to back in their football team days. Then the dialogue veered a little, and I tried to pry gently into his private life but he was restrained on the topic, giving nothing away.

'What about you?' he asked. He was brave enough to be more direct. 'Is there a husband, a boyfriend waiting in the wings?' He did a comical look over his shoulder and around the room. 'Should I be worried?'

I waved a hand. 'No. I haven't been with anyone for a while. I've had dates now and then, but no one has come along that's impressed me enough to want to move them in with me.' I sipped my cider and raised an eyebrow at him. 'I suppose I've always enjoyed my own company and I get a lot of satisfaction from the work I do, so finding the right man has never really been a priority. Although... I have been thinking lately...'

'What?'

'Well, I'm going to be uncharacteristically open here. My biological clock is ticking. I don't have children but I don't want to end up childless... You know. The sort of thing that women start to think about when they reach a certain age.'

'*Tell* me about it.' He spoke with a tone of experience.

'There's a retreat I've been getting involved with recently. It's a place for couples to stay at where they prepare themselves for parenthood, both physically and mentally. I'm going to be endorsing it when it properly opens, and it is just... well, such a contrast to normal life. Mountains, fresh air, wildlife. I love it. I go there and question what I'm doing with my life, and then I don't want to come home.'

'I know what you mean. I'd love to spend some time off the beaten track, simply exploring and feeling physically worn out at the end of the day. There's nothing like that feeling. I used to do a lot of backpacking during my uni days but... well, it's not easy to continue if you're with someone who'd never go camping or hostelling, and couldn't cope without a hairdryer. Or a phone.' He laughed. 'Your five-a-day thing doesn't help.'

'I used to be like that,' I said. 'But it feels like my priorities are changing. Some days I really can't be bothered with all the Instagram stuff and it just seems so meaningless. It feels like I need to make some big changes in my life. I suppose I shouldn't be telling you this, but, you know...'

'There's nothing wrong with honesty.'

I smiled and looked deep into the inky pools of his eyes. Something made me want to pour everything out, because it felt like he would listen and validate me and have answers and advice for all the things that worried me. Something else entirely made me just want to get my knickers off for him.

He dibbled his finger into a wet ring of cider on the table without breaking his gaze from mine. 'You know, it's funny. I thought you would be a bit unapproachable because you're like, a celebrity really. So, it's nice to find that... well... you're just so easy to talk to. Normal. I feel like I would be comfortable telling you about literally *anything*.'

'We must be soulmates, then.' I floated the idea with an enigmatic expression.

'Yeah. We must be.'

'Are *you* one of my followers? Just out of interest.'

He laughed. 'God, no. I don't do any social media. I've got better things to do with my life.'

I stretched my leg out and touched the toe of his shoe with the tip of mine for a few seconds. He broke the spell by reaching into his pockets and jangling his car keys. 'Sorry to be a party pooper.'

'Am I still OK for a lift with you?' I finished my drink and picked up my bag.

'Absolutely.'

I followed him out to the car park. Every cell in my body tingled in anticipation. He zapped his key fob at a vehicle in the corner and the indicators winked. My skirt rode up too far as I slipped into the passenger seat.

I ran a fingernail on his knee and a little way up his thigh. 'Let's get going, then.'

The car juddered as we drove off.

TWENTY-TWO

ADDIE

Was it the illicit nature of our relationship that made it so incredible? I wasn't sure. But it must have been, because I didn't know then who Reuben's elusive partner was; he was always keen to keep that area of his life completely separate. I reminded myself that we had similar interests, that we enjoyed each other's company. That he was achingly, stunningly hot. But really, I think that what aroused me the most about it all is that I enjoyed being *bad*.

Our time together was limited and we spent a lot of it having sex. It was usually in his car. Sometimes the front seat, sometimes the back seat: there was no specific pattern. I would go out to one of my Instagram assignments – cocktail bar or pizza restaurant or coffee lounge – and spend a short while sampling the menu and making a video review. Thirty minutes before leaving, I would text him with a location – a car park or a farm lane or the edge of a forest – and arrive with a pounding heart and a smouldering between my legs to slide silently into his vehicle. We didn't spend a lot of time on romantic small talk or foreplay. A quick, wordless fuck was the thing that seemed to do it best for both of us, and our main utterances were moans of pleasure, before we adjusted our clothing and took our separate routes home.

Were we actually in a relationship? It was difficult to put a label on what we were doing. We never discussed or analysed our sordid liaisons, yet I was confident that things had started to move in the right direction.

We began to talk more, particularly about our pasts, although I'd edited mine quite severely, unable to bring up the difficult subject of my previous love, Christopher.

He'd talked about his parents, and I'd gauged that they were healthy, normal people, neither of them carriers of genetic disorders. We'd expressed our likes and dislikes, our cultural preferences and favourite films. It was a very promising development.

The more I thought about it, the more I realised that he would be the perfect father for my child. And although time was ticking by, I couldn't rush this, I couldn't risk scaring him off.

He was gorgeous, a real head-turner. He had that striking combination of olive skin, light hair, and eyes so dark that they looked as if he was wearing eyeliner. In his left earlobe he wore a minute silver stud which had a rebelliously youthful quality about it. T-shirts and jeans hung well off his athletic body, and I made the assumption that he was a careful eater as he never seemed to put on excess weight. Intellectually, he was suitable. He had a degree in economics and marketing; he used the correct punctuation in his texts.

He definitely ticked all my boxes.

Dreams started to fill my head. Family scenes that included him and a ravishingly cute toddler that had inherited those enviable sable eyes of his. The three of us in a lush garden, laughing abundantly at some funny thing the child had just said. The three of us cosy in a crumpled bed, opening Christmas gifts. The three of us sitting on a beach eating ice cream.

What was going on in my mind?

I'd had goals for a few years now but they hadn't previously included a baby. They were just fame and fortune scenarios, the usual mansion with a swimming pool kind of thing.

But now...

I wanted it all. And I wanted Reuben's baby.

The Instagram life wasn't enough any more. My heart had been pulled in a different direction. But I couldn't mention any of this, not to someone who thought we were only having a fling, a series of seedy sexual meet-ups with no strings attached. I couldn't *tell* him that I wanted his baby.

I was still taking the contraceptive pill at this point. There was deception and then there was *Deception* with a capital D, and I couldn't do that. Well, certainly not yet.

I decided that I would give it until February.

If things hadn't naturally moved on by then, if I hadn't managed to capture him completely for myself... well, I would just take what I wanted and have his baby anyway.

TWENTY-THREE

ADDIE

It was around October time that everything changed. That was when I found out about Reuben's partner: the one he'd been planning to marry, the one he'd been trying to have a baby with.

I'd had a number of strands going on in my life, all separately simmering along while I watched and waited, engaging at the appropriate times. All the Instagram stuff: the reels and comments and messages. Then there was my work with the retreat, which was progressing but still in the development stage. Then there was my love life/sex life/no strings relationship. Then there was my ever-burgeoning yearning to become a mother, preferably before I reached the age of thirty-six, which didn't give me long.

October was when everything changed.

Finding out by accident just who it was that Reuben lived with turned me around and brought all those strands together.

It had been an unremarkable morning. I'd dealt with my inbox, recorded a reel for my Beautiful Buttocks routine and took in a delivery of parcels. Fruity bath bombs. Ultra shine hair conditioner. Stick-on nail jewels in the shape of tiny elephants. Some kind of frothing gadget. Lime green pyjamas in thin satin, printed with lemons. More CDs from bands I'd never heard of.

My God. The endless conveyor belt of pointless stuff had gone beyond burdensome. It all needed to go. So, I'd packed up everything that I had reviewed in the last few months. Some of the clothing I had worn out in public, but most of it was unused. I couldn't be bothered with listing everything on eBay despite its value. I just wanted to be rid of it.

I'd put it all in the car and driven to the charity shop that I always donated to. In and out I went, through the back delivery door; the volunteers all knew me and were grateful for how much money my goods raised.

My car was parked in one of the spaces at the front of the shop. As I got back into the car my phone rang, and, noticing that it was Carys trying to contact me, I sat and took the call. An irate driver, desperate for my parking space, beeped his horn, and so I indicated to him that I was on the phone. Other cars came and queued and still I sat there, chatting to Carys about website design and menu branding and the questionable practicality of putting chandeliers in the bedroom pods where the ceilings might not be high enough to make the right impression.

We'd been talking for around twenty minutes when my attention was drawn towards a couple at the door of the charity shop where I'd just deposited all my unwanted paraphernalia.

The woman outside the shop was engaged in a dialogue with the man beside her. Remarkably, I noticed her first, because there was something in her bone structure, her mannerisms and the way she swung her handbag onto her shoulder that I thought I recognised. But then... oh gosh, it wasn't, was it? No!

I sat up in my seat, transfixed. The man. It was *Reuben*!

A bemused expression pulled itself across my face at the memory of our last liaison. His shirt undone, tie loose as I straddled him in the back of my car.

I turned and looked at the very seat where we'd been, before returning my focus back on the couple. Carys's voice was still rattling from my phone.

'Hang on, I'll have to ring you back later,' I said. 'I'm in a car park and there's an issue.'

The woman was definitely his partner. She was strikingly attractive, more than I wanted to admit, even though I couldn't see her face straight on. Her hair, very similar to mine, was thicker and glossier, and was draped over the collar of a grey coat. She wore jeans with heels, like I often did when I was out and about, and carried a square handbag, the very type that I'd demonstrated six months ago.

A worm of anxiety squirmed inside me. I felt like I knew her. Maybe she was away from her normal environment; maybe she worked in a shop and I'd encountered her as she'd scanned my purchases. Hmm. Never mind, it would come to me.

I watched them interact. They made an attractive couple and there was that familiarity between them that spoke of years together, of an intimate relationship.

He rummaged in his pocket and handed her something – cash maybe? – and she laughed and gave him a gentle punch on the arm before venturing into the shop. I considered, at that point, sending him a text to let him know that I was watching him, but then dismissed the idea as creepy, thinking that he might view me as a bunny boiler.

Another car turned up and beeped, blocking my view of Reuben waiting outside the shop, but I waved it by and pointed to a vehicle whose reversing light had just come on.

He was still standing there, idly browsing the display in the window: a trio of mannequins in mismatched winter coats and hats. Sauntering a few steps away, he then ventured next door to the pharmacy where he stood and read a poster decorated with a Halloween pumpkin.

Suddenly, I remembered. My heart jolted; my breath caught in my throat. I felt the blood drain from my face.

I *did* know that woman!

It was *her*.

Gemma Morgan.

The realisation left me reeling and I gasped inwardly as I remembered her from twenty years ago: that confident toss of hair, that buttery smile, that captivating way she'd had of attracting everyone who was anyone into her circle of friendship.

I'd been in her class at school for a brief time, until it was decided that I couldn't be around people any more and I was taken away from it all. I wondered if she remembered anything of our school days. How often did the events of those times pop into her mind? I was certain that she wouldn't remember *me*; I'd never called myself Addie in those days, and everything about my look had changed during the intervening years.

Christ, it was like a lifetime ago...

Suddenly, she was in the doorway of the shop again, making her way back outside.

'Are you all done?' Reuben asked her – I was able to lipread his question.

She nodded and reached into a bulging carrier bag of bargains she'd acquired, pulling out some sports gear – leggings and a top – to show him.

A bubble of a laugh escaped involuntarily from my lips, and a speck of saliva hit the steering wheel, glistening like a jewel for a moment. Those were *my* clothes, the ones I'd literally just donated.

She shoved them back into the bag and took his arm as they walked away, past the chemist's, towards the precinct.

I laughed again and took my phone out to send a location and type a text.

Hey, I'm in need of fun. Meet me at 7?

From my driver's seat in the car, I saw the couple right before they disappeared around the corner. That slight jump as Reuben got the notification on the phone in his pocket. That discreet way of retrieving it, tilting it sideways so that he could read it without her seeing.

My body resonated with unfettered glee.

My phone pinged with a reply.

TWENTY-FOUR

ADDIE

Seeing them together as a couple outside the charity shop agitated yet galvanised me. This new knowledge changed everything. *Everything.*

I pondered how to handle it.

Should I tell Reuben that I'd seen him with his partner and let the conversation about her identity and their relationship spill out organically? He was unlikely to know that I had past history with his girlfriend. Hmm. I considered my reputation as an influencer and wondered if stirring things up might be too damaging.

I could just watch and wait; I could just leave them alone. Or I could download a dating app and find someone else to hook up with instead.

But...

He was gorgeous. We had a lot going together, and it genuinely felt like things would work well if our relationship progressed. I couldn't bear to lose him at this point.

He'd replied to my text immediately.

Yes! See you later x

Then he would have deleted everything from his phone; he was careful like that.

I manoeuvred out of the car park and went home to consider my options. Despite having to make decisions around this new curveball, the news that Gemma Morgan was Reuben's fiancée seemed to make my body even more desperate for vehemence and vigour; I craved the physicality of my insides clenching, his body grinding on mine until I stung. My mind lusted after what I shouldn't have; it was an adrenaline-rush of immorality.

We met up on the outskirts of the city, on pot-holed waste ground behind a car tyre warehouse. It was unlit and strewn with broken bricks, the sort of place that might attract drunks and drug dealers. A rusty white van, seemingly empty, was parked near the building, and a stringy stray whippet nosed around for a while, but apart from that, we had the place to ourselves.

I slipped into Reuben's back seat – it was more spacious than mine – and he clambered over the gear stick to join me. Within seconds, my shirt was open, bra loose, skirt up to my waist. Fevered with horniness, we clawed and sucked, kneaded and tasted each other's salty skin until I straddled him and we rocked frenetically, the vehicle's suspension going with our rhythm, condensation running on the windows, until it was done and we buckled softly around each other to let our racing hearts subside.

'God, that was good.' He rested his head on my shoulder and pressed his lips to my neck. 'I often wonder what it would be like to have you in an actual bed.'

A deep-throated laugh frothed out of me. 'You want me to take you home with me?'

'Well, I wouldn't turn down the offer.'

'A full night? I can rustle up a decent breakfast.' This was surely an opportunity to test him.

'Hmm. I thought our agreement had always been a mutually beneficial no-strings-attached series of sex gigs... I got the impression that you didn't want me in your house.'

I climbed off his lap, rearranging my clothes. The temperature had dropped. 'What if I've changed my mind?'

He lifted his eyebrows. 'Tell me more. I like the sound of this.'

'Well... we're getting into winter. The nights are cold; our cars are not the most comfortable. I have a big bed that is cosy and welcoming.'

'Ooh, just think what we could do in all that space.' His index finger stroked a trail from my neck down to my breast.

'Exactly.'

There was a pensive moment of anticipation. Was he suggesting that we go back to mine *now*? I tried to remember if the bedroom was tidy, if I'd picked up my clothes from the floor of the en suite.

There was a ping on his phone. He rummaged in the pocket of his trousers, which were on the floor of the car, and checked his text discreetly.

'Everything all right?' I asked, after he'd let out a spontaneous sigh.

An intake of breath accompanied a furrowed brow. 'Yeah, it's just...'

'What?'

'Don't worry about it. She's just so bloody needy sometimes.'

I felt a chance to probe presenting itself. He didn't normally offer this information up willingly. 'If you want to offload...'

He shook his head. 'Look, I don't want to spoil our time together telling you about *her* woes.'

'If it helps...'

But he didn't reply. He wriggled back into his clothes without mentioning her again. The vibe had soured.

'How about we go for a quick drink somewhere?' I suggested, mainly to break the silence.

He brightened. 'OK.'

We drove in our separate cars to a big chain pub next to a retail park, where we found a quiet corner away from the carvery station. I kept my back to the other drinkers and diners, and he returned from the bar with two small glasses of red wine which we eked out for an hour.

'Any news from the trenches?' I enquired with the ghost of a sneer on my face, but it turned out that he'd switched his phone off anyway because he hadn't wanted another diatribe while we were here.

We talked. It was something we hadn't done properly since that night at The Cider Barn. We chatted about my Instagram account and the weirdness of my fans. I told him about my involvement in the retreat and all the fantastic plans for it, and when I said where it was located we did that middle-aged thing of discussing routes and speed restrictions.

'So, it's a couples type of place?' he asked.

'It's a fertility retreat. Quite a niche idea really. But it's aimed at couples who are trying, or thinking about planning to have a baby.'

He went quiet and stared at his outstretched fingers for a worryingly long time, until I reached over to caress his hand and ask if he was OK.

'Have you got children?' he said.

'No. I've never been married or had a long-term partner. I keep thinking that I ought to, because my youthfulness is running out, isn't it?'

'Well, same here.' He gave a hollow laugh. 'I'd like to be a father. In fact, I'll be honest with you, we've been trying for a while. It was her idea at first, but I got swept along too, and it's been about eight months now but nothing seems to be happening for us. The text earlier was to let me know that the most recent test is another negative one. That means she's going to be in tears when I get home and hassling me again about IVF.'

Was I supposed to commiserate with him on the news that his partner couldn't get pregnant? It seemed ironic that he was planning to father a child with someone else while we were regularly meeting up for sex in our cars. But the thought now of having Reuben's baby had suddenly become even more attractive. To have the very thing that Gemma was also desperate to have... It was the perfect challenge.

'I don't know what to do about it all.' A resigned breath puffed hopelessly out of him. 'We were supposed to be planning a wedding and... I don't know. I'm not even sure if I want to spend the rest of my life with her.'

Well.

This additional revelation left me reeling. I made some pitying noises and fondled his hand in between sips of the hideous wine. He clammed up again, as if he'd already said too much.

The pub thinned out and staff came to wipe tables and switch off some of the lights even though it wasn't yet nine o'clock. My glass was still half full: I'd lacked the appetite for drinking in this soulless place.

'Time to go, I'm afraid,' I said, checking my watch and downing the rest of my harsh Shiraz.

'Did you say something about a warm bed at your house?'

I blinked in surprise.

'I mean, I can't stay for the full night, but...'

It didn't matter that the bedroom and en suite might be in a state of untidiness. I had to grasp this fortuity before it passed me by.

'Follow me,' I said as I got into my car and he got into his.

I reversed out of my space and set off with Reuben behind me.

THE RETREAT

TWENTY-FIVE

GEMMA

Reuben? How can it be him? How can he turn up like this after all these months? How can he be married to Addie? So this must mean that... no, oh no, it can't be. My stomach clenches in pain. It's true, isn't it? It means that Reuben is the father of her baby. Oh my God, how is this nightmare happening?

My limbs feel floppy; my soul is crushed. It's like Addie has stormed into my life and stolen everything from me.

I'm the only one still sitting, while everyone else stands around with a variety of expressions on their faces. Matt appears to be baffled by everything.

There's a pause which is beyond awkward. Even Jozef stiffens behind the bar, a wet glass frozen in his hand. Addie is the only one still smiling.

Finally, Tom speaks. 'Well, this is a surprise.'

Reuben scratches his head and looks at Addie. 'I didn't know... I wasn't aware that you... all you lot were here. I mean...'

'Do you know these people?' Addie asks him with an air of innocence.

Sophy steps forward, her body latent with stroppiness. 'Of course he knows us. Because the love of your life has turned out to be Gemma's ex-fiancé, hasn't he? The guy who cheats and then disappears without any sort of apology or explanation. Isn't that right, Reuben?'

'What?' There's a crimson stripe rising up from Matt's neck. 'So, *you're* her ex?'

'Look, as I said, I wasn't aware...' Reuben holds out his hands ready to fend off our attacking party.

'And now you've turned up here, *married*? Married to *her*? Having a *baby*?' Sophy has moved in closer. 'We were supposed to be your friends and you blocked us all and then we find out like this...'

'It was complicated.' Reuben tries again. 'It was like...'

'You're a fucking *snake*.' Sophy's voice has risen at least three tones. 'How do you think Gemma feels about all this? She was *heartbroken* when you left.'

Matt tugs at his shirt collar before striding off to go and stand at the bar with his back to us all. What must he think of this chaos?

'Hey. Hey, let's try and be sensible, shall we?' Tom reaches for Sophy's arm. 'Let's sit down and behave like grownups.'

Sophy slaps Tom's arm away. 'Was it you?' She points at Addie. 'Were you the one that he was seeing behind Gemma's back? Did you instigate it?'

Oh God, I can't bear this. I can't bear to be here, unable to speak for myself, sitting in the centre of what can only be described as a catastrophic fuck-up.

'Sophy, don't,' I say. 'It doesn't matter. I've got Matt now and it's all good. Let's just leave it alone.' I stumble to my feet hoping that no one can see the tears in my eyes. Oh God, this is all so embarrassing. And agonising, too. To think that all those months of me and Reuben trying for a baby to no avail, and then he's here with her, flaunting their fertility for all to see. It can only mean that it must be me; it must be my fault. I'm *never* going to get pregnant, am I?

I push past everyone and head for the door. Outside, I gulp at the air and make my way along the footpaths and through the pergolas to arrive at the seating around the firepit, where I slump onto a bench. The sun still shines, burning the back of my head, and insects chatter in the undergrowth. Buzzards circle overhead. Beyond my chaos, life goes on normally.

It feels as if everything has culminated in my humiliation. Matt must despise me now. Reuben will have zero respect for me. Tom and Sophy pity me.

And Addie... How could I have been so full of admiration for her? So willing to follow her advice? So *trusting*? I feel conned, tricked. It almost seems as if she intentionally organised this meet-up just to demean me.

There's the sound of footsteps, flip-flops slapping along the path, and I hastily pull in some deep breaths to try and regain an element of composure.

'Oh God, there you are!' Sophy rushes to envelop me in a hug as if she'd expected me to have thrown myself off a mountain. 'Are you OK?'

I hold my palms out. 'A surprise like that is probably the last thing I expected from a week at a fertility retreat.'

'I can't believe it. And for them to stroll in, so blasé like that: *look at us, we just got married...*' Sophy puts on a silly voice, and I have to smile at her.

'It did seem like a surprise for Reuben, too,' I say. 'You didn't need to shout at everyone, Soph. It made it seem as if I'm still upset about him. And I'm not; I'm happy with Matt now. God, how must *he* feel about the whole scene?'

We sit silently together for a few minutes, in a state of shellshock.

'What do we do now?' says Sophy. 'We've got to spend the rest of the week here, all of us together.'

.   .   .

Matt is perched on the end of the bed when I return to our room. 'It was great to meet your ex like that,' he states flatly.

I stand in front of him and touch his shoulder. 'I'm sorry. What else can I say? *I* didn't plan it.'

He watches his feet as his heels kick at the polished wooden floor. 'You obviously still have strong feelings for him. That's the impression I got.'

I throw my arms into the air and pace towards the door. My whole body is jittery with distress. 'I don't have feelings for him! Not at all! It was a bombshell after not seeing him for months. After not knowing where he went or who he was with.'

'I can get that it was a shock. But you seemed upset about it, and it's like Sophy knows that you're not over him, and that's why she got angry... I just felt so stupid being there in the middle of it all.'

His words touch a nerve in me. 'Matt, I'm sorry. I love *you*, not him. Look, it's really crap that he's turned up and I don't know how it's happened, but I'm with you and we're married now and we're here because we want to start a family and—'

'Yeah, right.' Matt stands and goes into the en suite, slamming the door behind him.

'Matt, please.' My pulse is hammering in my ears and I feel sick because we haven't eaten yet, and all the earlier conflict has stirred up my adrenaline to the point of exhaustion.

'I'm getting the feeling that you only wanted me so you could get pregnant.' His blunt statement, with the bathroom door between us, chokes me so that I can't reply.

Through the window I see Tom and Sophy in the distance, in deep conversation, striding back to the dining area. My stomach gurgles with hunger, and I'm reminded again of how the six of us were supposed to be dining together and having an enjoyable evening socialising. What a farce it has all been. I should get out of this ridiculous outfit and wash the make-up off my face and pull myself together even though I feel like shit.

I strip out of my dress and drag on leggings and a loose T-shirt.

'Matt.' I knock on the bathroom door carefully. 'Matt, please. I need the bathroom. And we need to talk.'

'Maybe we should go home.' His voice sounds gravelly, like he's been crying.

'Please, open the door.'

'I don't know why I bothered agreeing to come on this holiday with you. You'd rather have been here with *him*.'

'Matt, please. I don't want us to be like this. We've had a lovely time so far...'

The door opens. The rims of his eyes are red and his lips are pursed.

'I'm sorry,' I say, holding out my arms. We have to find a way of sorting this out because we can't have Addie and Reuben getting between us.

I hug him hard until he hugs me back, until there's some kind of warmth regenerating.

'We should leave,' he says as we sit down, side-by-side on the bed. 'We should pack up our stuff and go. There's no point in staying.'

'Sophy and Tom will have to go too,' I remind him. 'We gave them a lift here.'

He nods. 'Yeah, but I can't imagine that they're enjoying the vibes after what happened earlier.'

I relent. 'OK. I'll speak to Sophy first, and we'll probably have to tell Jozef or someone so that the buggy can come and pick us up.'

'Ahh...' Matt grimaces. 'I don't know if the situation might have changed, but it couldn't get through before because of a fallen tree.'

'Well, I'll check anyway. If we have to walk, then that's what we'll do.' I'm determined to make things right with Matt, who has been caught up in the aftermath of my heartbreak through no fault of his own.

I unravel the French plait in my hair. Anger begins to fill the cracks in my heart. How could Addie do this? What is she trying to achieve?

'Can I ask you something?' Matt grabs my hand. 'And will you be honest with me?'

A jolt runs through my body. 'What?'

'Are you hiding something?'

My breath catches in my throat and makes me cough. 'No, what makes you think that?'

He stares into my eyes. 'I don't know. Just the feeling that you're keeping a big, big secret.'

Spasmodically, my eyes blink as I press the soles of my feet hard into the floor.

I force a smile onto my face. 'Of course I'm not.'

I don't want to lie to him, but sometimes life requires it.

TWENTY-SIX

ADDIE

We sit alone – Reuben and me – in the dining area as Jozef moves one of the tables to the edge of the wall, rearranging the place settings for the two of us rather than six.

'Why didn't you tell me?' Reuben asks. He's been rubbing despairingly at his face and his neck since the whole episode half an hour ago. 'I would never have come if I'd known that *she* would be here.'

I reach for his hand and pull his fingers to my lips so that I can kiss the stress out of him. 'Darling, I didn't *know*. It was a randomly generated giveaway, a promotion where thousands of people applied and one name got picked. How could I have guessed that your ex would be the one who won? I run these kinds of things all the time with no problems.'

'She followed you obsessively, though. There was a possibility that this could have happened. You should have told me who was going to be here, and I could have headed it off.'

'But I didn't know who she was! You hardly talked about her, and in fact I don't recall you ever telling me her name! Did you expect me to be telepathic? And, as I said, thousands of people applied.'

He groans and pulls his hand away from me to pluck helplessly at his own lips. 'Do we really have to be around them for the full week? I feel like it won't end well.'

'Calm down,' I tell him softly. 'For now, let's eat. We can keep a low profile and have different mealtimes to them. It will probably blow over when they all realise what a fuss they've made over nothing.' I realise that I still have yoga sessions scheduled for the rest of the break and wonder how they might play out in these fragile circumstances.

Jozef approaches our table with a platter of tapas dishes and a comforting smile. 'I hope things are all right now.'

'It's fine, thanks. Just a misunderstanding.'

Jozef returns to the bar, and Reuben stabs at the food. 'OK. I don't want to get embroiled in anything else. They don't know the rest, do they...?'

'Oh gosh,' I reply. 'You mean the baby? I'm so sorry, Reuben. I told them all earlier. It was just going that way.'

The door clatters open, and I turn to see Sophy and Tom pacing towards the bar without looking towards us.

'Excuse me, could I take our food out so that we can eat it elsewhere?' Sophy says to Jozef in a clipped tone of superiority.

They wait in silence by the bar, their backs to us, until Jozef returns about ten minutes later with a tray of plates, cutlery and plastic tubs of food. They sail past our table, and Sophy holds the door open for Tom to carry everything through, hissing 'enjoy your meal' at us on her way out.

'So, *they* used to be your friends?' I ask Reuben as I raise an eyebrow.

He huffs and spears a piece of chicken. 'Yeah, I know. But people take sides when couples split up, and they took hers. I suppose I can't blame them. They're just angry about what happened. Maybe I shouldn't have been such a coward; I should have faced up to her and done the right thing.'

'It's over now,' I tell him. 'Don't beat yourself up. Relationships break down and people move on; it's all part of life. And she's moved on too. She's married to Matt and they want to have a baby.'

Reuben sets his cutlery down, an anguished expression on his face. 'She can be difficult, though. She often got jealous for no apparent reason...'

'Hey, look, it's been a shock for everyone, meeting up like this. But we're grownups, aren't we? We simply need to bite our tongues for a few days and try to be civil. It's part of my contract that I deliver the yoga sessions and be on site for the week, so I can't leave early. And, really, if we do stay here it's not like anyone is going to die, is it?'

Reuben laughs. 'No. No I suppose it isn't.'

We both laugh.

I pick up my fork to resume my meal. We have to stay, whatever happens. I can't go now I've come this far.

There's so much more fun to be had.

TWENTY-SEVEN

GEMMA

Sophy and Tom are heading past our room with a tray of food as I open the door.

'I've got our evening meal,' she says. 'Let's go and eat around the firepit, away from the others.'

I follow them along the path with Matt trailing behind me. We can have dinner, then we can make plans to leave the retreat.

'Are you OK now?' Sophy asks me quietly. 'Are things all right with Matt?'

'I don't know. It's all turned out to be a disaster, hasn't it? He wants to go home.'

'Really?' Tom seems disappointed. He puts the tray down on one of the benches. 'I suppose that means...' He looks towards Sophy, who gives a vague shrug.

'It won't be easy staying with an atmosphere hanging over us, with those two here as well. And it's not fair on Matt either.'

They share out the food between the four plates.

'I know that means you'll have to leave too, or make other arrangements for travelling home later, so that's a bit crap and I'm sorry...'

Matt comes and picks up a plate, sitting meekly at the end of the bench.

'Don't we need to organise that guy with the buggy to come and get us?' says Tom.

'He won't be able to,' Matt replies. 'Remember, the track's blocked.'

'Oh great, so we'll have to walk?' says Sophy with some sarcasm. 'Like moving about in this heat is fun while being pregnant and carrying a massive rucksack.'

'It's all turned out a bit shit, hasn't it?' I say to Sophy, who is making the most of the olives and hummus and ciabatta.

'Look, we don't have to go. We could stay and try to keep out of their way.'

Tom chips in. 'Have you considered that they might be feeling as awkward as we do?'

'Maybe it's time to bury the hatchet,' says Sophy. 'Some people end up being friends with their exes, don't they? And now you're both married to different partners and getting on with your lives...'

'But what about Matt?'

We all turn to look at him. He's definitely not comfortable with the situation.

'I can cope.' His voice is stiff. 'As long as Gemma's not fawning all over him.'

'Oh God, why would I do that?' I protest. 'I'm done with Reuben. I'm here with *you*, to try and have a baby!'

We all look around at each other, trying to read each other's minds.

'How about we give it a couple of days?' says Tom finally. 'See how it goes, and if any of us aren't comfortable with the situation, we'll decide to leave then. That way, we might be able to get the buggy back to the car park if the fallen tree is moved.'

'Good idea,' Sophy replies. 'How about it, Gem? Just a couple of days?'

I meet Matt's eyes, and he shrugs. 'Up to you.'

We were doing so well here. I had such high hopes for us.

'OK,' I say. Maybe there's still time for me to get pregnant. 'Let's see how things are by Tuesday and make a decision then. Anyway, they might decide to leave in the meantime.'

'Well, that would be the ideal scenario.' Sophy smiles before her expression turns serious. 'You know, I think it might be a good idea if you don't follow Addie's account any more when you get home.'

Sophy is right again. She always seems to know what's best for me.

'Yeah, when I get my phone back, I'm going to delete Instagram. And the rest of my social media. I've realised that it's not good for me.'

What would I get from Addie's Instagram anyway? Information about the progress of her pregnancy, and how fantastic it is to be married to Reuben? No, I would definitely be better off not knowing. I don't care about her recipes and fitness routines. Or any of the other things that I copied for over a year. Hair, fashion sense, lifestyle hacks. How could I have been so gullible?

On the face of it, it seemed like I was trying to steal *her* life, but then she came along and stole mine instead.

The husband I almost had. The baby I wanted more than anything.

How *could* she?...

'Shh.' Sophy puts a finger across her lips.

We freeze on the bench as we hear footsteps.

Suddenly, Addie appears through the vegetation, to stand in front of us. 'Gosh, here you are. I came to check that you're OK. It turned out to be a bit of a surprise earlier, didn't it?'

'You could say that.'

'Oh, gosh, how can I apologise? I feel terrible.' She puts her hands over her chest and gazes up to the sky with welling eyes. 'I'm so, so sorry. Really I am.'

'You weren't to know,' says Tom.

'I never realised when I arranged it all.' Addie looks straight at me. She must think that I can't hear the insincerity in her voice. 'Reuben never ever spoke about you, so I didn't even know your name. It seems so unprofessional, doesn't it, and I normally wouldn't have let anything like this happen.'

I shrug as if I don't care. As if I don't mind knowing that I mattered so little to Reuben that he never bothered to mention me. How long had he been seeing her? Weeks? Months? A picture flashes into my memory of a selfie on Reuben's phone, of him with his arm around Addie, at that time when he got her to do the personalised video for me. Was that the start of their relationship? So she knew he wasn't single, didn't she? She knew that she was stealing him from someone else.

'You must be devastated,' she says.

I stand up to face her. 'Actually, I don't care at all. I'm blissfully married to Matt who's a million times better than *him*, so I'm quite happy for you to have Reuben, and the best of luck to you both.'

'Oh, darling, I'm so pleased that the whole episode hasn't upset you; I was worried that you'd want to leave.' She reaches to stroke my arm, and I flinch at the condescension in her touch.

'*We're* not going,' I say, wondering why no one else is joining in with the discussion. 'We're going to stay and make the most of it.'

'Gosh, that is literally the best news. I'm so pleased. We'll make it work, won't we? In such a beautiful place as this, how could we fail to get on with each other? The thought that there might be conflict was making me worry about this little chipmunk in here.' She cups her hands over her tiny abdomen. 'Stress can have such a negative effect on a pregnancy.'

'It's all gonna be great,' Tom says. 'So don't worry about us. We're fine.'

* * *

'Patronising cow,' I say, when Addie has left the group and is out of earshot.

Tom laughs as if I'm being ridiculous. 'Patronising? She was only coming to try and smooth over the situation, and check that she hadn't offended us.'

'She's having a baby, too, remember,' Sophy adds.

'But she just seems to make such a drama out of everything. It's like everything always has to be about her.' I can't help loading my tone with bitterness.

Matt gives me a sympathetic look but doesn't respond.

'I thought you were her biggest fan?' Tom really seems to be gunning for me now. He's switched sides. He's been turned by Addie's charms. 'You follow her on social media and you ended up getting this free holiday, but now you've gone all weird and taken against her—'

'Gone all weird?' I puff out my chest indignantly. 'What d'you mean, *gone all weird*? I don't care that she's with Reuben. It really doesn't matter to me.'

Matt stands up and holds out his hands. 'Hey, let's be friendly. We're here together on holiday and I think all the fertility stuff and the group dynamics is a bit of a tricky mix.'

'I'm only saying... Addie wasn't doing anything wrong. She came to make peace and check we were all right...' Tom shakes his head. 'Is it because she mentioned her pregnancy again?'

Sophy glares at him. 'Leave it, Tom.'

'We're at a fertility retreat, though. People are going to be announcing pregnancies, aren't they?'

Matt comes to crouch by the side of me and wrap an arm around my knees. I take some long breaths instead of retaliating to Tom's comment. Doesn't he realise how inadequate I feel around all these women with their unborn babies blossoming inside them?

Sophy goes over to Tom's bench and there's a brief discussion in hushed tones. Eventually, he comes to put a hand on my shoulder.

'Sorry, Gem. I wasn't thinking. No hard feelings, eh?'

I shrug and mumble in response. There's no point in continuing the argument: Sophy and Tom are my only real friends and I wouldn't want to jeopardise our relationship. In fact, Sophy and me have been totally solid since we were at school, covering each other's backs against every purported threat possible. I'd quite feasibly *die* if I didn't have her in my life.

Matt stands up and presses his hand to my belly. 'Come on, Gem,' he whispers. 'It'll all be OK. By the end of the week, we could have our own little one in here.'

I smile at him. I have to be positive.

'Yeah. By the end of the week, who knows what might have happened.'

TWENTY-EIGHT

GEMMA

Breakfast is a sheepish affair of almond croissants and strawberries, with Addie and Reuben sitting on their own table at the far side of the dining room. We all speak quietly and behave genially, subdued by yesterday's embarrassment.

Just before we've finished, they venture across to our part of the room, where Addie reminds us that yoga will be happening again at eleven o'clock and that she hopes we will all be joining her. There is no mention that Reuben will be involved.

'Great,' says Tom with a genuine spirit of enthusiasm. 'You can count on us.'

A graceless pause provokes Reuben into scratching his head and embarking on a statement. 'Guys, about last night. It was just one of those... well, situations I suppose. I want to say that I'm sorry about how I dealt with the whole' – he waves his hand towards me rather than say my name – 'episode where I did a moonlight flit from you. But it's great to see that you two' – he waves his hand between me and Matt this time – 'have got something going, and you're moving on, and I really hope that we can let bygones be bygones so we can be friendly and have a good week.' He inhales deeply, looking towards Addie as if seeking her approval.

I clench my jaw and look at the crumbs on my plate. It's Matt who responds.

'Well, that's what we want, too. I don't assume that we'll end up being best mates, but if we can get along OK while we're here, then that will be enough.' I half expect him to offer a handshake, but his arms stay firmly folded.

Addie claps and beams, doing a strange sort of bow towards us as we remain seated at our table. 'Well, that's fabulous. I'll see you all at yoga.'

I watch as she turns and walks away with Reuben, and something stirs in me, like dust being kicked. Something in her tone, or the way she moves, or a facial gesture... I can't say what it is exactly, but it gives me a shivering sense of déjà vu.

'Sophy.' I touch her arm, thinking that she might have experienced it too, but she's busy pouring herself another cup of tea.

We all arrive back in the dining room later. If it had been up to me I wouldn't have bothered coming, but everyone else thought it politically correct to attend.

Addie is standing, facing us all, a seriously mindful expression on her face. Thankfully, this time, I'm not wearing the same clothes as her. And I'm happy to see that Reuben is absent.

'Hi, everyone.' She taps her Fitbit and doesn't meet our eyes. 'Let's loosen up. It's only going to be a short stint this time, but it will be fun.'

I've done all the sessions from her 'Yoga For You' series, so I know the type of moves and flows she is likely to throw in, and I'm fairly confident that I won't make a fool of myself.

But once we've warmed up she's demonstrating the Crow Pose, which I know I definitely can't do without falling and breaking my nose, and the Scorpion, which has all of us floundering pathetically on our mats.

Matt and Tom are in hysterics.

'I used to be able to do a headstand, but this is impossible,' says Sophy, toppling over for the third time. 'Can't we do something easier?'

I'm trying as hard as I can to balance, but my arms are shaking, and within seconds I have collapsed to the floor again.

'Keep practising, and it will come. You need to tone up your bodies.' Addie moves towards me and bends my legs into a pose that I'm unable to hold for more than a second. 'I think you need to do some serious work on your thighs.'

'Yes! Yes, you've nearly got it.' She attends to Matt then, who has somehow got himself into a Crow, and she puts a commendatory hand on his back.

I look away to stop myself from reacting. She's trying to provoke me, isn't she? And there is nothing about this session that is worthwhile. My shoulder is aching and it feels like I have a bruise on my knee. She shouldn't be trying to make us do all this advanced stuff: it's not only dangerous but it makes us feel stupid and useless. It's as if she wants to show off her own fitness instead of helping us. And anyway, how is this supposed to improve fertility?

Annoyance bubbles inside me like lava, and I'm glad when the session finally ends.

'That was fun, wasn't it?' says Matt. 'I think she did a great job of distracting from all the bad feeling last night and getting us back on track. She certainly knows her stuff, doesn't she?'

I clamp my mouth shut and push the door open to go outside.

Matt and I are on our own, sitting beside the empty firepit. Sophy has changed into a long cotton dress and wide-brimmed hat, and she and Tom have romantically gone off to explore the footpaths on the other side of the mountain.

I don't want to be with them. All the pregnancy talk makes me feel so inadequate. I just want to stay here, to wallow and think, to visualise my ovaries as healthy organs waiting for the right sperm. In our room is a book about manifestation, about claiming things that we truly want, and how that can happen. Positive thinking, basically.

I need to do more of that, I tell myself. It *will* happen. I need to embrace the fact that this week I am ovulating, and we are in a special place that is properly geared up with all the nutritious food and mindful therapies in a stunning location, and there is no reason at all why I shouldn't be returning home without a tiny scrap of a baby – *my* baby – snuggled inside me.

'Do you fancy going inside?' I ask Matt.

'Is that a proposition?' He wiggles his eyebrows, then he's up off the sun lounger within a fraction of a second.

We lock the door of our pod and tear off our clothes. It's cooler in here, more pleasant on the skin and on our intentions. I throw myself on top of the duvet and wait as Matt switches the privacy setting on the glass door.

'How about I read some love poetry?' He puts on a low, throaty voice and selects a book from the shelf. 'Get us in the mood.'

'Go on then,' I reply salaciously.

He flicks through the book and a piece of paper drops out, fluttering to the floor.

He stoops to pick up the paper. 'Here's one. It's called "Wild Nights", by someone called Emily Dickinson. Have you heard of her?'

'Yes.' A long time ago, during my school days. Poetry was only something that I engaged with for my English exams. But the surface of my memory is scratched somehow...

'OK. It seems quite relevant, so I'll go with this.' He smiles and sits beside me on the bed. Here we are, in our nakedness, with a typed poem on a dog-eared wisp of paper, ready to initiate our passion.

Matt smiles and begins to read the poem to me. And then the words... they somehow needle into my recollection.

My chest is rigid and tense. 'Stop it. Please. I don't think...'

But Matt is in the moment, putting on a performance for me, and he's enjoying himself too much to stop until he's recited the final line. '"Might I but moor tonight in thee!"'

Suddenly my stomach caves in. Cold sweat breaches my forehead, and I jump from the bed to run into the en suite, hanging over the toilet basin as I vomit up my breakfast.

Then Matt is in the doorway. 'Oh wow, Gem, do you think...?'

I turn, with sour strands of saliva dangling from my chin.

'Do you think you've got morning sickness already?'

I can't reply. It's a ridiculous question anyway; does he know nothing about pregnancy? Breathless, I spit into the toilet as fear starts to take hold of me and my face crumples, then I'm sobbing uncontrollably, sinking to my knees on the cold marble floor, totally overwhelmed by everything.

Matt comes to me, to pull me up into his arms, to try and calm my convulsing body.

'What is it?' He holds me and strokes my hair. 'Darling, what's wrong?'

I can feel his heart thudding as we're pressed together, but I can't stop myself crying for long enough to try and explain. It's as if everything has rolled like a snowball into a monstrous orb of stress.

'Please, tell me. Is it *not* morning sickness? Has something else happened that's upset you? Is it something to do with all the baby announcements? Is that what it is?'

Well, those have certainly contributed to my state of mind. Both of Sophy's attempts to get pregnant have been effortless, and even though she's my best friend I can't help feeling jealous. And then there's the fact that I wasn't able to make a baby with Reuben yet Addie has. But it's not just that; it's more a culmination of things that are cramming into my mind and making me question everything, examine everything, opening up old wounds and fears so that I feel like I'm on the verge of craziness.

'But you're not normally ill like this, are you? Not to the point of vomiting.'

He's continuing his persistent probing even though he can see that my body is stricken with involuntary sobs.

'I wondered if it might be the pastries we had earlier, because that almond thing didn't sit well with me either and I ended up leaving mine, but you're not usually a sickly person, are you? That's why I'm thinking it could be morning sickness. You could be pregnant. We could be having a baby.'

I shake my head to indicate that I don't think he's right, it's too early for any pregnancy symptoms and far too soon to be hopeful and start thinking like that...

'Why don't you do a test? There are some free ones in the welcome pack. That's how Sophy and Tom found out. And then if you are, we can all celebrate together, can't we? We can announce it at the evening meal to the others.'

I gasp in a lungful of air. He moves away from me to squat on the floor and rummage through the basket of complementary stuff that contains things like herbal tea sachets, vitamin capsules and scented intimate wipes.

'No, I can't do a test yet. I'll do one the week after we get home.' I manage to squeak out the words before retreating to the en suite to press my face with a cold flannel.

He appears, waggling a long, thin box. 'We could do one now and then we'd know, wouldn't we? It says that these are early detection ones.'

'It won't work yet.' I push away his hand that is holding out the box. Doesn't he realise that it's too soon to find out? We need to wait. We need to give this week everything we can while we're here, but we won't know for at least another ten days if it has worked. Does he know nothing about ovulation?

He stares at me, the test held loosely in his dangling hand. 'Is anything else wrong? Is it just the baby stuff you're upset about? It's nothing *I've* done, is it?'

I wrap myself in the silk dressing gown. 'No. It's nothing you've done.'

'Is it your ex? Is it something to do with him?'

A sob catches unwittingly in the back of my throat. 'No.'

Matt steps forward. His body is soft and vulnerable in its nakedness. I don't want to see him like that. 'It is, isn't it? It's about him...'

'No!' Oh God, how much longer do we have to bat these questions backwards and forwards? 'Just leave me alone.'

I push past him to go and slump onto the bed, hurling away the poetry book that is waiting in my space. The scrap of paper with the Emily Dickinson poem sits innocently on the duvet and I grab it to scrunch tightly in my fist and toss onto the floor.

Matt watches me from the bathroom entrance, where he switches off the cold tap that I have left running. 'Do you want me to get dressed?'

I shrug. 'Do what you want.'

Closing my eyes, I sink back into the bed and curl into the foetal position. I hear Matt opening drawers and moving around the room, then minutes later he is gone and I can finally scream fearfully into my pillow.

TWENTY-NINE

ADDIE

I stand behind the privacy glass of my pod and watch Sophy and Tom stroll hand in hand through the site and away, up the mountain path that will take them beyond the waterfall.

They look like a fairytale couple with an aura of happiness shining around them. She's in a floral dress that sweeps the foliage on the ground, a floppy-brimmed hat perching glamorously on her head as if she's doing a holiday advertisement. He's wearing shorts and a baseball cap, his bare chest and shoulders slathered with sun cream.

When I checked them out on social media after discovering that they too would be part of the giveaway prize, I saw that they had a ten-month old daughter, Olivia. A pretty girl, with dark curls and a wet, toothy grin. Obviously, they couldn't bring the baby here, and I was surprised that they thought it would be acceptable to leave her behind. But looking at Sophy and Tom and the way they are with each other... well, it's clear that they have plans for more children.

I'm like a mind reader sometimes.

I look at my watch and run through today's itinerary. Plenty of time to be lazy and enjoy the retreat while Reuben is having a massage with Eloise. Plenty of time to better get to know the guests. A stroll in the direction of Sophy and Tom might be a good idea.

I leave it ten minutes before I set off: I don't want to look like I'm following them. Once I'm higher up, around the sweep of the path, I get a panoramic view of the landscape and it's easy to spot where they are. Two tiny figures, on the other side of the waterfall, are reclining on a flat pocket of grass in the rocks, hands contentedly behind their heads, their footwear kicked off. I keep them in my sights as I head in their direction, watching as Tom casually rolls onto his side to caress Sophy's face, to kiss her lips, to jostle her feet with his.

The sun is scorching. On previous visits to the retreat the weather has always been cool and mixed, unpredictable. But this... the temperature has been rising every day and a record-breaking heatwave is expected by the end of the week.

Over the ridge of the hill, I notice a route where I can drop down on the couple so that they won't see me approach. It's a bit of a scramble, and by the time I can see them properly – Tom with his hand slipped inside the bodice of Sophy's dress, and her biting gently on his bottom lip – I'm breathless with the effort. The steep descent has pulled at my calves and hamstrings, and my legs are trembling as I close in on them. When I'm within a few feet of their little haven, I feel it's only polite to make them aware of my presence, so I kick at some of the rubble and let out a laboured groan.

'What was that?' Sophy is startled and sits up quickly as Tom looks around.

'Oh gosh, I didn't mean to disturb you.' I put on my best influencer voice as I make a show of hobbling into their grassy encampment. 'I've just climbed down from the ridge and it wasn't as easy as I expected. I don't think I'm as fit as I'd like my followers to believe.' My laugh cuts into their befuddled silence.

Tom and Sophy shuffle across the grass to make room for me, and I sink to the ground next to them.

'We just came across that way, along the footpath,' Tom says, pointing out the direction in the distance. 'No climbing involved.'

'Well thanks for the advice. That's the route I will be taking back to the site.' I remove my trainers and socks to sit cross-legged, realising that I'm encroaching severely into their personal space.

'Great view from here,' says Sophy, adjusting the bodice of her dress.

'Yes, I love this place so much.'

'So quiet. It's like being on another planet.' We maintain the small talk for a few minutes.

'Is your accommodation OK?' I ask. 'If you need anything...'

'It's amazing. We couldn't wish for better. Everything is lovely and we're really grateful. Gemma was so lucky to win because you must surely have had millions of people applying.'

'Well, not quite millions. But yes, over ten thousand applications from people all over the world.'

'How did you pick?' Tom asks. 'What did you do: just choose a name that you liked the sound of, or what?'

Sophy nudges him in the ribs. 'Don't be nosey. It doesn't really matter, does it? We ended up being the lucky ones.'

'I shouldn't be telling you this,' I whisper and lean in. 'But before I even announced the giveaway, I'd decided that the winner would be the fourteenth person to comment on the post. That's all it was. And Gemma was the fourteenth person. Actually, I was pleased that it went to someone local rather than some unknown person in, like, Australia or wherever.'

'Fourteen?' Tom laughs heartily. 'So, all the thousands of comments afterwards were pointless and you ignored them? That's so funny.'

'Why the number fourteen?' asks Sophy. 'Is it your lucky number?'

'Oh gosh, no,' I reply. 'Not *lucky*. But it is significant. Yes. Fourteen.' A picture of a calendar pops into my head. The fourteenth of February, Valentine's Day. I remember how I'd written 'Date Night' in the empty space, so carefully, purposefully in my neat, teenage hand. Obviously, the number is meaningless to Sophy now. I rub a hand across my face and stare out across the grey and green undulations, the slanted sunbeams, the hazy mushrooms of steam being coaxed out of the ground by the heat. 'Sorry. I got all mystical then, didn't I?' I smile and attempt to lighten things by demonstrating a namaste sign with my hands in prayer at my forehead. 'It's good. It's all wonderful.'

Tom has turned away for a moment and is whispering to Sophy.

'Hey!' I click my fingers. 'Hey, do you two fancy being in a video? I need to record some shots for my Instagram while I'm here.'

Sophy has a cynical ridge between her eyebrows. 'I thought phones weren't to be used here? We wanted to bring one to keep in touch with our daughter but weren't allowed. All we've got is some kind of radio system where staff will pass on a message in an emergency.'

I wave away their concerns that I get some kind of preferential treatment. 'Oh, this is just for filming; it's part of the agreement for my endorsement. Although I can't use the internet or anything. You can't get any sort of signal out here: it's just one big blackspot.'

'Well, we did wonder about that,' says Tom.

I stand up with my phone, adjusting the settings to take in the stunning sweep of the mountains against the horizon.

'Would it be OK to include you in a short reel?' I ask them

again. 'You two look so happy with each other and it would be a great advert for the retreat.'

'Well...' Tom grins and slides a hand over Sophy's belly. 'Shall we tell her?'

'Oh God, you're rubbish at keeping secrets, aren't you?' Sophy rolls her eyes. 'We can't not now.'

It's so obvious what is going on. I pretend to look surprised, pressing a splayed hand to my own womb and gasping as Sophy announces that they have just – like *genuinely yesterday* – found out that they will be having another baby.

'That is such superb news!' I screech a little to show how delighted I am. 'And what a perfect place to unveil that wonderful information.'

Tom puts his arm around Sophy and pulls her into him. Before they object, I've switched my phone into video mode, recording their show of joy, their wide smiles and sparkling eyes as they sit in the most idyllic surroundings, a secret corner of paradise, to share with my followers the revelation of their pregnancy. I will be able to add in my own happy news with a follow-up reel when we get home.

The film is only twenty-nine seconds long, but it's a brilliant piece of advertising for LunaBliss. There are no actors, no fake grins. Here we have a great-looking couple announcing their conception at a first-class fertility retreat and it is all real. *I'm* even tearful too!

'Amazing! That is absolutely spot on.' I do the squealy thing again and crouch down to hug them both together. 'Congratulations. We really must keep in touch after this week and...'

'And you want to feature our baby on your Five-a-Day?' Tom jokes. 'He's a celebrity before he's born.'

'He?' Sophy replies indignantly. 'It might be another girl.'

'Oh gosh, I would *love* mine to be a girl!'

We're in the middle of all the cooey clichéd baby talk when Tom looks away and points towards the waterfall.

'Hey, isn't that Matt down there?'

'Yes, it is. Strange that he's on his own.'

We all peer at him until Sophy suggests that we head back towards the site to go and join him.

'What did you think of the yoga session?' I ask as we follow the path.

'I loved it,' Tom replies. 'Will you be doing some more tomorrow, too?'

'Absolutely. I mean, no one needs to take it seriously. Some of the poses are easier than others and it's just a piece of group fun, just a laugh.'

'Yes, but could you at least throw in a tree or a chair pose because I can do those without looking like I'm totally unfit.'

The sound of our voices and laughter carries over the lake, and Matt waves in our direction before lobbing a stone into the water.

'Everything all right?' Tom asks when we reach him.

Matt puffs out a long sigh. 'Yeah, well... I don't know. Gem's a bit up and down at the moment, triggered by the slightest thing. She wanted some time alone so I thought I'd come out for a bit. Give her some space.'

I link my elbow through his. 'Let's go for a walk around the pond. I can show you the other path and there's a cave near the waterfall, and then by the time we get back Gemma might be in a better frame of mind so that we can all eat our evening meal together.'

Everyone agrees with my suggestion, and I lead the way with Matt hanging on to my arm. I turn and smile at Tom and Sophy behind me, swinging my glance up the side of the mountain.

Something catches on the perimeter of my vision and I have a feeling of unease, another sense of being watched. A human figure with something flapping around the edges – surely it can't be the retreat staff: they only ever stay in the main site areas –

and as my breath sticks in my throat for a few seconds I realise that it is Gemma, wearing the complementary white silk robe. Watching us.

When I look again, only a minute later, she is gone.

THIRTY

GEMMA

I wake with a start, a pang of dread. What happened earlier? And where is Matt?

The bedroom is muggy and oppressive; my neck is clammy with sweat. I swing my legs off the bed and see the discarded poetry book on the floor, the screwed-up poem.

Something is quivery in my body. Something here doesn't feel right, doesn't feel normal. It's not only about Reuben turning up. This whole situation of us winning a free week in a luxury retreat, it's starting to make me obsess over all sorts of silly little things. Things from the past I thought I'd moved on from. What is going on? I need to talk to someone who can convince me that I'm safe here, that I'm not paranoid.

I put on the white bathrobe and run outside to Sophy's pod to hammer on her door. I press my face to the glass but the room is empty, the bed unmade.

Here I am, up a mountain, in the middle of nowhere. Alone.

I race up the path towards the waterfall with my feet bare. 'Sophy! Matt!'

Breathless and panting, realising with horror that there is no immediate way of contacting the emergency services if anything terrible happens, I scramble along the track towards the sound of crashing water. Around the side of the mountain, I emerge to look down on the natural pool in the rocks, its glassy hue shining up to dazzle me for a moment.

Suddenly, I hear a shriek. Shrill, high-pitched: the sound of people having fun. I cast my gaze to its direction and see them all on the far shore of the lake. Sophy and Tom. Matt.

And Addie.

She has her arm linked into Matt's, her head tipping into his shoulder as she laughs at something he's said. Her actions look false, attention-seeking.

Then Tom points and makes a remark, and her strident chortle pierces the air again. I stand, frozen, watching the four of them. What are they doing together? What are they talking about? Are they discussing *me*, laughing at *me*?

Hurt and rage churns inside me. Just when I need someone to talk to, they have all gone off together to enjoy themselves without me. I can't shout out to them. I just can't. I turn around and flounce back along the path to my room, and all I can hear is their laughter.

In the dining area, our evening meal places have been configured so that Addie and Reuben can be with us. We arrived to find name cards for the place settings already laid out.

Addie is at the far end – the head of the table – with Matt and Reuben on each corner of her. Next to Matt is Tom, and next to Reuben is Sophy, then I am next to Sophy. Where there should be a setting opposite me, the chair has been removed and a lavish pickle tray with a plate of poppadoms has been put in the gap on the table.

'Surely we can move so that we're opposite our partners?' I protest, ready to move my plates and glasses and cutlery. 'Then I won't feel so out on a limb.'

'It's probably easier for the waiter to bring all the food if we leave it like this,' Addie says from her prominent position, as she puts on a charitable smile. 'It's not causing you a massive problem, is it?'

I ignore her and start moving things around.

'Whoa!' says Sophy, grabbing her glass of mango juice as the tablecloth ripples and drags. 'You nearly knocked it over.'

Addie claps a hand over her mouth. 'Oh gosh, not the juice again. We don't want a rerun of Saturday night's embarrassment, do we?'

Matt glares at me. 'Just stay there. It doesn't matter really, does it?'

'It seems stupid though, when you're all up at that end and I'm down here...' My argument fades out pathetically, and Addie is already talking over me, saying something that Tom finds hilarious.

I reluctantly sit beside Sophy and arrange the table back to how it was.

'Something smells nice,' she says. 'I think it's curry.'

Smiling weakly, I lower my voice to ask about the events of the afternoon. 'Did you have some kind of activity with her, down near the pool?'

'Activity? No, we only went out for a walk and bumped into each other. She's actually all right when you get to know her properly. We told her about the new baby and she made a reel of us for her Instagram. How good is that?'

'Great.' I find it difficult to hold back the sarcastic tone. So Addie gets to find out before Sophy's own mother and family.

Sophy frowns at me. 'Is there something wrong?'

'Oh, I don't know.' I grit my teeth and turn away so that she can't see my expression. 'Maybe it's my hormones.'

Our food arrives. Individual balti dishes heavily garnished with fresh coriander, and ramekins of wholegrain rice and lentils.

Matt leans over to enthusiastically sniff the food with a smile on his face. 'This looks gorgeous,' he says.

'It's one I've tried before, and I specifically asked for it to be on the menu here,' Addie tells us. 'It's only medium spiced, so it won't blow your head off. Aubergine and tomato curry with a few secret ingredients in it. You just try it. It's delicious.'

I stare down at the balti dish as everyone else tucks in, loading up their plates with rice and chutneys. This can't be happening. This must *mean* something.

'Sophy?' I give her a nudge. 'Look.'

'Hmm?' She's got her mouth full already. 'This is lovely, isn't it?'

I nod towards the food and whisper. 'Aubergine curry. Remember?'

'What?'

'You *know*. Oh, God, do I need to spell it out?'

Addie looks up.

'Everything OK, ladies?'

'This is bloody lush,' says Sophy. 'There's like a velvety background to it.'

'Have you never had it before?'

'Not that I remember. It's so creamy.'

'Coconut milk and peanut butter. They're the secret ingredients.' Addie pops a forkful into her mouth with pride.

'So, did *you* make it?' Matt asks.

'No, no.' She laughs and waves a hand. 'I just helped Carys to develop the retreat menu and gave her this recipe. One of my favourites.'

'She's a fabulous cook,' Reuben tells everyone. 'Everything she makes is stunning.'

I can't eat it. I don't want to listen to everyone else praising it. All I really want to do is get up and run out of the room and get away from this place because things here are increasingly freaking me out.

'Gem? Gem?' Matt is looking at me with suspicion from the other end of the table. 'Are you going to try it? You're not still... you know?'

I shake my head and take a deep breath to dissipate my ridiculous thoughts. Carefully, I push the food to one side so that I don't knock over any glasses and break off a piece of poppadom to force into my dry mouth.

'That was amazing,' says Sophy as she puts down her knife and fork beside her empty dish. 'Great recommendation for the menu, Addie. I *need* that recipe.'

I can't believe what Sophy is saying. Does she not remember?

Can't she connect all the bizarre clues like I can, the clues that are screaming out to tell us both that someone here knows something about what happened all those years ago?

THIRTY-ONE

GEMMA

Matt has insisted that we make the most of the sunken jacuzzi bath instead of joining Sophy and Tom for an evening swim in the pool. There are scented candles lit around the edges. The special manifestation music is playing in the background. He spotted that things weren't right with me after the curry. He saw how I refused the food, sitting stunned and mute while everyone else laughed and joked and commended Addie's menu choices.

'Someone needs a bit of a pick-me-up,' he said as he sorted everything out in the bathroom.

He helps me undress and step into the steamy water. We settle into the bubbles and I breathe in the herbal aroma. There's an anticipation that I need to deliver an explanation.

'I know we said about waiting to see how things were going after what happened the other night, but I do really think we'd be better off going home.' I have realised that no amount of ambience and scenic views will make me want to stay now. The only thing that will improve my sanity is to get back to normal life, to our little house and our daily routines. To safety.

'Yeah, unfortunately that's not happening,' says Matt.

'What? Why?'

'I talked to Jozef earlier about our options. He managed to radio through to Erik, but he's away somewhere until Friday. And apparently the track's still blocked. They're waiting for tree surgeons or someone to come with a special type of chainsaw to sort it out.'

'But that doesn't matter! We can walk, and I don't care if we have to carry our own stuff. It shouldn't be that difficult to make our way back to the car park, should it?'

Matt shakes his head. 'We'd have a wasted journey. Apparently, the car park gate is locked and the key is in the office, which is also locked up, so we wouldn't be able to get the car out. Not to mention that our phones are stuck in the safe in the office, too. No one can get hold of Carys because she's out of the country and her flight isn't due back until tomorrow night.'

'Oh God. What are we supposed to do, then?'

'Wait. That's all we can do. And anyway, we're all fine with each other now. Why do you want to go home?'

'I don't know. There are just things here that make me jittery.'

He splurts out a laugh. The candle flames jump and dodge at the same time. 'Like what? It feels like the nicest place on the planet.'

'There are things around that seem like – I don't know – like they're trying to expose me. And I feel as if I'm being watched.' I'm embarrassed as soon as the words are out of my mouth, and I slide my head under the water for a few seconds so that I don't have to hear him laugh at me again. But when I resurface, he's staring at me with a serious expression. He's questioning my sanity, isn't he? He's wondering if it's a bad idea to have a baby with me.

'*Expose* you?'

Oh shit, why did I say that? It was the wrong word and he's going to think...

'Look, I didn't mean... It just seems like Addie hates me.'

We look at each other for what seems like ages before he breaks eye contact with me to lean over and switch off the water jets.

'Are you ready to get out yet?' He douses his face and hair with water.

'I could manage another ten minutes.'

'OK, then. I'll leave you to it.'

I watch, feeling rejected as he climbs out and wraps himself in one of the huge fluffy towels. He's having second thoughts about me – about us – isn't he? He's thinking he shouldn't have rushed into a marriage without knowing *everything* about me. He's going to start *delving*.

I wallow about in the water, instinctively knowing that my cortisol levels are rising again, when it's so important that I should stay calm for my body to be in the right condition for growing a baby. Although... should I be thinking about having a baby with someone who seems like he is changing his mind and might not want to stay with me when we get home?

Oh God, everything is causing me stress. I need to stop obsessing so much. I know I do. But this is all Addie's doing. If she hadn't turned up...

Suddenly I have the startling thought that things could be running much deeper. Reuben was with me for five years. All the conversations, secrets, drunken blurtings, overheard snippets between me and Sophy... Maybe I talked in my sleep, mentioned black lilies, the 'Wild Nights' poem, even something as innocuous as a curry recipe. Maybe Reuben collated these bits of information and worked out a version of the truth. Maybe that's why he left me.

Reuben *knows*.

Matt opens the door. 'Gem, honestly, is there something more to all this? Is there something you're not telling me?'

'No!' I put my hands over my face so that he can't see the shame that is written there.

'Well, something is obviously wrong and I feel like I can't help you. I think you should talk to someone. I wonder if the woman who does the meditation and massage treatments might also do counselling. How about it?'

'No. I can't. I just can't.' I don't want to talk about all *that*. I just want it buried, left alone. That's the simplest thing.

'Well, maybe *I* should go and talk to someone, then.' He stares hard, unblinking, into my eyes. 'Something needs to be done.'

'Matt, please. Let's just go home tomorrow. That's all I want. Then everything will be OK.'

He shakes his head slowly. He thinks I'm mad, doesn't he?

'I'm going to go out for a walk. I'll see you later.' He hangs up his wet towel before he leaves, and the door clunks shut behind him.

* * *

My future hangs precariously on the side of a mountain. Everything is crumbling.

Matt doesn't trust me; he thinks I'm hiding something from him.

Sophy and Tom have been captivated by Addie and think that she's amazing.

And Reuben *knows*.

I shiver despite the heat of the water in the jacuzzi. What can I do? How can I prevent my secret from being laid bare?

I scramble through the steam to find a towel, and pad into the bedroom to look through the glass doors of the pod. Matt is out of sight. I should go and find him, talk to him, try to convince him in a sane, logical way that being at home is preferable to being here. I need to get him away before he finds out.

My hair is still wet, my face flushed, as I dress quickly in my loose yoga wear and trainers. There is an impending dusk in the sky and a cacophony of insects in the air as I make my way through the pergola and along the footpath towards the pool. The temperature has hardly dropped since the stifling heat of the afternoon.

In the distance I see two figures – men, I think – standing high up on a crag, gazing down towards the waterfall. I freeze, trying to work out who they are.

No, it can't be!

It is Reuben, with Matt, seemingly locked in conversation by the look of their hand gestures. What are they talking about? Are they being friendly or hostile? Am I the subject of their discussion?

There is no one else around; maybe Addie, Sophy and Tom are socialising around the firepit or swimming in the pool.

I creep towards the men, grateful for the camouflage of the shadowy twilight. They are too far away for me to hear what they are saying and I need to get closer. But even as I approach them through the outcrop of rocky boulders, I still cannot catch any of their conversation.

Suddenly, Matt strikes out and hits Reuben flat on the shoulder. Oh God, are they starting a fight? Reuben moves out of his space, dodging this way and that, and Matt steps towards him again to waft his hand aggressively near his face. Then Matt stumbles on the uneven ground before righting himself with an embarrassed skip. Something is said: some grunt or mumble, though I can't work out what it is. But whatever has happened is over now, and Matt is striding away from him, away from me, to go further along the track around the top of the waterfall. I watch as he disappears into the far distance.

I move to try and keep Matt within my sights, and there's a scurry of pebbles onto the path as I accidentally kick a rock.

Reuben turns. There's a look of something – disinterest, disdain? – on his face as he walks towards me.

'What are you doing?' I ask. 'What was all that with Matt?'

'What business is it of yours?'

'I saw you up there, having some kind of scuffle.'

Reuben laughs and rubs a hand over his mouth. 'Yeah.'

'What was it about?'

He laughs again. 'Did you think we were fighting over *you*?'

'Have you said something to him about me?'

'About you? Like what? Ahh, you mean all your secrets?'

A stone of dread wedges up in my throat. 'What have you told him?'

'Are we talking dirty stuff here, like your bedroom preferences or what?' His eyes are so black in this gauzy light, so terrifyingly, threateningly black.

'God, you haven't, have you?'

That look again, which was in fact, disdain. 'Of course not.' He starts trying to walk past me, to get back down the path to the site.

'So what was it, then? Did you say anything about lilies? Or poetry?'

He turns his back, guffawing with ridicule, as I reach to grab his sleeve.

'Reuben, please! What have you said? And have you been telling Addie all this stuff, too?'

He shakes my hand away. 'Get off me, you mad bitch. Just leave us alone. Go and sort your relationship out with Matt, because I have the feeling he's got concerns.'

I watch the silhouette of him disappear briskly down the track as I try to contain my rising emotions. It was inevitable, wasn't it? My secret had to come out at some point, didn't it?

Karma is going to come and get me.

THIRTY-TWO

GEMMA

I can't sleep. It's so hot, so unbearably humid, where everything feels heavy, weighed down. My mind is a conveyor belt of images and thoughts and blind panic. My skin is crawling with non-existent insects that continually make me fidget and writhe.

Where the hell is Matt?

I get out of bed again, to pace around the pod, to the en suite and back to the glass doors, looking for a shadow or the flicker of a torch beam outside, listening for the slightest scuff of a footstep. But there's nothing.

'Matt!' I squat on my haunches and yell into my hands. Where the hell is he?

Too much has happened. I knew we should have gone home earlier, when I said. Even with the tree blocking the track: we should have at least *tried*.

Something happened with Reuben, didn't it? Up on the edge of that cliff. What were they talking about? That is the key to the whole thing, isn't it? That's why Matt is missing.

I grab his pillow off the bed and pull it into my face, to howl for a few seconds. Oh God, what happened? I've waited and waited and he hasn't come back. Again, I go and open the doors to stand outside and listen – was that the crack of a twig just then? – to confuse the nocturnal voices of the owls with the pained cries of my husband.

I can't bear it.

Oh God, where is he?

THIRTY-THREE

ADDIE

Have I gone too far? It isn't easy to know how to strike the right balance because I've never been a bully before. I've always made the effort to be likeable and accommodating. Measuring the impact of my actions is impossible, though. And I only intended to continue until I knew that she was completely broken. Still, I am having a lot of fun planting all the little clues. Each one gave me such a burst of adrenaline just from imagining the panic it would cause.

My favourite so far was the curry we had at our evening meal earlier. Gosh, her face when I mentioned peanut butter! And the way she pushed her plate away. I could see that I was definitely messing with her head.

I go out for a walk to mull over the events of the last few days. Have I done enough? Too much? At which point should I deliver the ultimate surprise?

I stand for a while above the waterfall, out of the view of Sophy and Tom, observing their tiny forms as they lap across the pool and back like insects on a pond. I thought all four of them would have been together, but Gemma and Matt aren't here.

Trekking further along the path, I reach the hidden mossy cleft, my special place. I'd found it on a previous visit – it was like a nest, a cupped palm of a giant's hand – and had spent time there luxuriating on a blanket under a clear sky.

Reclining on the ground – that oval spot holds my form perfectly – I breathe mindfully, telling myself that what I am doing is justified.

Gemma Morgan deserves this.

She's been out of my social circle for twenty years. She has a job and a house, and she's had Reuben. She could have gone unnoticed into middle age. She could have had a child with him.

But then... one fell swoop, her click on the *follow* button on my Instagram, and all our paths merged. It seemed like fate itself had tempted me to take action.

I muse on these thoughts for a while, before getting up to stroll again to a vantage point on the far side of the water that has the most incredible views, particularly as dusk is falling.

Standing back from the edge of where the land drops away into a marshy valley, I let the breeze swish my hair around. The setting sun is still glowing warmly on my face, and an urge comes that I should bless my body with a yoga flow – to do it for myself and my unborn baby rather than my Instagram followers – so without thinking, my body naturally falls into a mountain pose, ready to raise my arms in an upward salute.

Inhale, exhale. I stretch and fold, breathing the pure air in and out, feeling how my core engages, how my hands and feet ground. The moment is divine; it is between me and the earth and the strawberry-sized foetus drawing life from me in the safety of my womb. I repeat the flow and focus on synchronising my breathing. The third time through, I am mindful of the earth's energy running through my limbs as I drop into the Cobra pose, connecting me...

Suddenly my flow is disrupted.

There is that feeling again.

Someone is watching me

From my position on the floor, I push up onto my elbows and look around.

'Oh gosh, I didn't see you there!' I give a cautious giggle and roll onto my side to squint up at the woman. Is it Eloise? She doesn't reply, which is a bit unnerving, and I shield my eyes from the glare so that I can get a better look at her.

Shit!

It is *her*. Gemma.

'Oh, it's *you*! Did you follow me?' I realise the irony of my question as I squirm on the floor, raising myself onto my knees to sit casually on my heels.

Her feet are firmly planted on the ground; her hands are on her hips; her chin is tilted dourly. Her stance is definitely threatening.

'There are things I need to know. So, yes, I followed you. I want answers.'

Something flips in my stomach. There is conflict in her tone. I should stand up, I tell myself, I should put myself on the same level as her; I should start walking briskly back to the site, back to Reuben...

'You give off this image of being down to earth on your Instagram,' she says, taking a step closer to me.

I am still on the floor and can smell some kind of floral aroma on her: deodorant or shower gel. I fix a smile on my face to bring an element of calm to the situation.

'You try to look like you're normal, like you're one of the girls and you're doing your best for us, but it's not true, is it? Not when you're stealing someone's boyfriend.'

I blink at her. If I stand up she might react defensively, I surmise. I decide to stay down on the floor while I defuse the situation.

'My Instagram appeals to all sorts of people, but obviously

it's not for everyone. And I didn't set out to get Reuben. I honestly didn't know he was with *you*.' It is largely true.

'And what about the other stuff? The snide comments? The things around the site to remind me...'

'Look, Gemma...'

'Has this come from Reuben? Something *he's* told you? What do you know? And what have you told Matt?'

I cast my eyes beyond her, to see if I can scramble up quickly and skirt around her to get on the path and away. 'Reuben? Of course it hasn't come from Reuben.'

Gemma takes a breath and looks up at the sky before speaking. 'What has Reuben told Matt? Are you both trying to destroy my marriage?'

'Hey, look...' I can't see a way past her; I am trapped with her looming over me.

She takes another step forward and reaches out her hand towards me. 'Why are you doing this?'

'Maybe before you have a child, Matt ought to know what you did.' The moment that the words are out of my mouth, I know that I shouldn't have said them, but I couldn't help myself. And suddenly she is angry, livid, the fury on her face unmistakable.

I flinch, but it is too late to stop her grabbing the collar of my shirt and twisting, pulling, yanking so that the smell of the Chanel No. 5 I sprayed earlier stirs up into my nostrils as her grip on me tightens and tightens...

I flail and topple sideways, yelling as she kicks me in the shoulder. Then she is on top of me, pinning me down with her knees, as she clenches harder at my collar, the fabric squeezing and closing around my neck and my thoughts – *I can't breathe, stop, I'm choking, panicking, gasping for air, please let go, what about my baby, please, I'm going to die if you don't let me g—* and then suddenly the last fragments of evening sun are on my face again, the breeze tousling my hair, the buzzards circling above me in the magnificent multicoloured sky, but I don't see any of it because everything is fading...

fading...

fading...

until everything is black.

THIRTY-FOUR

GEMMA

By the time dawn breaks the morning is screaming with birdsong. I've had no sleep; instead I have worried and wept here in my room, and roamed around the site in the dark. Did I really attack Addie last night or was it just a bad dream? I see the swelling on my thumb, the dirt under my fingernails. It was real, wasn't it? Oh God, but it was just a moment of madness, it wasn't intentional. And she must be OK because I went back later to the spot where she was doing yoga and it was empty. She's fine. She must be. But Matt, though... At one point I hung around in the early hours outside Sophy and Tom's pod, inexplicably unable to knock and ask for their help, or to check if he was there.

Still, he hasn't returned.

I watch through the privacy glass of my door as steam rises from the ground. The temperature is threatening another record-breaking heatwave; already the mountain heather is dry and crisp, devoid of moisture.

There's a graze on my elbow and a deep scratch down my leg. My face feels swollen and my throat is parched. I need water. I take my glass and fill it at the bathroom sink, then gulp it all down greedily. Pacing back through to the bedroom, I open the glass door and look outside. A blindingly bright sun blasts its rays down, and the wood of the newly erected pod cracks and creaks in discomfort.

Where *is* Matt?

My chest throbs with apprehension, with fatigue. I should go out again and search for him. He might be in danger. God, we could all be in danger. Who knows what could happen after the events of last night?

'Matt!' I cry out his name and whimper again. What has he found out? What must he think of me? Is there any hope left for us at all? Matt, please. Just give me the chance to explain. It's not what you think.

Maybe... Yes, maybe...

What if Matt has tried to get back to the car?

With a spark of hope in my heart, I leave our room and make my way along the path to the ridge that overlooks the ravine where we travelled in the buggy with Erik. The ground is already hard and cracked from the heat; the vegetation shrivelled and desiccating. Sweat trickles from my head and neck and armpits as the sun slows my efforts.

I scramble with hands and feet over smooth, shiny rocks. Below me is a hidden cleft of a valley where the trees are spindly and tall, reaching up to the light. I look down at the sheer drop into the gorge, but there is no sign of Matt. Maybe he's somehow made his way back, and he's sitting in the car, waiting for us all.

The office is somewhere down there. When we arrived, Erik brought us along a track through that ravine, but I can't see it from here. It's too risky to descend from my current location, so I edge carefully in a different direction to try and scout out our original route.

The air prickles and purrs; it's thick with thrips. My hair is frizzy and swollen from the humidity, and the stifling morning is glaring at me from all angles. I realise that I have no sun cream on.

What am I doing, clambering around on all these rocks so high up? Have I gone completely mad? One wrong footing and I could be down at the bottom with my head smashed in. I need to go back to our room; Matt could be there, wondering where *I* am.

It's just before seven o'clock when I return, but he's still not there. Even though I left the door unlocked there's no sign that he's been back while I was out. I sit on the bed, and exhaustion puts an uncontrollable tremble in my limbs and a surge of nausea in my stomach. I drink more water but it doesn't help. It must be the lack of sleep. The stress. My cortisol levels.

Matt! Oh God, where has he gone?

Suddenly I'm shivering, then I'm needing to pee but when I go to the toilet I can manage no more than an eggcup full. I'm dehydrated; I must be. I put my face under the tap and slurp from the stream of water, and even though I'm covered in sweat I'm still trembling so I get in bed and cover myself up with the duvet, unable to keep my eyes open.

Finally, I sleep.

TWENTY YEARS BEFORE

THIRTY-FIVE

SOPHY

Me and Gemma. We were always popular at school, the ones wearing the most fashionable shoes, the shortest skirts, the coolest make-up.

Everyone followed us. Everyone followed Gemma.

We were fifteen years old. Brash and beautiful, with fresh skin and long, luscious hair, a trail of boys behind us. If there had been Instagram in those days, we would have been influencers, going viral, showing off to the world how everything should be done.

The only person I'd say was more popular than us at that time was Christopher Bray.

Christopher was tall and striking with high cheekbones and dyed coal-black hair. Unassuming and with a leisurely air of mystery, he ranged the corridors with his arms full of literature and his head full of music. The Cure, Bauhaus, Joy Division, and Siouxsie – bands that most of us had never heard of, having exited the charts years ago – were the usual choices that he hummed, seemingly in a world of his own. He was different to all the other boys in school, pensive and arty, uninterested in sport and the laddish curriculum of fights and farts and practical jokes.

Christopher Bray was a Goth.

He had most of the girls swooning. Maybe it was his confidence, or his cryptic smile, or the way he often – as a Goth evangelist – chose any random person that wasn't on any kind of popularity scale, just to get into intense conversation for a few days, where he would swap books and music and recommend poems that spoke to their soul.

Almost everyone wanted to be that unwitting person. They wanted to sit in a chair next to him in the dinner hall and listen to him bestow the virtues of Edgar Allan Poe as they gazed at his backcombed hair and his full lips, hoping that he would slide one of his paperback classics towards them, so that they could later press their face into the pages and inhale him there.

Gemma had never had any issues getting the boys in school to like her, but Christopher was a different story. She'd never been on a date with him, as hard as she'd tried. She'd flirted to the best of her ability while trying to play it casual and hard to get, as if it didn't matter one way or another whether he noticed her.

Initially, Gemma saw Christopher Bray as a challenge. She couldn't bear the thought that he would engage so positively with the geeky-looking girls with glasses and greasy hair yet walk past her in the corridor without a second glance. She wanted to be noticed. She wanted to be wanted.

When she started carrying around a copy of *Dracula*, I knew immediately what she was up to. Although it was a new book, she had flipped and battered the pages, bending the cover and throwing it around in her bedroom to make it look like she'd read it hundreds of times. And then her make-up changed. A thicker strip of eyeliner; paler foundation; darker lipstick. Oh, I knew what she was up to.

We were hanging around the cafeteria one lunchtime when Christopher finally made a move. The ubiquitous *Dracula* book was displayed like bait at the end of the table while we ate our pasta salads. And then, next thing, he was there. Nudging the novel with his thumb, flashing out a rare smile as Gemma languished under his gaze and tried to swallow her mouthful of food.

I made an excuse, as had been the plan in the event of this scenario, and left them to it. Christopher took my seat and began his spiel about Gothic literature.

'So, what happened?' I asked later as we sat together in Maths.

Nothing, apparently. No date had been arranged; no numbers swapped. Gemma said that she didn't care but I could tell otherwise. They'd had a difficult discussion about Bram Stoker, tricky because Gemma knew nothing about Bram Stoker and had been mortifyingly aware of appearing ignorant. She hadn't even read the book and didn't know the names of the characters in the story. But at least the ice had been broken with Christopher, and initiating conversation with him in the future would be so much easier.

She was right.

In the days that followed, they hung out together at break time and Christopher introduced her to the music of Siouxsie and the Banshees. By the weekend, Gemma was wearing black nail varnish and a lace choker and had started saving up for a pair of Dr. Martens. A date had been arranged.

Within those few days, Gemma became besotted with him.

I observed as her obsession became even more irrational. After their date, which was at a gig in a grungy cellar bar in the city, where they had to use fake ID to gain admission, she didn't want to leave him alone. There were further liaisons: walks around ancient churchyards, takeaways in the park, a trip to a specialist Goth shop where she bought a studded belt. Later, Gemma invited him back to her house, where she encouraged his thoughts on how she could revamp her bedroom in a cool way, and her parents were horrified to return from shopping one Saturday to find the ceiling painted dark red with the vast mural of a raven dominating the wall above her bed.

At lunchtimes, Gemma would insist on meeting up with Christopher to eat and make plans for the weekend. This didn't seem to fit with Christopher's idea of a relationship: he still wanted the freedom to discuss his beloved literature and poetry and art with anyone else who was interested. Gemma, though, wanted him all to herself.

I witnessed this imbalance play out throughout the late autumn term. It was ironic that Halloween seemed to mark the point where Christopher's commitment to their romance began to wane.

He started to become more unavailable, citing family meals that didn't involve Gemma, or lengthy pieces of homework, or dyeing his hair. He made claims that he had joined a post-punk band as their bassist where he was expected to practise four times a week.

But Gemma's obsession with him wouldn't let her believe that she was being rejected. She would telephone his house constantly and write long letters that included quotes from *Wuthering Heights*, which I had to deliver to him. I tried to advise her, to let her down gently, describing to her Christopher's facial expression – one of obvious tedium and annoyance – as he received these love letters to cram, unopened, into his blazer pocket. I really did try to tell her, for her own good.

She wouldn't accept this spurning, though. She continued, despite the ghastly change in the weather, to wait, shivering, in the bus shelter outside his house in the hope of catching him returning home with his bass guitar, so that she could hold him and press her freezing lips to his for a few seconds.

By the time school resumed for the January term, it was totally over.

Christopher Bray, in an effort to make it perfectly clear to Gemma, had told her in person during morning break while also handing over a letter stating briefly but succinctly that they were no longer an item, and requesting that she didn't ring his house or use the bus shelter as a watch station any more.

Devastated wasn't the word. Gemma was beyond herself with absolute grief.

But that wasn't the worst of it.

On the first day of term a new girl had turned up in our class. Her time at our school didn't last long, though.

She was called Dina.

Her surname was Peacock, I remember.

But this girl, and the impact of her arrival, changed everything.

THIRTY-SIX

SOPHY

We dubbed her Peacock Girl. Not to her face, but simply to everyone else's, because they seemed to find it funny and quite relevant on account of the striking make-up that she always wore.

I think that if it hadn't been for her turning up when she did, then maybe Gemma's infatuation with Christopher would have fizzled out organically. She would have retreated, licked her wounds and found someone else to fall in love with. She always loved to be in love with someone.

But the arrival of Peacock Girl inflamed a deep and implausible anger within Gemma that she refused to shake off.

You see, Peacock Girl was already a Goth when she arrived at our school. A proper, authentic Goth, with the mysterious mindset and a longing for the ethereal, a genuine passion for the eerie, chugging music, and a dress sense that verged on Victorian. She dripped with silver jewellery: studs, skulls, crosses and a tangle of chains and bracelets that clinked and jangled everywhere she went.

This irked Gemma immensely. It had become obvious to everyone who knew her that her own poor efforts were superficial, and that she had only taken on certain aspects of the look in order to attract Christopher.

Our immediate thoughts were that Peacock Girl wouldn't get away with all those piercings: nose, eyebrow and at least six studs in each ear. She had a web of backcombed black hair and huge tragic eyes made-up on a porcelain face, and her rosebud lips were immaculately symmetrical and always painted purple. She wasn't that tall but she was slender framed, and carried a style and confidence with such ease that the attention of Christopher Bray was captured effortlessly. The magnetism between them was prompt and palpable, and everyone watched to see how it would play out.

Everyone watched, too, to see how Gemma would react.

By that first mid-morning break Christopher and Peacock Girl were a corresponding pair, backs against the science block walls as they laughed coyly, matching off their interests and experiences. We watched them from a distance, Gemma simmering with resentment as they swapped books.

At lunchtime they ate together, picking like birds over their chicken and mushroom risottos. Gemma suggested that we go and sit with them, but, after a long and circuitous argument, I managed to convince her that it could appear passive aggressive and wouldn't be wise.

By the time afternoon classes came around, they were whispering together at the same desk at the back of the room, their dark eyes locked. We turned and watched as they passed notes between each other, as Christopher willingly gave her the answers to all the history questions on our worksheets.

Their relationship became a soap opera, an addiction.

. . .

During the days ahead, with Christopher by her side, Peacock Girl showed no inclination to interact with anyone else.

Of course, me and Gemma found this bizarre. Why would a new student, with all the opportunities to make friends and influence people, actually *choose* to become such a social hermit rather than gravitating towards us, the girls in the popular cliques, the girls having fun, the obvious choices?

We never really got an answer. We just watched, perplexed, as this fascinating pair of characters became embroiled with each other to the exclusion of all others.

Yet despite seeing how captivated Christopher Bray was by this new interloper, Gemma wasn't ready to give up on him. Why on earth did she still think she was in with a chance? I pleaded with her to leave him alone, knowing that her efforts would be wasted, but my words were ignored.

For the next few weeks, she maintained her efforts at gothic fashion by flaunting a stiffly pleated black skirt, perfecting the use of liquid eyeliner and loading up her arms with silver bangles. With *Dracula* abandoned and a similarly abused copy of *Frankenstein* in her hand, she continued to pursue Christopher Bray as unobtrusively as she could, but all her efforts were worthless. This time he did not take the bait. Of course he wouldn't. He was smitten with Peacock Girl.

Gemma had been my best friend for as long as I could remember, and she had always been the type of person who would get what she wanted eventually, even if it didn't come easily. When she was focused on a challenge, nothing would stop her. And this situation with Christopher Bray had wormed its way into her head, making her unable to back down. She couldn't understand how a new girl could simply walk in from nowhere and have that control over him. And she also couldn't believe that the pair wouldn't want to hang around in our group when it seemed like everyone else was clamouring to.

'Leave it,' I told her. 'It's not worth the mind space.'

I didn't care that Christopher had a new girlfriend. Good luck to them, I thought, secretly pleased that I would have Gemma back and we could seek out boys to go out on double dates with.

But Gemma seemed to talk of nothing else, and their relationship turned into a running commentary. In fact, her obsession over their movements started to piss me off. We didn't need them around us; we could co-exist quite easily around school without having to know what they were doing or who they were talking to. Gemma could have literally gone out on dates every weekend, with almost anyone she wanted to, yet she still craved the attention of Christopher.

The endless brush-offs and dismissals and snubs from him did nothing to stop her. Her skin grew thicker and she motored on.

And then she switched her tactics.

I couldn't understand her. After weeks of hating Peacock Girl, she suddenly made it her mission to wheedle into her confidence. It soon became obvious though: her intentions were to sever the fresh young heartstrings binding the couple together.

Irritated by this new strategy, I reluctantly trailed along with Gemma as we followed her around, sitting behind her on the bus, picking up the pens she dropped, reminding her when homework had to be handed in.

'I wondered if you might want this.' Gemma handed Peacock Girl a half-bottle of black nail varnish. This generosity was apparently part of the second stage of her plan. 'It doesn't really suit me, but it would look great on you.'

It got to the point where it seemed as if Peacock Girl was starting to like us. In some ways, *I* quite liked *her*. If it hadn't been for Gemma, I could genuinely have been her friend. She appreciated our glowing comments regarding her pencil drawing of a spider trapped in a web laden with raindrops. 'Oh my God, that water is transparent; it looks so realistic; aren't you talented?' We complimented her hair, her teeth, her skin, and she always gave the impression that she thought we were being authentic when she received this flattery. Attempts to entice her into our group for science were largely successful, and she took up a place on the end of the bench even though she didn't join in with the gossip and bitching that overrode the biology experiments.

But the main thing was, we were on speaking terms. She started to take us into her confidence. Sporadically, she fed us the information that Gemma was so hungry for: she told us about the previous weekend when she'd been on a date to the cinema with Christopher; she told us how he was involved in writing songs for his band; she told us that he was allergic to nuts. She even showed us the poem by Emily Dickinson called 'Wild Nights' that Christopher had written out onto handmade paper for her, telling us that she was going to put it in a frame beside her bed. Every detail that we elicited from her about Christopher's life was snatched up and hoarded, ready to be used if and when necessary.

We continued with this game, with this farce of pretending to be Peacock Girl's friend, until I began to wonder why we were bothering. It wasn't achieving anything and there were other, more interesting, boys that we could be focusing our efforts on.

'Let's leave it,' I reiterated. 'It's getting boring and we're not into the goth scene anyway. We could be going to parties at the weekends where they play music that we actually *like*, instead of having to pretend to read old books and stuff.'

But Gemma was stubborn. She declared that it was only a matter of time. She was still in love with him and wouldn't give up until Christopher and Peacock Girl's relationship was dead and buried, whereby he would become single and available again.

I didn't *get* her fascination with him. There were better-looking boys than Christopher in the school that would have dated her. Maybe it was that she hated being a quitter, or that the new girl in the school, swooping in like a beautiful bird of prey, had somehow beaten her and she needed to uphold her status.

Looking back, I regretted not being more assertive with her. I could easily have set up a blind date and led her towards a relationship with Josh Millet or Tyler Humberstone. But I didn't. I allowed Gemma to continue with her vain campaign regardless.

And look how it ended.

THIRTY-SEVEN

SOPHY

We were in Food Technology class when the first seeds of an idea took root. Our assignment was to plan and cook an Indian meal, and we had already been given the base recipe for the Aubergine Curry around which we were to theme our food.

'I feel a date night coming on,' Peacock Girl declared. She had apparently never cooked for Christopher before. 'Dimmed lights, candles, romantic music in the background...'

'The soft and subtle tones of My Chemical Romance,' I said with a wink, and Gemma doubled over laughing.

'So, there are things you can tweak.' The teacher held up the A4 copy of the recipe. 'There's a list at the bottom, of additional ingredients you can add in depending on how you like your curry. Extra chillies if you like heat, or chickpeas if you want a bit more texture. And then you can choose three sides. Either rice or chapati will need to be used as your main side.'

'I don't get it,' said Gemma. 'Can't you have both?'

'No,' I told her. 'You make the curry and then choose either rice or chapati. So then you'll need two more things from the list, so for example pakora and mango chutney.'

'Oh, OK.'

We read all through the sheet again, and I could tell that she'd had a lightbulb moment because her mouth fell open at the same time as she turned to look at me.

'What?' I said.

'So you can put extra things in the curry. That's right?'

'Yes.'

'Look at this,' she whispered, pointing to one of the additional ingredients.

I read the line above her fingernail.

Add one tablespoon of peanut butter to give a thick and creamy consistency.

'Yeah?'

'Christopher Bray is allergic to nuts.'

'Yeah? He's not cooking, though.'

'But Peacock Girl is making the curry for him, for their date night.'

What was Gemma trying to say? I didn't understand where she was going with this. 'So she'll know not to include peanut butter in it, won't she?'

Gemma gave a shifty smile. 'Will she though? Imagine if she forgot about his allergy and served it to him and he had a reaction. She'd be so mortified, wouldn't she? And he'd probably be embarrassed about it and... well, it wouldn't be such an amazing date night then, would it? It could even be the thing that puts an end to their little romance.'

I gasped. 'But it could be dangerous.'

'Nah. Most people with allergies... they just come out in hives or their lips swell up a bit. It's not like he'd die, is it?'

'But he might.'

'But everyone carries an antidote thing around with them. Medication or an EpiPen or whatever they're called. So there wouldn't be anything to worry about. But imagine the humiliation. Imagine how Peacock Girl will freak out.' That creepy smile smeared itself across her lips again.

'But, as I said earlier, she will already know not to put peanut butter in his food. So, if you're hoping for their date night to end up being a disaster with them splitting up from the embarrassment of it, then it's unlikely to happen, isn't it?'

Gemma looked away and giggled. Something about her behaviour made me twitchy.

'Oh, never mind,' she said, flapping her hand at me. 'You don't get it.'

'Get what?'

'Nothing. It was just an idea, that's all.'

I didn't have chance to enquire further. The teacher said that we were causing a distraction with our chatter, and Gemma was moved to the other end of the room. But something had unsettled me.

Later, on the bus home, I quizzed her about her comments regarding Christopher's allergy, but she breezed over the subject, instead talking about the forthcoming half-term disco and what she planned to wear.

It was only a week later, when we turned up to our Food Technology class again and took the ingredients out of our bags for the Indian Meal Assignment, that it hit me what Gemma was about to do.

THIRTY-EIGHT

SOPHY

During the run-up to our Food Technology assignment, Gemma tried to ingratiate herself around Peacock Girl as much as she could. Asking about the Brontë sisters and which books were considered the most Gothic. Asking about her hair: what type of black did she use; did she dye it herself; and 'oh my God, it looked so much better than how it would be done if she went to a hairdresser'.

It was all very cringeworthy to watch.

'When's your date night?' Gemma asked Peacock Girl.

'Yeah, it's next Wednesday, Valentine's Day, the same day as our Food Technology assignment. I told you, didn't I? So, I'm going to use the curry that we make in class, plus get some other stuff – all the trimmings – and we'll get dressed up and maybe have a glass of wine too.'

'Will this be at your house or his?' Gemma knew the answers to all these questions because she'd already been through the itinerary with her last Friday.

'Oh, it's at mine. My mum's going out so we have the place to ourselves.' Peacock Girl winked her heavily mascaraed eye. I wondered if she intended to seduce him into bed.

'Ah bless. I bet Christopher will love it.' Gemma's voice was so spuriously sickly that it made me want to retch.

I pulled her away and we strolled by the tennis courts.

'What is all this about? Why are you so interested in their date night? Is this something to do with the recipe, with the peanut butter?' I had to know exactly what she was planning, because my theory about Gemma's strategy to wreck their evening and risk Christopher's life was keeping me awake at night.

She dismissed my quizzing with a laugh and a flick of her hair. 'Don't worry,' she said. 'Banter, that's all it is. I'm not going to *do* anything.'

On that Wednesday, we arrived in the Food Technology class with our ingredients. Gemma was usually the sort of person who forgot things, but today she had everything and more. I watched as she took it all out of her bag and placed it on the worktop. Aubergine, onion, coconut milk, curry paste, fresh coriander, peanut butter.

'Peanut butter?' I said. 'That was one of the extras, wasn't it?'

'Yeah.' She smirked. Her eyes glinted.

I recoiled at her intentions. 'Gemma, you're not, are you?'

'What?'

'You're not going to put it in Peacock Girl's curry, are you, knowing that she's going to serve it up to Christopher?'

She burst out laughing. 'No! How do you think I'm going to secretly get a tablespoon of peanut butter into her pan while she's cooking?'

I slackened in relief. 'Well, thank God for that. I was worried that you were going to sabotage her food...'

She leaned in to whisper. 'I'm just going to swap them afterwards. It will be easy seeing as we've all got the same plastic tubs to take them home in.'

I stared, open-mouthed. Was she joking? Would she really get the opportunity to swap the food? I realised that the last period of the day was netball, where we would leave our bags unattended in the changing rooms. Oh God, she really meant it, didn't she?

'Gemma, you can't do this. What are you thinking? It's dangerous.'

'Don't be silly. It's not as bad as you think. Just one spoonful of peanut butter in a pan full of curry won't make much differ-ence. The worst that can happen is that he'll end up being sick, and Peacock Girl will be embarrassed about her cooking and their date night will get ruined. Next week, it will all be over for them both. You wait and see. Just one tablespoon will do it.'

'I'm not sure you're right.' I shook my head slowly.

'OK, I'll compromise. Just a teaspoon, then. That's all. It's just to have some fun.'

Feeling uncomfortable about everything, I took a chopping board and began to cut up my vegetables, following the recipe. My head was a mess of worry. I wondered whether to warn Peacock Girl. Or even tell the teacher. But I knew that if I did it would cause a massive scene and then Gemma would go mad and accuse me of being disloyal and fall out with me. Which wouldn't be ideal, because I was supposed to be going on holiday with her and her family to a Spanish villa at the begin-ning of summer, and my dad had – very grudgingly – already paid for my flight.

I continued with my cooking, along with the rest of the class, along with Gemma who was using the gas ring next to mine, stirring her saucepan with a devilish expression on her face. Defiantly, she picked up the jar of peanut butter.

'Do you dare me?' She waved it in my direction.

'Of course I don't dare you,' I snapped. 'I think it's a bad idea.'

She mimicked my concerns in a mocking voice, before picking up a teaspoon. 'Half a spoon, that's all. That's my last offer.' She dug a blob out of the jar and held it up for me to see.

'You're deranged,' I told her. 'It's a stupid risk to take.'

But she ignored my words and stirred the sticky brown lump into her simmering pan until it left the spoon and dispersed.

'I can't believe you've done that,' I said, clearing up the peelings from my chopping board.

Gemma had a stupid look on her face and she hummed an unrecognisable tune as she ran hot water into the sink.

What could I do? We'd been best friends since nursery school and although she could be infuriating at times, I loved her like a sister. I really didn't want to jeopardise our relationship at this point, just because of a curry and what was basically a practical joke. How bad was half a teaspoon? It was unlikely to kill someone, wasn't it? It would probably evaporate in the sauce, wouldn't it?

He wouldn't *really* die, would he?

THIRTY-NINE

SOPHY

We didn't find out about Christopher Bray until we got to school the next day. Morning registration was chaos. Our bus had been diverted around a flooded road, and me and Gemma filtered through the classroom door ten minutes late to find our teacher crying, a wad of tissue held against her swollen, red nose. No one was sitting at their desks. Students stood around in a state of bewilderment, most silently gawking at each other; some of the girls weeping openly.

A spasm of misgiving clawed my insides. What was going on?

I honestly never considered at that point that it would be anything to do with Christopher: I had gone home from school the previous day satisfied that he would not be in danger because I'd done everything possible to prevent it.

'What's happened?' I asked a girl quietly. She was standing, fingers clenched around the back of a pulled-out chair as if she'd been turned to stone in the middle of sitting down.

'He's dead.' Her eyes didn't move. Her lips didn't move.

'Who?' I gripped Gemma's hand as we waited for further information.

A piteous wail came from someone at the back of the class who was pressing her face against the desk, arms outstretched on the pitted Formica surface.

'Who's dead?' Again, I asked the girl beside us, but in a more urgent tone. Instead of replying, she scrunched her eyes shut.

'Oh my God, I feel sick.' Gemma's hand trembled in mine. Her face had turned ashy.

I held my breath. My eyes flicked around the room to see who was missing. Where was Peacock Girl? I couldn't see her anywhere. Please, please, don't let it be...

'Christopher Bray.'

It was only a murmur and it came from the far side of the room, but my ears picked out the name amid the sobs and subdued chatter.

I turned to Gemma. 'Christopher?' I dug my fingernails into her palm and although she stared at me with an expression of absolute terror, she left her hand there to be impaired by mine. 'What have you done? What the fuck have you done?'

'It wasn't me!' Her breath started to rag and catch as if she was having an asthma attack. 'It wasn't me.'

I dragged her out of the classroom and we went and locked ourselves together in a toilet cubicle, where we put our hands over our faces and whimpered into them. At one point Gemma threw up into the toilet, splashing the seat with slimy orange flecks which she didn't even wipe off.

'I didn't do it. It can't have been me!' She continued to insist that whatever had happened yesterday had no bearing on this tragic result. Something else must have killed him. Maybe it was something that Peacock Girl had done, either deliberately or accidentally. 'They do weird stuff, don't they? All that fascination with horror stories and blood and the supernatural. We don't know what happened at all, do we? God, here we are worrying, and we could go back to the class to find that he died in a car accident or something.'

She did have a valid point. No one had told us yet *how* he'd died. We'd just assumed that it had been something to do with the curry.

We drenched our faces with cold water and reapplied our make-up before returning to our classroom. Some semblance of order resumed and we all sat in restrained silence as the teacher explained in a small, scratchy voice that Christopher had died the previous night after a fatal anaphylactic episode. It was a dreadful accident that had happened very quickly, she said, and although emergency services had been involved, they had been unable to save him. His family had requested for Christopher's friends to give them some space for a while, and school would be informed of funeral arrangements in due course.

We were expected to continue with our classes as normal, but no one could concentrate. And then the next day, the Friday, there were even more students absent. About a third of the class stayed at home, shocked and grieving. Peacock Girl was still missing.

The following Monday was when the police arrived in school. Those of us who had been in the Food Technology class were asked to go back there, and so we nervously, hesitantly, turned up to inhabit the places where we'd prepared our ingredients and cooked our curries.

'You're not in any trouble,' an official-looking woman said to everyone. 'We want to recreate the scene and get some information for the coroner, to find out how this incident could have happened, because it's not quite as straightforward as we originally thought.'

The head teacher, who had also made an appearance,

leaned forward to make an additional comment. 'We need to ensure that something like this will never happen again.'

The Food Technology teacher stood at the back, her face scarlet, her eyes to the floor. With a shaking hand she opened the window to let in fresh air.

Despite the fact that some of the students were missing, we were all quizzed on which cookers we had used, where we had done our preparations and what ingredients we had brought with us.

'They're trying to track down anyone who had peanut butter,' I whispered, to Gemma's alarm.

The official-looking woman came around to chat with us all and make some notes.

'OK girls, so you both made the curry last week. Can you tell me if either of you brought any form of nuts in your ingredients?'

'No, I didn't,' I replied.

'No,' said Gemma.

I turned and gave her a hard stare. Whether she thought me a snitch or not, I wouldn't sit here and let her lie about it. 'You brought peanut butter, didn't you?'

'Oh yes.' Gemma gave a childish laugh. 'Sorry. I thought you just meant, like, nuts.'

'So, peanut butter in a jar?'

'Yes.'

'And was it only you that used it? Or did you offer it to anyone else?'

'No. It was just me. Just half a teaspoon, actually. Only a very small amount, so nothing dangerous.' There was a small twitch in Gemma's eye as she answered the questions.

'A tiny fraction of a teaspoon can be extremely dangerous to a person with a nut allergy.' The official-looking woman didn't look up as she was writing.

Gemma swallowed visibly and plucked at the fabric of her skirt.

'And, I assume that you know Dina Peacock?'

'Yes.' Gemma nodded.

'Did you take any container or implement that might have contained even a small amount of peanut butter anywhere in the vicinity of where Dina Peacock was cooking? For example, your saucepan, or a spoon, or even the jar itself?'

'No,' said Gemma firmly. 'No, not at all. I stayed here.'

It was true. I backed up Gemma's statement. We had stayed here all along.

The official-looking woman, satisfied with our accounts, moved on to the next pair of students, and me and Gemma looked at each other without speaking. Had we got away with it? We'd answered all the questions and technically hadn't told any lies. They just hadn't asked the right questions.

'Phew,' said Gemma at break time later. 'That was scary, wasn't it? I thought we were going to get done then. Thanks for not saying anything else.'

I bit my lip and looked away. My hands trembled in my pockets. I wondered then, if at some moment in the future it might all come back to haunt us.

THE RETREAT

FORTY

ADDIE

I splutter and cough: my chest is on fire. There's a prickle, a stabbing itch as my face is pressed into a patch of dry grass, and I writhe on the ground, feeling a jag of pain in the back of my shoulder. My arms are heavy as I flounder around to push myself up to a sitting position. I open my eyes.

What just happened?

Trembling and alone, I sit, gasping, trying to make sense of it. All my energy has gone. I touch my neck and my throat which is sore and bruised.

Did Gemma really try to kill me? Did she strangle me and leave me for dead? Did she actually do that?

I accept that I have poked and provoked her over the last few days, but I honestly didn't expect her to retaliate to the extent where my life would be at risk.

Where is she now? Am I still in danger?

I crawl to the edge of the hill and look out towards the pool, to where I can still see Sophy and Tom swimming laps back and forth across the water. The temperature hasn't dropped yet, even though most of the light has gone, leaving a mystical gloom behind. There is no sign of Gemma; no sign of anyone else.

Am I OK to stand? There's still a shakiness in my legs. It must be the shock. I'd shout out for Reuben but I don't want to alert Gemma. Maybe she thinks I'm dead. Gosh, is that what she hoped would happen?

Breathe. Breathe. Breathe. Everything's all right now. I'm still alive; I don't have any broken bones. Oh no, what if my baby has been harmed? What if... I tentatively touch my belly, spread my legs. Thankfully, I can't see any evidence of bleeding and there's no pain. It must be OK, it must be. I just need to get myself to safety. That's what I must do. And then somehow alert the police to come and deal with the situation.

Come on, Addie, I tell myself. Just get yourself up and back to your room, where you can lock the door and nestle in the care of Reuben.

I stand cautiously, like a newborn foal. My heart is still fluttering. I brush the dusty detritus off my clothes and out of my hair. I'm OK. I can walk. Ten minutes down the path and I'll be back in my bedroom and everything will be fine.

FORTY-ONE

GEMMA

'Gemma!'

I'm stuck on a cliff and Sophy can't reach me, and Matt is on a different cliff, and Addie and Reuben are at the very top threatening to kill us all.

'Gemma!'

Sophy is shouting my name, and even though I'm trying to move my hands and feet, I can't get anywhere and now she is hammering something but I can't see what it is.

'Gemma, wake up!'

Disorientated, I snap out of my dream and shove back the duvet. 'What?'

Sophy is in my room, standing by the door that I'd left unlocked for Matt. 'It's half past nine. Have you had breakfast already? Me and Tom were concerned that you didn't join us for a swim last night, and then there was no sign of either of you at breakfast. What's going on?'

I sit up and furiously rub my eyes. My memories of the last twenty-four hours are tangled in my head and I try to pick them out. Swimming? Why didn't I go swimming? Something happened, didn't it? Oh God, yes, I did something... Addie was on the floor... and Matt didn't come home, did he?

Something *did* happen.

'Have *you* seen him?' I ask her. My head is still groggy.

'Who?'

'Matt. He's gone missing,' I tell her. I run my fingers through my dishevelled hair and swing my legs out of bed.

'Missing?' Sophy gives a little laugh of disbelief.

'I was looking for him earlier because he didn't come back.'

'No.' Sophy has a deep groove of unease between her eyebrows. 'What happened?'

'He went out for a walk and then I saw him with Reuben. It looked like they were arguing and then he went off. I tried to follow him and then... Oh God, he never came back. I've been waiting all night and I don't know where he is, or if he's gone to the car or something.'

'What have you done to your arm?' Sophy comes across to touch the nasty abrasion on my elbow.

'I think I fell. Last night, just as it was getting dark.' I bend down to touch the scratch on my leg, too. 'Honestly, I've been scrambling about looking for him everywhere and I'm so worried...' My voice fades into a tremor as my throat clogs up.

Sophy goes to speak to Tom who is waiting outside the door. I pull on a pair of shorts. My T-shirt is damp and crumpled but I can't be bothered to change it. In the bathroom, I splash cold water onto my face and garner my hair into a scrunchie. Sophy and Tom are still mumbling in low voices.

'So, are you on your way to get food?' I join them outside.

'Gemma, we've already had our breakfast. We should really go and look for Matt.' Sophy glances at Tom as if there is some kind of conspiracy going on.

'Where was the last place you saw him? And what time was it? And were him and Reuben actually getting angry with each other?'

Tom's questions are suffocating. It's bad enough being in this heatwave without having to remember everything else.

'It was getting dark and they were up on the side of the cliff above the waterfall. And... I don't know... they were discussing something and then they were, like, pushing each other. And then Matt went off and didn't come back.' I try to remember the shadowy scene but with my state of mind after having almost no sleep, it's all quite blurry. 'So this morning, I went up on the ridge near the track that goes back to the office. I wondered if he could have gone to the car.'

'What time was that?'

Christ, what is this? An interrogation? It's as if they suspect me of some kind of foul play. 'I can't remember. Early, like around six o'clock.'

'And did you see the car?'

'No! That's why I came back. I think I went the wrong way.' Flustered, I wipe the sweat from my forehead.

Sophy begins to stride away. 'Well, we need to find him. Why would he stay out all night? I mean, it's not even as if he was drunk or anything, is it? And to be wandering around in the dark on *mountains*. It's a bit worrying.'

'Come on.' Tom follows her and pulls on the sleeve of my T-shirt. 'Let's all go to the car park and see if he's there.'

I scurry behind them, a migraine pulsing on the edges of my vision.

We pass the dining area, where Jozef has cleared the tables and is nowhere in sight. Everything seems desolate. We skim around the perimeter of the retreat site and take a different path to the one I'd tried earlier, an uneven trail between the rocks and heather. Heat is blasting down on our heads and I realise that we haven't even brought a bottle of water.

It has been half an hour since we set off. Already, we are sticky and jaded, disheartened with our lack of progress. Despite stopping every few minutes to look, there has been no sign of Matt, and nothing visible of the outside world. No buildings, roads, or the elusive car park. Just rocks and trees and mountains.

Sophy cups her hands around her mouth. 'Matt! Matt!'

Her shouts bounce around the hills. We wait some moments for a response, but there is none.

We are part-way down the mountain, our calves aching from cautious steps. Any unpredictable slip could have us hurtling to our deaths. I swab my forehead with the back of my arm. My eyes are stinging with salt.

'You know, she's not how I expected her to be.' My armpits are dripping with sweat as I follow Sophy.

'Who? Addie? You're not still going on about her, are you?'

'Well, she seems so nice and normal on her Instagram reels, but there's just something about her in real life that freaks me out. She honestly scares me.'

Sophy laughs. 'Scares you? I mean, I know the whole scene where Reuben turned up was a shock, and I can understand that you were embarrassed about your fashion calamity and spilling the juice, but I'm not sure what there is to be frightened of.'

'She picked me out in the yoga class and said that my thighs aren't toned. Literally humiliated me. And then there's all the other stuff. The black lilies and everything else. I'm wondering if Reuben is in on it.'

Sophy actually stops to double over and cackle. 'Oh, Gem. You take things far too seriously. And as for the black lily connection: who else would know about that? No one.'

'You don't think that it's some kind of campaign against me?'

'Of course not. It's just a coincidence. And as far as the way she speaks to you: you've got to remember that Addie's like a celebrity and those kinds of people can sometimes come across as a bit superior. She probably doesn't even realise she's doing it.'

Tom is out in front of us, scraping his way through the bracken. Suddenly he stops.

'Oh fuck.'

'What?'

We stand and look at the view before us. A jagged mass of rock, each pinnacle almost vertical.

'We can't get down to the track from here. It's impossible. We must have gone the wrong way again.'

My spirit sinks. 'Oh no. Sophy, can't *you* remember how we get to the path to the car park?'

Sophy doesn't reply. She's blinking out the sun, turning away, focusing on something behind us.

'What?'

'I'm sure there's someone following us.'

'Where?' I gaze in the direction of her eyes but can't see anything.

'Actually, I think it was Addie.'

'I can't see anyone.'

Sophy scans the tree line. 'She's gone now. Maybe she was out for a run.'

My head is woozy; my legs tremble. My chest is pounding.

Dejected, we scan the area for a way into the ravine that will take us back to the car park, but the more we look, the more we realise how inaccessible it is.

'Matt! Matt!' Sophy yells again, loud enough to send a flurry of birds up into the air.

Tom puts a hand on Sophy's shoulder. 'Come on, darling. It's only going to get hotter. We should go back.'

We reluctantly turn round. The sun beats down harder as we summon our last morsels of energy to clamber slowly, resignedly, retracing our steps along the ridge. It feels like hours before we reach the edge of the retreat again. Our faces, necks and arms are crimson from the effort: we are burning up with the heat and the rays. Exhausted, we all flop inelegantly onto the baked ground.

'We're never going to get out, are we? We're trapped here, aren't we?' I am close to tears. 'How are we going to find Matt?'

'We need to get Jozef to use the emergency radio. They might be able to send someone to look in the car park or get a mountain rescue team to come and search.'

Suddenly, there is a breeze, a rush of sweltering air. There's a familiar cosy smell carried on the edge of it that reminds me of tranquillity, of toasting marshmallows.

'I can smell burning.' My words have an excited tone, because – foolishly – I have the idea that the wood smoke might be coming from a house, a chimney.

'Oh my God. Look!' Sophy grabs my arm and points down to the ravine, to the track we have been trying to reach which will take us back to the car park.

Plumes of black smoke are ballooning from the trees: orange flames lash like ribbons into the air.

'Fuck,' says Tom. 'It's a wildfire. We really do need to raise the alarm.'

FORTY-TWO

ADDIE

Our pod was empty when I stumbled back in my shaken and dishevelled state last night. Reuben had left the door unlocked, returning twenty minutes after me with steaming mugs of hot chocolate that he'd got from Jozef in the bar.

'What is it?' There was consternation on his face as he saw the state of me: the terror and agitation. 'Has something happened?'

'She tried to kill me,' I told him with my chin wobbling and tears in my eyes. 'Your ex. She attacked me and strangled me until I passed out and left me for dead.'

He inspected my throat, but the red welts that had definitely been there earlier had already faded.

'I can't believe she'd do anything like that.' He shook his head, his expression astounded.

'Well, she did. I'm not lying. She's deranged.'

'When was this? Because I thought I heard some kind of argument outside when I went out to the bar.'

'It was about half an hour ago. Out on that hill that overlooks the pool. We didn't really argue. She just went for me like a lunatic.'

'Well, there was definitely a major argument going on. Yelling. Screaming. And I'm sure I heard a man's voice, too.'

'They're all as bad as each other,' I said savagely. 'I wish I'd never picked them for the giveaway. I certainly never expected to be attacked by someone who'd won a free holiday from me.'

'Look, shall I go and speak to her? Sort things out?'

'What? *Sort things out?*' I was dumbfounded that Reuben didn't seem to be taking it seriously. The bitch had tried to kill me!

'Well, what *should* I do?'

'We need to go to the police. Have her arrested.'

Reuben came to circle his arms around me and kiss my sore neck.

'I'm so sorry. It feels like I'm the cause of all this. I shouldn't have run away from our relationship in the way I did, and maybe if I'd faced up to her instead of disappearing then she wouldn't be so angry.'

'Why are you defending her? She tried to kill me. You think she's a psycho because of the way you dumped her? Let me tell you, it runs much deeper than that.'

'Babe, I'm not defending her, I'm feeling guilty about how all this has played out for everyone. And as far as going to the police, well, let's be rational about it. It's dark now and you can't actually get a phone signal until you go back to the car park. We don't want to walk down there in the dark, not knowing if the track is accessible yet.'

Despondently I slumped onto the bed and ran my fingers around my bruised neck. 'We're trapped here, aren't we? With *her.*'

Reuben went to the door. 'It's OK. Really, it is. We can lock ourselves in. And I'm here to protect you. It was probably just a moment of madness on her part. I mean, emotions were running quite high earlier at the meal, weren't they?'

'It's not simply emotions running high,' I said harshly. 'She's evil. She's an absolute monster that ought to be locked up.'

Reuben sat down and stared at me for a long time before leaning over to kiss my forehead. He didn't know the whole story. I couldn't tell him that I knew her before. And I couldn't tell him that I deliberately invited her here to the retreat.

From that first moment when she clicked *follow* on my social media, I was triggered. I baited her to put her trust in me. Then I waited.

I'd had no plans to kill her. No, of course not. But I'd definitely wanted to torture her. Oh gosh, the pain she would feel when I revealed that her ex-fiancé, the one that had broken her heart, was *my* husband. The torment that would burn through her with the knowledge that I was carrying Reuben's baby, after she had been trying unsuccessfully for months.

And I'd wanted to terrify her with all the little signs around the retreat indicating that someone knew about the terrible thing she'd done twenty years ago.

What I'd wanted to do was break her down, bit by bit, until she was paranoid and completely ruined.

Until she was only a husk of a woman with nothing to live for.

That's what I'd wanted.

But now... Had I pushed her too far? I hadn't bargained for her fighting back, had I? I'd never considered that my actions would lead to her wanting *me* dead.

Perhaps I had done all I could to Gemma, and maybe that was enough to keep her looking over her shoulder for the rest of her life. Perhaps this was the point where I should stop, because I didn't want to put me and Reuben and our unborn child in danger.

He came to me and pulled a blanket around my shoulders. 'You're safe now. I won't let her harm you. Let's chill out and sleep on things, see how we feel in the morning. We could always leave the site early: I'm sure Carys would understand. Then you could make a statement to the police in a couple of days if you're still upset.'

He stroked my hair for a while, and I calmed down under his touch. Had I overreacted? Had Gemma really been as violent as I'd thought? There didn't seem to be the damaging bruises around my neck that I'd expected to see. Had she really strangled me, or had it been merely a bout of pushing and shoving that had taken me by surprise? Maybe I'd imagined a different version of events...

Still, I didn't want to leave anything to chance.

'Lock us in,' I told him as I made myself cosy on the bed, warming my hands around the mug of hot chocolate. 'I won't be able to sleep if I know that she can get to us.'

I watched as he first opened the glass door and stood on the step for a few minutes, aroused by something outside.

'What is it?' My senses were still on high alert.

'Shh.'

I listened. There was a brief noise, a high-pitched keening. Was that the sound of animals roaming the mountains? Or was it something to do with her?

Reuben took a few steps away from the door and onto the path. The glass door drifted shut. I waited, bracing myself for some trauma, some incident...

Minutes later, he was back, inside, turning the key behind him.

'Everything OK?' I asked.

'It's nothing. Probably a fox.'

'So what was the argument you heard earlier? What were they shouting about?' This must have been something that happened after Gemma left me for dead.

'I don't know. I couldn't tell who it was. Definitely a man's voice.'

'What were they arguing about?'

'Well, I didn't get the gist of it. Shouting, swearing maybe. It was in the distance. I mean, it could have just been someone larking around. Don't worry about it.'

He smiled at me, but I could tell it was fake. He didn't want to scare me.

I decided then, that I would go and contact the police sooner rather than later. I would get up early in the morning and take my phone, to go back down the track to the office car park where I would be able to get a signal.

And then I would tell them everything.

FORTY-THREE

GEMMA

The fire could be half a mile away but we're not sure. We don't know how fast it is travelling, or which direction it will take next, and we don't want to hang around to find out.

Frantically we stumble, with pounding hearts and stinging lungs, over the boulders and along the ridge to get back. Our clothes are drenched in perspiration. The days of jogging through the city park have not prepared me for this journey of blind desperation, where slapping one foot in front of another in a freak heatwave isn't just an endurance test but a matter of life and death.

Gasping and panting, sagging almost to our knees, we burst through the door of the dining area.

Jozef looks up from mopping the floor. 'Everything all right?'

'There's a fire. Down in the ravine, along the track that exits the site. You need to contact the emergency services.' Tom is short of breath.

'How close is it?'

'It's hard to tell. But everything is so hot and dry out there, and we don't know which way it's going to spread.'

'We can't find Matt either. Have you seen him since last night?' Sophy adds.

'No.' Jozef puts his mop in the bucket and skims it towards the wall, joining us as we all head outside again. He scans the direction of the ravine. 'I can't see any fire.'

Sophy's tone is urgent. 'Smell it! Just smell the smoke in the air.'

A muted acridity has crept in to tinge the atmosphere. We might not be in imminent danger but the fire is certainly heading our way and blocking our exit from the retreat.

'OK. I'll make some calls through the office radio,' says Jozef. 'You'd better go and alert the others.'

I slant my eyes towards Sophy, who catches my aggrieved expression.

'Forget about your issues with her and Reuben,' she says. 'Everyone is in danger. We need to let them know.'

'I'll go.' Tom shrugs and goes to make his way to Addie and Reuben's room.

'What did you think we should do?' Sophy hisses. 'Leave them behind to burn?'

I can't reply. I pace around and tug at my hair as I watch the sky for each little cloud of smoke that is carried on the breeze.

'Maybe we should go and pack our stuff,' Sophy says.

I'm too distracted to do anything. I want to turn back the clocks and have Matt here by my side. Oh God, what if he's left me? What if he's somehow managed to get home and he's taken his belongings out of the house so that when I get back all trace of him will be gone, just like Reuben did?

Sophy is walking up and down the path, trying to monitor the progress of the wildfire. There is a definite whiff of bonfire on the air now, and I'm sure that we can hear a distant crackle even though the flames aren't visible yet from the site.

Jozef appears, with Eloise behind him, a crinkle of anxiety squished across her face.

'OK, so I've been in touch with the emergency services. I told them about Matt and they're going to alert the mountain rescue team,' he says. 'With the fire, they can't get a truck anywhere near, obviously. But they're going to put some kind of monitoring in place and have told us to make our way to the other side of the site. The thing is, by doing that it means we won't be able to keep in touch with them because there's no phone signal around here, and the radio equipment is set up in the staff quarters.'

'So what do we do?'

Jozef continues. 'We need to find a different route out of the retreat. I don't know what kind of terrain is over the other side though, because we've only ever used the track and never planned for it being totally cut off. I can't even find an ordnance survey map anywhere on site. And as far as we can see, there are hills and mountains in every direction. It's probably worth packing a few things to take with us.'

'What about Matt, though? We can't leave,' I say. 'He's still missing.'

'But you've looked for him already?' says Jozef.

'Yes. I thought he might have tried to go down the track to the car.'

Jozef scratches his head. 'I'm sorry, but we can't risk the safety of the whole group to wait for him. Maybe we'll find him on the way, or the mountain rescue services will track him somehow.'

'Oh God. Look at that!' Sophy suddenly gasps as a thick plume of black smoke sails past.

Fear takes me then, and my pulse kicks fiercely in my throat. The perfect week away that was supposed to bring me and Matt even closer, with the hope of going home pregnant, has become a hellish nightmare.

Is this really all a series of dreadful coincidences?

Or is someone out to get me?

FORTY-FOUR

ADDIE

'Is this some kind of trick?' Reuben holds the door open a crack, with his foot behind it.

I hear Tom's voice but can't make out what he's saying, and I'd rather hide away back here in the bathroom than go and see any of their group after what happened last night.

'And how urgent is it?' says Reuben.

What are they talking about? Is this something to do with Gemma?

'No, we haven't seen Matt.'

Matt? What's happened with Matt? I step closer, into the bedroom, to try and catch the topic of their conversation.

'No, *I* didn't have a fight with him. She's lying.'

There's more mumbling from outside.

'No, mate. I'm not joking. She's a bloody nutter. You should see what she did to Addie last night.'

I tiptoe another two steps towards Reuben and touch his arm. 'What's going on?'

'There's a couple of issues.' He turns around to face me and widens the gap of the door. 'Matt has gone missing. And there's a fire.'

'Oh gosh. Matt's missing? Since when?'

Tom nods his head towards Reuben. 'Apparently since he had a fight with your husband last night, up near the waterfall.'

'That can't be true!' I turn to Reuben. 'You didn't have a fight with him, did you?'

'Of course I didn't. If we're talking about fights, then let's talk about Gemma attacking Addie.'

'What?' Tom eyes us with some uncertainty. 'That's not the story I got.'

'Have you seen this?' I tilt my chin up and point at my neck. 'I've probably still got bruises from what Gemma did last night. She went for me. Throttled me until I lost consciousness and then left me there on the floor until I managed to come round and get myself back here.'

'Oh, really?' Tom moves in to examine my neck. 'Bruises, you say? There's nothing noticeable.'

I glare at him. He thinks I'm lying, doesn't he?

'So, was Matt around when this happened?'

'No! I went out to do some yoga in a nice peaceful spot at sunset, and then *she* came up and attacked me. I don't know how long I passed out for, but there was no one around afterwards. You and Sophy were swimming in the pool. Didn't you see or hear anything?'

'No,' Tom replies. 'It's too noisy when you're near the waterfall.'

'Well, it's true. She had her hands around my throat. I could have died.' I see the disbelief in Tom's eyes. It's disappointing to see how he automatically takes Gemma's side rather than mine. I was under the impression that I'd won him over a few days ago.

'Look, I'm not trying to defend her, but Gemma is stressed that she can't find Matt. I think there's been a lot of memories dragged up since Reuben arrived here, and also there's the underlying thing about her being unsuccessful at getting pregnant. I mean, poor thing, she's not really herself at the moment...'

'Not *herself*? She's a monster!'

Tom scratches his head. 'Addie, please. Let's consider the other issues here and put Gemma to one side. I know this is difficult, and the group dynamics aren't great. But this is an emergency. There's a fire outside and Jozef says we need to move to the other end of the site because it's heading in our direction.'

'Darling, he's right.' Reuben strokes my arm. 'We should go. Whatever happened with Gemma isn't going to happen again with all the rest of us around, is it? And I'll be looking after you.'

'OK.' I relent. I go to the wardrobe and pull Reuben's rucksack out to pack up our belongings.

'See you up there,' Reuben says to Tom. He puts on his reasonable voice. 'Just give us a few minutes.'

He closes the door, and we prioritise which of our belongings to shove into the bag. I fill up my water bottle; grab the sunscreen.

'How bad do you think it is?' I say. 'Wildfires can be devastating, can't they? I bet Carys doesn't know what's going on. She's probably on her way to an airport. And she could come back later and find everything burnt to ash. God, what a thing to happen after all the time and effort of building it up.'

'Look, it probably won't get to that.' Reuben is good at being positive in critical situations. 'The wind could change. And the ground up here might be too damp for the fire to take hold. But we need to follow procedure, that's all.'

He bucks the rucksack onto his back, and we set off towards the group who are waiting outside the dining area.

'Where are the flames?' Reuben says, turning a full circle on tiptoes to scour the landscape. 'I can't see any.'

But I can smell the smoke. My nose prickles; my eyes water.

There's definitely a fire nearby. And I have no doubt it's spreading fast.

Gemma is watching as we approach. But she won't scare me; I won't let her. I stare menacingly at her, unwilling to break eye contact. She can blink first.

Reuben takes my hand and grips it tightly. I lean my head into his shoulder and rest my other palm on the place where our baby is growing.

Just the merest hint of a vindictive smile on my lips is all that it takes for Gemma to blink and turn away.

FORTY-FIVE

GEMMA

There is no one coming to rescue us, no fire engines are able to access the site. We are on our own, monitoring the now visible barrage of flames that creeps ever closer, the fat clouds of smoke in the sky. Maybe this is Addie's doing. After all, Sophy saw her this morning when we were trying to find the exit track. Perhaps she's progressed from taunting me and now she's actively trying to kill me.

'The fire's almost up to the ridge. You can see all the trees alight from here.' Tom is monitoring the path of the flames. The hidden crevice that leads into the retreat is now a blazing fissure, totally inaccessible. I can taste the heat at the back of my throat, hear the crackle of the inferno's advance.

Jozef packs bottles of water into his rucksack. 'OK, let's go. We'll head for the waterfall.'

'They'll send a helicopter or something. Surely they will?' Eloise is such a positive soul.

'Maybe. But we don't know when that will be.' There is a crack in Jozef's voice. 'And we may have to consider that the only exit now will probably be down a rock face. So prepare yourselves for some climbing.'

None of us want to hear it even though we all know it is true.

The space between us and the ferocious blaze shimmers like an optical illusion. I watch as Reuben mops the gleaming sweat from his face, the ash in the air leaving stripes on his brow. Addie stands close to him, her cheek pressed against his shoulder, an arm around his waist. She's trying to provoke me. That's what is going on.

Jozef strides away, having established himself as the leader. Maybe he's had training, but it's hard to tell.

Whoosh!

Another cluster of dry vegetation in the distance is consumed in a beat, and then suddenly we can feel it, really feel the fire sear our skin so that we have to close our eyes and breathe through cupped hands. We can't stand and watch any longer; we have to go. Our week of bliss has come to an abrupt and unexpected end.

Tom has his arms full of bed sheets that he's pulled out of his pod and is stuffing them into his rucksack. 'You never know. They might be useful.'

We all scramble behind Jozef up the mountain path, past our accommodation that may soon be nothing but ash, around the side of the mountain, towards the waterfall and lake – still beautifully clear and inviting – an implausible reminder of how we all thought this place was some kind of paradise when we first arrived.

The thick air wraps around us, trying to hinder our escape. My hair feels singed, crispy; my eyes are smarting with the smoke.

Tom ploughs ahead, the white linen trailing out of the rucksack on his back. He is intent on saving us.

Reuben and Addie stride up front with Jozef, while Sophy trails arduously along the track, groaning with the effort. Eloise is still scanning the sky, still hoping for a hero to arrive.

'Hang on a minute,' Sophy pants, stopping to press a hand to her side. 'I feel like I'm going to suffocate.'

I grab her arm and hold her for a while, and the others disappear around the bend in the path. 'What the fuck is going on here, Soph? I don't mean only this, the fire, but *everything*. Just when I thought my life was so happy and I had such hope for the future, there's this. And Matt... Oh God, I've got the horrible feeling that he's left me. He's done the same thing as Reuben, hasn't he? He's done the same thing that everyone does to me. I'm going to get home – *if* we get home after all this shit – and find his wardrobe empty and his stuff gone, aren't I?'

'Gem, I don't know. I mean, it's probably nothing, and there's a simple explanation for Matt...'

'Everyone leaves me,' I wail. 'Why does no one want to stay around and be with me?'

'Gem, look, you're obsessing. Sometimes you really do obsess too much – you always have done ever since you were at school – and, well, you know...'

'You're trying to say that it's my fault? That *I* make things happen? That everything bad that's ever happened has been because I get obsessed with people?' My heart is hammering so hard that I'm light-headed and out of breath. 'Are we even talking about...'

Sophy puts a finger over my lips. 'Don't go there. We're not going back to that. We're calmly trying to follow a safe route away from the fire, and we'll find out where Matt has gone. Let's not panic, and stop overthinking everything. We need to focus on getting away and making sure we're all OK.'

I close my eyes and exhale. Christ, what is wrong with me? Why can't I be normal? Is this what keeping a secret for twenty years does to someone's head?

'Come on.' Sophy pulls me to walk again before everyone gets too far in front.

Around the side of the hill, the others are waiting for us.

This had been the quietest part of the retreat. Silent, apart from the click of insects in the grass, the *tsip-tsip* of meadow pipits, the whisper of the breeze through the rushes in the boggy valley. It had been somewhere to breathe in the pure air and be truly mindful. But now...

The fire crackles and cackles in the distance. It's difficult to tell if it is gaining on us. Birds scatter up into the cobalt sky, leaving us behind.

Addie and Reuben scowl as we reach the group. I am convinced that they know something about Matt's disappearance. I know what they've done: they've tried to discredit me; they've advised him to leave me; they've even helped him to get away. They know something. And I think that they know about more than they're letting on.

Addie's gaze is fixed onto mine again. But *I* won't be the first to look away. No, I won't.

'Everyone OK?' Jozef asks. 'Anyone need a rest?'

But we're all good, so we carry on walking, and eventually, the path runs out and we reach the edge of the mountain, the steep precipice where in some distant past the land has fallen away.

'How can we possibly climb down there?' I look fearfully over the cliff.

Addie mutters. Perhaps it's only meant for the others to hear. 'Maybe jump and see what happens.'

Jozef points to where a scrubby hill rises up from the valley. 'If we can aim for that, I'm guessing that there might be a road behind it.'

'But you don't know that, and it's miles away,' Sophy proclaims. 'Let's just face the obvious fact here. There's no way down. We're trapped.'

'Babe, you're being fatalistic. There's no need. We're all going to be fine.' Tom has a sheet between his teeth, ripping it into wide ribbons. I suddenly realise what he's doing, and watch from a distance as Reuben joins in, his biceps flexing as he yanks the fabric apart.

'Great thinking,' says Jozef. 'We can knot the strips together and plait them to make a rope, then use it to get down the cliff.' He eyes up something to tie onto: a jutting rock; a sturdy tree trunk.

'Who dares to go first, then?' Tom asks. 'Anyone?'

I am overwhelmed by a need to get away from here, from this poisoned place. I need to escape from all these people; I need to escape from myself. There's no other way out.

My hand rises first. 'I'll do it.'

'You sure?'

'Yes. I'll do it.' I pick up the end of the fabric and tie it around my waist. 'Don't let me fall.'

'You'd better get a move on,' says Tom, looking back towards the smoky sky as he starts to wind the other end around a solid rock.

'Ready?' Jozef asks.

Addie drills her eyes into mine until I relent and look at the ground.

'Ready,' I say.

FORTY-SIX

GEMMA

I shuffle backwards towards the edge of the mountain. Although it's daytime now and everything looks different, I remember that this is close to where I found Addie doing yoga last night. This is where it all *really* started to go wrong in a big way.

'Hurry up,' says Tom. 'The rest of us need to get down, too.'

'Is this secure?' I need Jozef to check before I go over the edge. What if the cloth doesn't hold? What if it has been tied wrong? What if I descend too fast and smash onto the rocks below?

Suddenly, there is a blast of heat. Sophy and Eloise shriek in unison and Tom squats, covering his face.

Jozef tugs on the plaited bedsheet around my waist. 'Don't look down. It's the golden rule if you've never done an abseil before.'

But I've already seen over the ledge. I've seen the sheer side of the crag, the dizzying distance to the bottom.

'OK. Ready.' I've got to do it. There's no other way out.

I drop backwards.

Scrambling, bouncing, with my teeth clenched and a gritty scream at the back of my throat, I cling on to that makeshift rope because my life depends on it. My knee scrapes on something abrasive; I unbalance and rebound, my shoulder slamming into the savage rock.

For a moment I drop my hold, and then I'm swinging, spinning, my cheek grazing a patch of something thorny.

Then I'm falling, as if the knot has snapped, and I yell and flail, grasping wildly at the branches and tufts as I slide down the cliff.

Sophy shouts my name and the echo bounces spookily around the mountains.

I hit the bottom and pass out momentarily, before realising that I am still alive, still breathing. I'm not injured; I'm just shocked. The ground is cold. Squidgy. Something squelches as I move my feet. I wriggle onto my side and open my eyes.

I'm in some kind of marshy, mossy bog. The wet, spongy surface has probably saved my life. My arms are scuffed and my face stings, but it doesn't feel like I have broken any bones.

Shaky and stunned, I push myself into a sitting position and look around.

I hear Jozef shout from the top of the cliff. 'Are you all right?'

I can't answer. A gasp is caught in my throat.

There is something beside me, butted up against my hip.

I can't speak. All I can do is scream.

A man's voice spills over the ledge. It could be Jozef's or Tom's. 'Are you all right? What is it?'

Oh my God, it's Matt. There's blood in his hair; there are scratches and bruises on his cheeks; there's a sharp piece of twig wedged under his wedding ring. His eyes are open but he's dead, and he's staring upwards as the sun burns onto his face. He's only got one shoe on.

'NOOO!' I scream again and put my head into my hands because I don't want to see this, I don't want to acknowledge what might have happened.

There is a clamorous humming: a busy sheet of flies hovers over the surface of his body. The unbearable heat shimmers around him and maybe it's my imagination, but it seems like there's already a putrid stench in the air. Repulsed, I scramble, crab-like, away. And then I realise: the others. They're going to come down here and see him too, aren't they?

Then they'll question everything about him and about us, peeling back the layers of my life until there's simply the truth, bare and exposed, and I can't keep it hidden any longer.

FORTY-SEVEN

ADDIE

My heart is pounding as Reuben stands on top of the cliff to see how the rope holds up as Gemma bounces her way down. GET BACK! I want to yell at him, because he could so easily fall. I imagine how he could lose his footing and slip, and it's only now that I am realising how dangerous this idyllic place really is.

I take a few steps away from the group and turn to see how far the fire has caught up with us, coughing with each breath of noxious air.

Suddenly, there's a scream. A dreadful, shrill bawl that bounces around the mountains as if it's in an amphitheatre. The others run towards the edge of the cliff. What's happened? Maybe it's Gemma. Maybe the makeshift rope broke and she has plunged onto the rocks and injured herself.

If only.

There's a babble of consternation, a fluster of questions thrown down to wherever she has landed. Some vocal toing and froing between Gemma at the bottom of the mountain and the rest of the group at the top. Then Jozef is pulling up the rope again, which looks intact. Sophy and Tom turn and look towards me but I can't decipher their expression.

'What?' I ask, but they don't answer and Sophy clamps a hand over her mouth with a gasp.

I move towards the group. 'What's going on?'

Eloise appears unaware of the panic that is spreading around everyone as she concentrates on tying the sheet around her waist, ready to descend the cliff.

Reuben, his face scrunched with apprehension, comes to put his hands on my shoulders.

'What?' I ask him. 'Has Gemma fallen? Is she hurt?' I try to restrain the tone of delight that threatens to stray into my voice.

He pins his eyes firmly to mine so that I can't be distracted. 'Addie, darling, you've got to prepare yourself.'

'I'm OK,' I tell him. 'I'm not a fan of heights, but this is an emergency so if I've got to get down that mountain then I'll do whatever it takes.'

'I'm not talking about that.' Reuben casts a look towards Sophy, who is standing by the edge, wrapped in a despondent embrace with Tom. Even from here, I can see that she is distraught.

'Addie.' Reuben rubs a hand on my back.

What is going on? I'm starting to feel nervous.

'There's a body at the bottom of the cliff. That's what all the shouting was about just now. Gemma is down there.'

'A body? Oh gosh, that's horrible!'

'We're all going to have to go down that way and see it. *Him*. It's going to be a shock for everyone. People will be asking questions, pointing fingers...' Reuben is squeezing my shoulders and everything is feeling strange, like I'm hovering in the air and watching myself down here with all these people.

'Pointing fingers?' What does he mean?

'The body... it's Matt.'

'What?' There's a sudden pain in my ribs, as if a knife has been thrust in.

'Everyone thinks that I was the last person to see him before he disappeared.' Reuben's voice breaks in a moment of discomposure.

'But *you* didn't do anything. Did you?'

'No! It's a horrendous situation...'

Didn't Tom say that Matt and Reuben had been fighting last night? Over near the edge of the cliff, maybe close to where we are standing now. And I had been alone in our room for at least twenty minutes after I got away from Gemma. Had it really taken that long to go and get the mugs of hot chocolate?

'Don't look at me like that,' says Reuben. 'I didn't do anything to him.'

'Well it was a pretty intense evening, wasn't it?' I can't keep the doubt out of my voice. 'And you weren't here when I got back, were you? What were you doing, arguing over Gemma?'

He tries to embrace me, to contain my suspicions. 'Babe, there was no argument. Nothing. We were chatting about the stars, the Milky Way. Matt's into all that sort of thing. He was telling me about one of the constellations and saying how he wished he'd brought his binoculars, that's all. That's as far as it went.'

I laugh loudly – too loudly – at the ridiculousness of his explanation. Jozef turns to look sternly at me. Tom catches my eye and shakes his head as he comforts Sophy. Maybe I'm coming across as a little hysterical.

'Addie, let's park this for a while and try to stay calm. Let's be respectful. We don't know what sort of state Gemma's going to be in. And on top of that we've all got to get safely down this cliff, and... God, we need some kind of emergency response soon. Not only from the fire service, but, I don't know, the police will have to be involved now that this has happened...' He babbles on and my mind drifts up to flitter away with the dusty clouds because it can't deal with the information that is trying to prise its way in.

Matt?

What, really? The husband of the woman I hate is dead at the bottom of this mountain?

Oh gosh, how did this situation get so out of hand? I know I wanted to taunt her, hurt her, wreck *her* life in some way in repayment for what she did to mine, but... Matt is dead?

I did not plan for this.

FORTY-EIGHT

GEMMA

I scream until my throat can't take any more. Then I retch violently at the foot of the cliff. Oh God, Matt. How did I let it get to this?

I step a little closer and squat down, taking shallow breaths with a hand across my face. His hands and arms are scuffed and scraped, covered with blood, the result of trying to grapple rocks and vegetation, the result of trying to save himself. The right knee of his trousers is ripped; his shirt is studded with thorns and twigs. But on his face...

What's all this? A busted lip. A bald patch the size of a coin where hair has been pulled from his scalp. Four long scratches across his cheekbone that look like they were done by robust fingernails. Just the sort of injuries you'd get from a fight.

Does this actually look like it was done *deliberately*?

My legs are shaking.

'Talk to me!' Jozef is shouting from the top of the slope. 'What is it?'

'It's Matt,' I yell into the air, a sob catching in my mouth. 'He's dead!'

'Check his pulse!' The instruction comes from Jozef.

I push myself back into a wobbly standing position and exhale loudly. I am dizzy, howling soundlessly deep inside my chest, gasping, tasting the foul air and the wildfire smoke that is gathering on this side of the crag now.

'He's gone!' I don't need to check a pulse. The flies, the lifeless eyes with the cold stare, everything I can see tells me that there has been no pulse for many hours.

Tom calls down this time. 'Is it Matt? Is it definitely him?'

'Yes!' My voice is cracking from the smoke and the shouting. From the hideous discovery.

They're all still up there at the top, their conversation a shocked rumble of noise, and I'm down here beside the body of the person with whom I was supposed to spend the remainder of my life.

'Gemma, the rest of us need to come down. You'd better move out of the way.'

Then there's a shriek, a smattering of loose rocks falling, as Eloise appears over the edge with the makeshift rope around her waist. Her hands and feet scurry beetle-like over the mountain face as she makes her way down, and with an undignified topple backwards, she drops with a groan onto the marshy ground. I watch numbly as she unties the rope from her waist so that it can be pulled back up again.

'What the hell?' she says as her eyes drift to Matt's body. The colour drains from her skin. She pulls her T-shirt up to cover her face.

'I know.' I bury my eyes into the crease of my elbow because everything is so overwhelming, and then the tears start to come, and I can't stop them. Hadn't Matt been the kindest, most perfect husband to me? Gentle, funny, inspiring, eager to please and so accommodating of all my whims and wishes. Our relationship may have been short and our marriage a whirlwind, but we were so right for each other. I was his yin; he was my yang. It was effortless how we clicked right from the beginning. I remember how, on our wedding day, we both smiled until our faces ached, thinking of all the wonderful times ahead of us. Thinking of the babies we would have together. Matt would have been the most brilliant father, but now he will never have the chance.

Eloise is staring, her body frozen like she's playing musical statues. Her mouth is locked open. There's a squeal from Sophy, who is descending the mountain, using branches and prominent rocks to feel her way down.

'I'm not going to look,' Sophy shouts as she nears the bottom. 'I don't want to see what's happened to him.'

She unties the rope, shielding her eyes from Matt.

'I can't believe it. Poor Matt. It's the most tragic thing ever.' Sophy comes to wrap her arms around my neck. 'God, what an awful thing for you to have to discover.'

I sniff and cry into her sleeve.

'How did he die?'

'I don't know.' I wipe my face and look at his facial injuries again. 'Maybe he fell or something.'

'Do you think it looks like he was attacked?' Eloise scrutinises me and there's a moment where we don't speak, but somehow we both *know*. We look up as Reuben climbs carefully, one hand on the rope, one hand seeking boulders and stumps to grab onto, as he zig-zags an elaborate path in our direction.

By the time everyone has descended, the fire has crept closer: we can smell the acridity in the air and the sky is now grey with smoke clouds. Luckily, we are protected somewhat from the callous heat by the slope of the mountain. A crescendo of sputtering is audible, the roaring of the impending flames. Spots of falling soot settle on our faces, smudging into the perspiration. We stand in a huddle, away from Matt's body.

'We should call the police,' Eloise says to Jozef.

I watch vacantly as Addie casts a look towards Reuben.

'We don't have any means of contacting the emergency services now. At least they know about the fire, and all we can hope is that they will be monitoring things. It's up to us to find a safe place where we can get rescued from. But just look... even a helicopter wouldn't find it easy to land around here.'

'It must be dreadful for Gemma,' says Eloise. 'The poor woman.'

Jozef moves towards me, to shepherd me away from the rest of the group. 'We need to walk on. Will you be OK to do that? We have to leave your husband here. Just for now, and then the police will deal with things later.'

I nod. Everything feels like it is happening in slow motion. I look around at everyone looking at me and I don't want to be the centre of attention any more, I just want to be normal and boring and away from here...

Oh God, the smoke, the smell. I retch again, spitting bile onto the ground.

Then I see them.

Just when I think that Addie's campaign against me has stopped, she takes Sophy's arm, pressing a sympathetic head against her shoulder. I can't hear what she says, but Sophy nods at Addie's words, treading forward, away from this scene of horror where we don't yet understand what has happened.

What is she saying? What is she telling her about *me*?

There is a sudden *whoosh* from above. Eloise screams, and we scramble away from the cliff as a tree on the mountainside bursts into flames, raining blazing debris down onto the ground.

'Come on!' Jozef takes the lead again. 'We've got to go!'

I watch as most of the group begin to run clumsily between the boggy clumps of grass, away from the cliff. What am *I* supposed to do? How can I just leave Matt behind?

'Gemma!' Jozef yanks at my arm. 'I'm sorry, but we need to leave.'

'Can't I stay with him?' But I know that it's pointless, however much I plead.

Jozef crushes me into a brief hug. 'He'd want you to be safe, wouldn't he?'

I nod, and a dry sob rattles out of my throat. Matt wanted so much for me, for us, and it feels like I've let him down. Resolutely, I pull my sunglasses down to cover up my puffy eyes and set off with Jozef to catch up with the others.

For five minutes we stumble towards a safer place, trying to outpace the smoke and sparks.

And it's then I see that Addie and Sophy have broken away from the group. They are further in front, arms linked, locked in conversation, in conspiracy.

They've locked me out.

FORTY-NINE

ADDIE

We stand around like we're at a funeral. Shock, grief, fear. The feeling as if time has slowed down. There's a background hum from the swarm of flies over Matt's body.

Reuben can't help but pace around. We're out of the direct sun but the heat is still intolerable. I fan the neck of my damp T-shirt to no avail. Eloise ties her mane of hair up in a knot. We all reek like steaming racehorses.

'Come on, let's get moving. The fire is going to catch up with us.' Jozef has just given some kind of motivational talk to Gemma, but now he's jittery, hitching his rucksack back on.

I put a hand to my belly, wondering if my child is safe. Would they be harmed by the smoke and the trauma? Sophy must be wondering the same, too. I step away from Reuben and sidle up to Sophy. Her face is pallid and drawn, spooked.

'Are you OK?' I ask, pressing up to her and taking her arm. 'Morning sickness?'

She pinches her lips together for a moment and shakes her head. 'I think I'm all right. Just hoping the little one isn't feeling the effects of all this madness.'

'Me too.'

A forced smile appears on her face. 'I know. It's a worry, isn't it?'

Is there a catch with the friendliness? I can't tell if she has another agenda. 'You must be devastated about Matt's death.'

'Oh God, it's such a nightmare. I know it's probably shock, but I can't take it in. Poor, poor Gemma. You don't expect something like this when you come away on holiday, do you? What an awful situation for everyone, but most of all for Matt. He was a good guy and didn't deserve it.'

A wry expression unleashes itself. 'You think some people *do* deserve it?'

Sophy doesn't get the chance to answer. The wind changes suddenly. A swirl drags the smoke around us and then we're coughing, blinded for a few moments, doubled over with choked lungs. We hear Jozef shouting to us to run; we hear footsteps like a stampede. Unable to see where the rest of the group are, we stagger away to where the smoke looks like it is thinning, holding the necks of our tops up to cover our faces.

'Hurry up.' Sophy pulls my hand, dragging me to go faster.

Eventually, we're clear, away from the stink, on our own. I link my arm through hers.

'Can I ask you something?' I'll risk a question now that we're separated from the others.

'What?'

'What do *you* think happened to Matt?' I watch her face carefully, to see what she might give away.

'I don't know. I couldn't bear to look at his body. Gemma said that he'd had a fight with Reuben, but – I don't know – there's also the chance that he got lost in the dark and fell over the edge of the cliff.'

'Reuben said he heard people arguing last night. Maybe Matt and Gemma were the ones who were fighting.' I watch for a reaction but she's not revealing any clues.

'She never said to me that they'd had a disagreement.'

'I think there's quite a lot that Gemma doesn't tell people. Like, did she tell you that she attacked *me* last night? Tried to strangle me? I had bruises all around my throat.'

I adjust the neck of my top and hold up my hair even though there's not much to see.

Sophy narrows her eyes. 'Really?'

'Really. Totally unprovoked. I thought I was going to die.'

Sophy doesn't respond to my information. She rubs at her nose and purses her lips firmly. It's obvious that she doesn't believe me.

'It's true. I'm not lying.'

'But Gemma said she went back to their room and Matt didn't turn up.'

I realise that Sophy is going to be a hard one to turn. 'You've always been very loyal to her, haven't you?'

'That's what friends are for,' Sophy says.

I wait for a while before speaking again. 'I saw Matt's body just now. His death was no accident. I saw the injuries on his face where he'd been assaulted. Those injuries weren't caused by falling down a mountain. What I think is that someone waited for him and then they had a fight which resulted in him going over the cliff.'

Sophy doesn't comment on my inferred theory and comes to a halt. The rest of the group are still trailing behind us. 'I'm going to wait for Tom. He's got water in his rucksack and I'm desperate for a drink.'

'Good idea,' I reply. 'I know the focus is very much on the tragedy with Matt, but we do need to look after ourselves and keep hydrated.'

'Oh God, look at the fire now,' she says, looking back to monitor the scene behind us, a hand clasped over her mouth in disbelief. 'It's going down the mountain. It's covered half the side of it and Matt's body is right there at the bottom. What's going to happen if the fire reaches him before anyone comes to help us?'

I tip a bitter smile towards her. 'I suppose they wouldn't be able to recover his body. And so they'd never find out what happened to him, would they?'

TWENTY YEARS BEFORE

FIFTY
SOPHY

Christopher Bray's death had a huge impact on everyone. His parents, who had doted on their only child. Pupils and teachers at the school who had found him to be an intelligent and dedicated student, liked by everyone. The local Goths and musicians who, with volunteers from the wider community, organised an allergy awareness gig in a city centre venue and played one of his songs to a tearful audience.

Distraught, the Food Technology teacher, having been scrutinised about her poor judgement in suggesting ingredients unsuitable for people with allergies, handed in her notice within days. She never returned to a career in education: instead she set up a dog walking business and sold sacks of pet food from her garage.

In the aftermath of that devastating event, me and Gemma kept a low profile. Everything about us was affected: the volume of our voices, our clothing choices, the subdued colours of our make-up. Any hint of Gemma looking like a Goth was removed and she even went to the hairdressers to have the black dye stripped out. We wrestled with our consciences, and Gemma constantly recited the mantra, 'it wasn't me; it wasn't us' until the words became meaningless. Neither of us could bring ourselves to discuss what had really happened that day in the Food Technology lesson, and our work relating to that particular assignment – along with everyone else's – remained unmarked. In our classroom, there were always empty desks where grief and anxiety took turns in keeping people at home.

On the day of the funeral, the school allowed us to mutely line both sides of the street as the hearse crawled through. We clenched our hands in our pockets, staring through our tears at the coffin that was decked with wreaths of black lilies, imagining Christopher's pale and lanky body inside, wrapped lavishly in satin. I speculated that it would have been red satin, taking inspiration from one of the covers of the classic books that he had been so passionate about.

The air was bitter for an early Thursday in March, cold enough to bring down flecks of snow onto the shoulders of our blazers, and we shivered expediently as the cortege passed. The black car that followed the hearse contained Christopher's parents who looked nothing like him. They seemed incredibly sad, but ordinary average people, with hairstyles just like our own parents'. Apparently, his mother worked in the local supermarket and his dad was a plumber.

We watched and waited, expecting to see Peacock Girl in the elite mourning group, but there was no sign of her. Later, we heard that she had not attended, instead staying at home, sedated by something that a doctor had prescribed.

With icy extremities and bloodshot eyes, we filed back into school with the rest of the students and went to the toilets to wash the mascara runnels off our cheeks.

Gemma braced herself over one of the sinks, breathing heavily. I wondered if she was going to be sick.

'If I'd have thought...' she began. 'If I'd have thought what might happen with that curry...'

There was a noise from the locked cubicle at the end of the row of toilets. I grabbed Gemma's sleeve and put my finger across my lips. This moment wasn't a good time for confessions.

The toilet flushed. Then the door opened, and a girl appeared, her eyes red and puffy. She was in the same year as us, a plain-looking student with a serious overbite, but I didn't know her very well. There had been occasions when I'd seen her in discussion with Christopher as they swapped CDs, so, obviously, she'd been a fan of his. Now though, she stood there, staring at us like we were some kind of freakshow, without making any attempt to leave or to even wash her hands.

'What?' said Gemma, touching the tips of her eyelashes delicately, one eye still on the mirror. 'What are *you* looking at?'

'I saw you.'

'What d'you mean, you saw me?'

'After the Food Technology class. In the changing rooms during the netball session.'

Gemma's jaw dropped. Her nostrils widened. She blinked about twenty-four times in the space of just a few seconds. She walked menacingly towards the girl to place a finger on her blazer lapel, under the line of her jaw. 'Just think carefully about what you might say next. Because it could have been someone else you saw, couldn't it? You could have been confused or mistaken, couldn't you?'

The girl's face flushed towards a shade of purple. She nodded.

Gemma moved her finger to hold it under the girl's chin. Things felt unsettling, threatening, and I was wary about how all this might play out.

'Gemma.' I had to intervene. 'Gemma, hey.'

'What?' Gemma didn't even turn back to meet my gaze, because she was too busy giving the girl her killer dead-eye.

'We *were* in the changing rooms after Food Technology, weren't we? We had netball, remember?' I spoke calmly.

Confused, Gemma turned, to quiz me with her expression.

'There were lots of us in the changing rooms for the netball session. She's right.'

'What?'

'Yes, she's right. We *were* there. She did see us. Just like she saw everyone else. All the girls from our class were there.' I gave a bright laugh.

I pulled at Gemma's arm. Pliantly puzzled, she followed me as we left the girl behind in the toilets.

'Why did you say that? What did you do that for?' she whispered urgently as we hurried back to class.

'Because trying to deny that you were somewhere when everyone knows that we *were* there is just stupid. It makes it look like we've got something to hide. And we haven't, have we?'

'No.' The excessive blinking thing was back again.

'So being aggressive with someone about it makes it even worse, doesn't it?'

'Yeah. I guess so.' She sighed and touched the tip of her eyelashes again. 'Yeah, you're right. Thanks.'

For a number of days after that incident, I worried whether the girl would have some crisis of conscience which would lead to her telling someone about our encounter in the toilets. A teacher maybe. The police. Or even Peacock Girl.

Perhaps she did; perhaps she didn't. We never knew. But whatever she did or didn't do, nothing came of it. And seeing us in the changing rooms didn't mean anything. After all, what evidence is a fleeting glimpse of two students finding somewhere safe to put their bags?

No, it was nothing to worry about.

But sometimes these little things linger, don't they? They

rumble along through the years, even decades, until the wind catches them and makes them fly.

FIFTY-ONE

SOPHY

'You know I won't say anything,' I reassured Gemma, time and time again. 'You can absolutely trust me not to tell anyone at all.'

I meant it. I meant every word, every time I told her. She was my best friend and always would be. I would always be loyal. Always.

Obviously, it was a subject that got brought up often, in those early days after the Christopher Bray Incident. We named it that because it seemed nicer than saying 'accident'. Although 'accident' had initially been safer than saying 'murder' which was actually what the whole thing had been, I'd pointed out to Gemma, since she'd basically planned it and provided the murder weapon.

'But I didn't do anything!' At first she'd protested her innocence, the way that all guilty people do. 'It wasn't me! It's not possible!'

I was gentle with her, despite her crime.

'Look, I'm not going to tell on you. Even though it was your peanut butter that you brought from your house.' I looked her in the eyes and we held hands. 'But believe me, I've got your back. Absolutely. Best friends forever.'

'I don't understand, though. How could it have happened?'

I genuinely believed her when she said she'd never considered that a tiny amount of peanuts could kill someone. I genuinely believed her when she said that she just wanted to cause some commotion, some humiliation at Christopher and Peacock Girl's Valentine date night. That was all. She certainly hadn't meant for anyone to die. Her only crimes were selfishness and ignorance.

She'd waited until she'd thought we were alone in the changing rooms and then – right before my very eyes – she'd taken the plastic tub of curry out of her school bag and swapped it for the plastic tub of curry in Peacock Girl's bag, knowing that Christopher was going to eat it that very evening.

In any other circumstances it would simply have been a practical joke. She'd tried to protest that that's all it was. A mischievous prank that had somehow, inexplicably, gone horribly wrong.

'Maybe so,' I told her. 'But it's not a practical joke when you know that the recipient has an allergy.'

'No one saw me swap it, though,' she insisted; she pleaded; she constantly tried to convince herself. 'That girl in the toilets, she only saw us in the changing rooms, didn't she? That was all.'

I reassured her for the millionth time. 'There was only *me* who saw you. And I won't tell. You know that I won't.' Despite what that student had said in the toilets about seeing us in the changing rooms, I was sure that no one had witnessed the actual act of Gemma putting her container into Peacock Girl's bag.

The Christopher Bray Incident shook Gemma up. Big time.

Her demeanour changed and she became nervy, shy, turning down dates until the offers stopped coming. She lost weight – too much – and lost sleep until her eyes looked bloodshot and sunken. She stopped wearing make-up, stopped doing her hair, stopped caring for herself. In the run-up towards the end of term, she didn't attend any of the revision sessions and made no effort to study at home either. During our final assessments she stared around the silent hall as if she didn't understand how or why she'd got there. It was as if she already knew that she'd fail most of her exams and have to contend with getting a dead-end job that she'd hate for the rest of her life.

It was as if she'd given up.

Just like Peacock Girl had done, too.

After weeks of absence, Peacock Girl arrived back in school at the start of the summer term, to sit at the desk she had previously shared with Christopher. Her face was paler than white, her eyes the blackest I had ever seen. Her piercings looked heavy and cumbersome. She took a picture frame out of her bag and set it in the empty space next to her. I assumed it was a photograph of Christopher, but it wasn't; it was the 'Wild Nights' poem that she had mounted in a glass frame.

All eyes were on her; she must have felt them burning as she sat impassively at the back of the room while everyone constantly stretched their necks around to see what she was doing.

Gemma kept her head down. It was as if she didn't want to see the empty shell of a girl that was the result of her rash jealousy. Quietly, unobtrusively, in a manner that mirrored Peacock Girl's, we got on with our work at the front of the class.

And then...

There was no provocation, no warning.

Peacock Girl leapt out of her seat and kicked it to one side. She upturned the table, a corner hitting the back of a student sitting in front of her. The framed poem smashed to the floor. Then she pulled her textbooks out of her bag and threw them into the air, screaming, while the teacher watched open-mouthed as pages fluttered out and spines broke open on the floor.

'You bitch!' She lunged towards the front of the class to where me and Gemma were sitting.

I ducked instinctively, but Gemma took the full force of Peacock Girl's rage. Her head was slammed down onto the desk as she snatched a handful of hair between her fingers.

'You fucking murderous bitch!' Peacock Girl was crying, sobbing out snot and saliva, and the slimy thin strings of it looped down to the back of Gemma's blazer to leave a trail that looked like a family of slugs had travelled across the shoulder. 'He was my boyfriend and you killed him!'

Cameron, one of the students sitting in the next aisle, quickly helped Miss Meredith to restrain Peacock Girl, prising a lock of Gemma's hair out of her hand. Unable to force her defiant body onto a chair in order to calm her down and extricate an apology, Miss Meredith instructed Cameron to assist her in getting the raging girl to the Head's office, so that her parents could be summoned. We heard the horrific shrieks as she was led away, feet dragging unresponsively on the ground, until she managed to escape their clutches and burst into the science department, where she threw a stool through a window.

The rest of us remained in the classroom, most of the students jostling for space at the window to witness the ensuing madness. I dabbed with a tissue at the bald patch weeping blood on the back of Gemma's head where her hair had been ripped out. A perfectly spherical haematoma on her forehead caused a mix of concern and hilarity with the jokers of the class likening it to a third eyeball.

The chaos eventually subsided and the classroom put right. Later in the morning there was an attempt at counselling the students through their adrenaline-fuelled confusion, and the school nurse attended to Gemma's head before sending for her mother to take her home.

In all the palaver, and beyond it, Peacock Girl's words that

Gemma was a murderer appeared to have been forgotten and no one ever asked why she'd made the accusation.

The school smoothed over the incident, and leaflets were given out to everyone about how to access young people's mental health services and grief counselling.

Peacock Girl never returned to our class. Someone told us that her parents and her older brother who was at sixth form college, had been on occasions to the school office to pick up coursework for her to complete at home, and then the next thing we knew was that an estate agent's For Sale board had been hammered into their garden.

More explosive information followed.

'Everyone's been trying to keep it quiet, but did you know that she killed herself?' I think it was Anna Skelly who broke the news to us. 'She put a long black dress on and lit candles all around her bedroom before taking an overdose. Her father found her, dead, clutching a picture of Christopher.'

'Oh my God.' Gemma was hyperventilating as we discussed the tragedy later.

'But people in the music room were saying different things. Someone even said that she was found on Christopher's grave, as if enacting a scene from *Wuthering Heights*. Someone else said that she was taken to hospital to have her stomach pumped but died the next day.'

Everyone discussed the rumours at length. No one found out what really happened. There was no drive-by funeral for the students to pay their respects this time.

But Peacock Girl, just like Christopher Bray, was dead and gone, and we never saw her again.

· · ·

We left school and bumbled through our lives. Things might have turned out very different for us all if Christopher Bray hadn't died, but he did so we just had to make the best of it. We had our jobs and relationships and our Friday nights out, and we did all the normal stuff like cleaning our houses and going on holidays and watching six-part drama series on Netflix.

We embraced technology to the best of our abilities. We got swept along by social media.

We followed influencers.

We really shouldn't have.

THE RETREAT

FIFTY-TWO

GEMMA

We lumber in what Jozef guesses is an easterly direction, carving out a path through the hills that tower around us. Turning now and then, we see the flames making their way to the cliff edge that we've left behind, feeling the frequent swathes of heat blowing across our backs.

The group has rearranged itself, forming different mini-cliques. Sophy is back in my possession now as we walk together, bringing up the rear.

'What was Addie saying to you?' I ask her. I can't handle the thought that their subject might have been me. Right now, I need her support, her loyalty more than ever.

'Nothing much. Pregnancy talk, that's all.' Sophy bites her lip and looks away.

There's more to it than that. I can tell from the way she is refusing to look at me. But there's something on her mind, a subject that she's deliberating on...

'Does Addie remind you of someone?' Sophy ponders. 'Someone from ages ago?'

'Who? Someone from school?' A nerve jars inside me.

'Maybe. I don't know. Actually, it's probably someone from

off the telly, not from school. I can't even remember most of the people that were in our class, can you?'

'No. I haven't kept in touch with anyone apart from you. And there are hardly any names from our year that I can think of.'

'Well, there are *some*, though, aren't there?'

My heart skips. 'Well yes. The obvious ones.'

The names Christopher Bray and Peacock Girl go unmentioned.

Sophy flicks her hair back and picks a leaf off her shoulder. 'Although it's not like we could keep in touch with *them*, is it?'

'So, who does Addie remind you of?' I can't leave this subject now that Sophy has started it.

'God, it's hard to think back twenty years, isn't it? People change so much, don't they? But do you remember that girl in the toilets, the one that you had an argument with? She said she'd seen us in the changing rooms on the day that we'd made the curry?'

'Her?' Of course I remember her. It's a face that has popped into my mind on many occasions. Something kicks and jolts under my ribs. A breath catches in my throat. 'You think... what? That might be Addie?'

Sophy rubs a hand through her hair and shakes her head. 'Nah. Maybe not. I'm just grasping at straws, making two and two add up to five. God, I'm overthinking like you here, Gem.' A laugh spills out of her and she playfully scuffles my arm.

I inhale deeply. The air is still tainted with fire, still tainted with Matt's death. She's set me off thinking now, putting my belly on turmoil setting. 'Really, though?'

'Forget it,' says Sophy. 'I wasn't being serious. I can't even remember what she looked like.'

I watch Addie, up in front of us, strolling along with her hand in Reuben's as if they are going on a picnic. Could she be someone from our past? Is it possible that she *was* the girl in the changing rooms? I wish I knew the truth. Whoever Addie might be, though, all I feel for her now is hatred.

We walk along, lost in our own dazed thoughts for a while, before Sophy speaks again.

'Do you think Matt died from falling down the cliff? Did it look like a head injury, do you think?'

I flinch at her question, at the way my mind has been forced into recalling the image of his lifeless, damaged body at the foot of the mountain. I don't want to remember him like that; I want to remember him laughing, looking stunning in his tweed suit on our wedding day. 'I don't know. But it must have been an accident. It must have been.'

'What if he had a fight with Reuben or something, and it got out of hand? You said you'd seen them in a dispute last night, and Eloise said that Matt had injuries on his face, scratches and things. She thought they didn't look like wounds from a fall, but more like he'd been in a fight.'

'Is that really what she said?' There's a sudden tightness in my chest. 'That it looked deliberate?'

'The police will have to be involved, obviously.'

I'm suddenly gripped by a wave of nausea. Maybe it's the repulsive fumes that we're breathing in; maybe I've been out in the sun for too long; maybe it's the stress of everything that has happened in the past twenty-four hours. It seems like my life is unravelling minute by minute. I stop walking and lean with my hands on my thighs, retching at the ground.

Sophy waits with me, rubbing my back sympathetically. 'Oh God, it's all awful, isn't it? I'm so sorry, Gem. I can't imagine the pain you must be feeling. He was a lovely bloke. Let's just hope that it was a horrible accident rather than something more sinister. I know that won't bring him back, but still... It's an easier thing to live with, isn't it, when you're picking up the pieces?'

A thought worms into my mind. 'What if Matt's body is lost

in the fire? All the evidence will be gone, won't it?' I wipe my mouth, unable to get rid of the sour taste of bile. 'There will need to be a funeral, won't there? But what happens if his body is gone? Could there still be a burial, like in a church? We never had a church wedding and I mean, we never talked about that sort of thing but...'

Sophy gives me a weird look. 'Look, Gem, I think you're in shock. We all are. Maybe we should just focus on getting out of here, and then we can let everything sink in when we're back home.'

'But how are we going to deal with all this *and* with the stuff that Addie's been saying...'

'Gemma.' Sophy grabs my arm as I begin to walk again. She must be able to feel me trembling. I realise that my babbling seems a little crazy. 'Are you OK? Do you *know* something?'

'No.'

'Tell me. Gem, if there's anything... God, we've been watching each other's backs all our lives, haven't we? Our friendship is practically built on secrets.'

What a thing to say. Is that really all our friendship is? I turn my head away so that she can't see the tears springing up. But she's right. All the stuff from our teenage years that could have destroyed us, and here we still are, looking after each other. To be fair, it seems like it's mainly been Sophy looking after *me* and I love her for it, because she's been so loyal and I wouldn't ever want to imagine life without her, and I know how much I'm going to need her again when we get away from here.

'Gem?'

'Oh Soph, I can't believe Matt's dead. I can't bear thinking about life without him. If only I could turn the clock back and do everything differently. We shouldn't have come here, should we? I shouldn't have followed her Instagram. Everything was going so well with me and Matt. He's been so kind and under-standing and I felt like our marriage was at the perfect point to have a child, but then... God, I can't get over how he ended up siding with Addie... you know, just like Reuben did.' A sense of unease grapples around my insides.

'Did something happen with you and him last night?'

Acid rises again in my throat and I gulp it down. The memory of Addie on the ground and my hands around her throat. The memory of Matt and Reuben together.

'No! I really wanted to go home but he wouldn't listen and we had a disagreement...'

'Shit. Gemma...'

'It wasn't *me*.'

'What wasn't you?' Tom has hung back so that we have caught up with him.

'Nothing,' I reply.

Flames dance on top of the cliff, hurling black spirals of smoke into the sky. Maybe it won't burn any further; it won't go all the way over the edge towards Matt's body. The air is certainly clearer here, and it's easier to breathe now we've put more distance between us and the retreat site.

My brain and legs feel disconnected, but somehow, automatically, I'm walking, stumbling along with Tom and Sophy, and everything is surreal, as if I'm playing a part in a disaster movie.

This can't be happening to us. It's not possible. Only a few days ago we were arriving at a fabulous retreat full of hope and anticipation, thinking how lucky we were.

But now...

Matt is dead and my world is falling apart.

'Hey! Hey! Over here!' There is a sudden uproar from the people who are a way in front of us. They're yelling and waving their arms, looking up to the sky.

'Look,' says Tom, pointing to a small black object circling in the sky. 'It's a drone.'

I could swear it's only a bird, but the heat is probably throwing my vision into confusion.

'Woo!' Sophy dances on the spot. 'Thank God for that. They've located us. They'll be able to send someone to rescue us now.'

While exhilaration buoys up the rest of the group, I sink to the ground. The fire is on the lip of the cliff now. How soon will the emergency services reach us?

I watch as the drone circles again, dipping, moving directly over me to get towards the blaze.

Tom comes to offer a hand and pull me up from the ground. 'Come on, Gem, don't give up. Looks like we're gonna make it out.'

I let him drag me up, all the while keeping my eyes on the drone which is now hovering over the marshy ground where Matt's body will have started to decompose. Sophy is watching it, too.

'Does it record things?' she asks Tom. 'Does it take photographs? Will it send them to the police, or forensics?'

But Tom doesn't know the answers.

Another flare of fire booms at the top of the cliff, spilling debris down the side, reminding me that we really do need to get away.

Will we actually make it out of here?

And if we do...

What then?

FIFTY-THREE

ADDIE

'How do wildfires start?' I ask Reuben. 'Do trees just spontaneously burst into flames?'

'I don't think so,' he replies. 'What we think of as wildfires aren't really "wild" at all. They're usually caused by unattended barbeques or people discarding things. Cigarettes and other stuff.'

'What sort of other stuff?'

'Well, for example, if there was a pile of grass or leaves and it was really dry, really combustible, and a small piece of glass ended up on top of it that caught the rays of the sun and directed them, then it could start to smoulder and catch fire.'

'Oh, you mean like a magnifying glass?'

'Yes, exactly like a magnifying glass.'

I'd got up at eight o'clock this morning. The room was in darkness, courtesy of the privacy glass which also acted as a blackout. In the bathroom I quietly changed into my running gear, leaving Reuben soundly asleep. My phone was in my pocket, charged and ready to connect to an available signal.

The morning was already hot. Steam hung over the ground; the insects were a rabble. Spiderwebs spanned the gap between the branches of the bilberry bushes. Even in my determination to do this dutiful deed I noticed all these things as I sneaked out of the glass door and along the path, past the empty dining area and out towards the ridge where the entrance to the track hid like a secret.

Because I had visited the retreat on other occasions with Carys to guide me around, I knew exactly how to get to it. I was no longer fooled by the trick of nature which deceived the eye into thinking that the dense cluster of vegetation beyond the hill was impassable, and that the path that forked to the left some twenty metres earlier would give easy access to the ravine and the exit away from the site. I had the confidence to continue towards the copse, to where the two sycamore trees bowed like a tunnel, and then all it took was a zig-zag through before I was jogging down the slope, on my way back to the car park and office.

Hidden in the cleft of the ravine, I felt secure with all the tall trees around me. It was highly unlikely that I would encounter Gemma along this route: their group had arrived in the dark and no one had shown them how to find the entrance to the path. I ran on, breathing in the clean morning air, motivated and purposeful.

This intended action would end it all, I told myself. All the ghosts would be put to rest; the grudge would be swept from my mind and I would be able to continue my life with Reuben and our child. It would mark the beginning of a fresh start. Because I wasn't just going to tell the police about what happened last night and how Gemma had attacked me. I was going to tell them *everything*.

There was a slight niggle in the back of my head about me creeping out without telling Reuben what I planned to do. But he didn't know the full story. In due course though, he would learn just how evil his ex-fiancée really was. He would thank me for his lucky escape.

I was about a mile and a half down the path. In the distance I could see the reason why Reuben had had to abandon Erik's buggy journey when he arrived here. As I approached, I realised the immensity of the tree that blocked the track, its trunk's girth being the size of a small car. Despite being horizontal, it was still in full foliage, a type of cedar, a majestic obstacle which looked like it would take some weeks to cut up and remove. Beside the track, a new cave gaped in the earth where the tree's roots had partially been pulled out.

There was no way to walk around it. I had to weasel through a network of branches before climbing onto the top of its vast trunk. It wasn't easy. Within seconds I had scratches on my ankle and a rip in my leggings. I edged carefully over the beast, trying to find the best way to get down, knowing that I would have to do all this in reverse later.

There. There was a space to get through. Between those branches that still held a tenderly crafted nest of one of the rare birds inhabiting the area. My cautious journey across the thin, shedding strips of bark was a tricky one, to the landing place that looked the least dangerous. I squatted and looked at the patch of rocky ground that I would jump on.

I launched myself off the tree and felt the tug on my thigh as my Lycra pocket became ensnared by an unscrupulous twig. There was a snap and a tear, and then the clatter and smash of my phone dropping onto the floor.

Fuck. Oh fuck, where had it landed?

I scrambled through more boughs, and sharp, broken spurs that snatched at my hair and sprang into my face. Where was my phone?

Pulling the greenery this way and that, I peered through the criss-cross of lichened limbs, kicking aside the debris. Finally, I saw it. I stretched my arm through the gap but it was out of my reach. Further down, I reckoned that I could slide my leg into a different space where I could kick my phone out and retrieve it.

Crunch.

I stepped on something that felt and sounded like glass. Oh gosh, no! Please, don't let my phone be damaged. Please, I just wanted to make one emergency call.

Rummaging my foot around, and nudging my heel against the phone, it eventually emerged face down.

I picked it up and stared in horror. Half of the screen was missing. The remaining half was broken. Grit and soil were encrusted in the workings of it. Shit, shit, shit.

Would it still work? I pressed the button and waited for something to happen. A vague buzz and a flicker over the surviving bit of screen gave me a morsel of hope. All I needed was to contact the emergency services. If I was only able to do that one thing, then everything would be all right.

I set off on a slow jog, away from the disruptive tree, my focus firmly on my phone. Nothing was happening. I tried to restart it and it gave another buzz and flicker. Maybe it would work properly when it was able to get a signal.

By the time I reached the car park I was sure that I'd be able to contact the police. I sank onto a grassy mound to concentrate my efforts on the task that I'd set out to do. The ground was so dry and crispy, and the heat was so glaring and laser-like that I couldn't sit for long. I held the gadget in front of my face as I blew at the dusty particles and shook away the loose bits of glass. I switched it off and on again.

Shit! I jabbed at the screen and another part fell onto the floor. Please, please, it couldn't be broken, it couldn't be! I had never experienced the devastation of breaking a phone ever before, but it felt like my world was ending right there in the car park. I pressed again but it didn't even buzz or flicker any more.

I was livid with the fallen tree and livid with myself for not being more careful. A yell spilled out of me, and I kicked out at the unrecognisable car beside me. This must have been the one that Gemma and her group had travelled in.

There was a rock near the front of the office, the one that Carys often used to prop the door open so that she could hear the birdsong. I stormed towards it, knowing that my journey couldn't be wasted: if I couldn't contact the police, then I had to do something else instead.

The rock was weighty, jagged, and went through the side window of the car without a problem. An alarm started to sound; the indicators flashed. The rock sat patiently on the passenger seat.

Fuck you, Gemma, I thought. I'm not done with you yet.

Recklessly, I grabbed a piece of the shattered window and threw it onto the ground. I reached inside the car to open the glovebox in the vain hope that their phones had been left there and I would be able to use one of them to call the police. What an ironic twist of fate that would be.

But of course they hadn't been so irresponsible.

I gave up on my mission. I dug out the rest of my phone screen before tucking the useless device into my bra. I set off back up the track towards the site.

The sun blazed down behind me, hotter and hotter. It bounced and twinkled and scorched all the facets of broken glass scattered around the car park. Some of them smouldered. Only one of them flared.

But that one was all it took.

FIFTY-FOUR

GEMMA

Sophy is a few paces in front of us. Tom is trying to motivate me to catch up with the rest of them.

'Come on, Gem,' he says. 'Just keep putting one foot in front of the other. You're doing so well, and it can't be much further.'

I grunt in response. What's going to be at the end of the track anyway? It's not as if Matt will be waiting for me. Then there will be the journey home, and opening the door to a house without him, knowing that he will never come back...

'It's a blow to us all, and it's going to take some processing.' Even Tom is tearful. He'd got on well with Matt right from the start.

I give a lengthy sigh. 'We should never have come here, should we? My expectations were too high and fertility is an emotional subject for me. You know how much I've been wanting a baby. But Matt was right behind the idea. He would have loved us to have a child, and I'd even started to believe that it was possible, I'd started to imagine that we'd be getting that flat-pack cot out of the loft and assembling it, and Matt would be painting the spare bedroom in nursery colours... But then everything – *everything* – has totally gone wrong.' My voice cracks and quivers. 'Oh God... Matt, just lying there. Did you see him?'

'Oh, Gem, what can I say? We're in an awful situation and can't even begin to think how we'll get over it.' Tom latches his arm through mine. 'But we will.'

'It's not only that, though. There's even more to it all than Matt's death.'

'How can there be more to it?'

'Things were so *weird*. There were signs all over the place.' I shudder.

Tom splutters. 'What do you mean?'

'Addie took against me. She used every opportunity she could to humiliate me.'

Tom wrinkles up his face and turns to look at me. 'What? But Matt's death is nothing to do with Addie! How can you think...?'

'I don't mean Matt's death necessarily. I mean the other things. You saw how she was. She wanted to make me feel small, so she put me right at the end of the table. And all that embarrassment with the spilt juice on my dress, after she turned up wearing the same as me.'

Tom shakes his head.

'Come on! Don't let your grief for Matt make you angry about all this other stuff. You can't blame spilt juice on Addie. You were clumsy. And you buy all the clothes she recommends on her account, but then complain that she wears the same things as you? Gemma, she actually seems *nice*. I don't know how you saw her as anything else.'

'But there's something definitely off with her. The way she looks at me. You know, I actually think that she picked *me* for the giveaway, out of thousands of people, because she wanted to bring me here for a reason.'

'Well, you're completely wrong about that.' Tom's sarcastic tone lets me know that he's still on Addie's side. 'I asked her yesterday how she'd chosen the winners, and she said that before she'd even announced the giveaway, she'd decided to pick the fourteenth person to comment because fourteen is a significant number for her. And that was you.'

I gulp at the same time as my heart skips.

'Fourteen? Is that what she said?'

'Gem, stop it. If you're trying to make some kind of connection, you need to stop it. I know you're devastated about Matt, but there's no point in overthinking everything else that's happened. It's just not relevant.'

I can't speak. I can't explain to him because he won't see it the way that I can. Fourteen is a significant number for me, too. Because Christopher Bray died on Valentine's Day, the *fourteenth* of February.

Tom scratches his head and gives up on the conversation. Picks up his tempo to close in on Sophy.

I try to forget about Matt for a moment as the space in my brain starts filling up again.

Fourteen. The fourteenth person to comment.

I think back to Addie's giveaway announcement on Instagram, and the long, endless registry of people who'd tagged their friends in the hope of winning. I visualise my own attempt, scrolling in my mind through the list, down, down, down to the next page, then the next. *Fourteen?* There was no way *I* was the fourteenth person to comment. At least fifty people had applied before me. Maybe even a hundred.

I stop in my tracks, a cold ribbon of sweat at the back of my neck.

Addie picked me and Sophy out of all those thousands of applicants. It was no coincidence; it was a deliberate act.

Oh God.

She knows what I did.

FIFTY-FIVE

ADDIE

Jozef gets us to step up the pace until I feel light-headed and have to stop again. Behind us, Eloise has slowed down to walk with Sophy and Gemma, while Tom is doing some strange and springy side-step movements like footballers do during training.

'Hey.' He catches up with me and Reuben. 'Have you seen any more of the drone?'

'No, nothing.' Reuben swigs from a bottle of water before passing it to me.

'I don't feel like I can keep going for much longer.' I smear a grimy hand across the sweat on my forehead.

'So much for a luxury retreat,' says Reuben. 'It's been more of a living nightmare, hasn't it?'

Tom pings the neck of his T-shirt to cool himself down. 'It's not how any of us would have wanted or expected it to end, is it? God knows what will happen when we get out of here. There'll be police swarming all over the place. We'll all need to give a statement.'

'Gosh, yes,' I say. 'Well, I'm quite happy to do that.'

Tom turns to Reuben. 'You were allegedly the last one to see Matt last night, weren't you?'

'What?' A ridge appears between his eyes. 'I don't think so. I'm pretty sure I heard him arguing with someone after that. Don't you remember me telling you, Addie?'

'Well...' I know that Reuben mentioned some kind of fracas outside, but I didn't hear it, did I?

'I thought it was you who had an argument with Matt?' Tom points his finger at Reuben. 'Gemma said that she saw you both fighting, up on the cliff.'

Reuben laughs in confusion. 'Fighting? God, no. We were chatting about stars and the Milky Way, that sort of thing. It was all friendly. He even wished me good luck with the baby.'

'Hmm. Differing accounts.' Tom widens his eyes to demonstrate the absurdity of Reuben's explanation. 'She said there was a scuffle. Some shoving and slapping before Matt looked like he was trying to walk away. That's what Gemma said she saw.'

There's a discomfort building in my stomach as I listen to Reuben attempting to defend himself. Should I be worried? Would he really have been talking about astronomy? I never knew that he had an interest in it.

'Well...' There's confusion in the way that Reuben shrugs his shoulders. 'She's lying.'

'I suppose though, if we all give a statement, then the police will work it out, won't they?' Tom looks between us and gives a twisted smile.

'Oh, wait. Hang on.' Reuben is having a lightbulb moment. 'No, I know how she must have been mistaken. There was an insect. Like a big mosquito or horsefly or something. It came buzzing around and we thought it was a wasp at first. Wouldn't leave us alone. Matt tried to swat it away but it came back and landed on my neck. Gave me a lethal nip that's been itching all day.'

Reuben pulls the collar of his T-shirt down to reveal an

angry red pustule, radiating a large pink circumference around it.

'Oh gosh, what a bite,' I say, reaching out to touch it. 'Looks like it might be infected. Are you sure it's not a wasp sting?'

'It might be a tick,' Tom suggests.

'Whatever it is, it's sore. And it's the reason that someone seeing us dancing about in the semi darkness might have thought we were having an altercation.'

Tom looks at me and nods. 'Yeah, I can see how that might have happened. You ought to see if Jozef has any antiseptic cream in his first aid kit for that.'

'My poor man.' I press my lips onto the livid spot to kiss it better. How could I have even considered that Reuben would lie about his encounter with Matt?

There is only one liar in our group that I know of.

FIFTY-SIX

ADDIE

'Come on, folks! Don't lag behind.' Jozef waves his hands in the air, walking backwards as he shouts out to us.

'You two go ahead,' I say to Reuben and Tom as we edge round the path of yet another hill. I need to take my shoe off to get a stone out. 'I'll catch you up.'

I hop and totter before crouching to untie my laces which have knotted of their own accord. Frustrated, I tug and tug, which doesn't help.

Suddenly, there's a freak rush of wind stirring up the dust, bringing in more clouds of smoke, and I wrap my arms over my face and eyes to protect them. I'm momentarily disorientated, then there are shouts from behind me and the sound of running footsteps.

'Owww!' Someone has fallen, and a hubbub of voices resonates somewhere around the other side of the hill, out of my sight.

Frantically, I prise the shoe off without undoing the laces. I need to remove the tiny stone that is digging into my foot before the rest of the group reaches me. Then the air is clearing again, and a rock behind me offers support, so I lean against it while I tackle the stubborn knot.

'Hey, look who it is.' The sarcastic tone can belong to only one person out of the trio that appears around the bend of the track. Gemma. She comes to stand in my personal space with one hand on her hip, having found a burst of assertiveness.

Eloise, seemingly uneasy and sensing confrontation, manoeuvres past us and increases her pace to catch up with the group of men in front. Sophy uses the opportunity to stop and swig from her bottle of water.

I stand on one leg, holding my shoe, my back against the rock. Although there's a vulnerability in my stance, I need to face her off; I won't be threatened by the likes of her. Even after what she did to me last night, I need to hold my ground and put on a show of confidence. If she attacks me again, I will be prepared. I'm fit; I'm stronger than her.

'What is going on?' Gemma's question cuts into the anticipation. 'Just tell us what is going on with *everything* here.'

Sophy glances at her indeterminately.

'Everything?' I can't help the leering smile that sneaks onto my lips. 'Do you mean the fire? Or are you talking about something else?'

'You know what I mean. *The fourteenth person to comment.*' Gemma puts on a silly voice. 'I wasn't the fourteenth person, was I? But you wanted to bring us here for a reason, didn't you? We didn't *win* anything. And now my husband is dead. So you've got some explaining to do.'

The moment is paralysing. Electric. I should have known that I would have to explain myself at some point.

Sophy visibly holds her breath, and Gemma glares in fury. I scan the enthralling scenery for a few seconds before turning back to them with a serious expression.

'*Everything*? Ahh, you mean Christopher Bray, don't you? That sort of everything.'

Gemma looks like her chest is about to explode. Sophy seems unaware that she is crushing the plastic bottle in her hand.

'I added some little touches to your stay. Did you notice? The black lilies. The Emily Dickinson poem. The curry with the deadly peanut butter. A killer of a dish *that* was.'

'What is this about? What are you trying to achieve? All that happened twenty years ago.' There's a wobble of breathlessness in Gemma's voice. There's fear. 'It wasn't me. It wasn't us.'

I gesticulate my left hand around my face and down the front of my body. 'You haven't recognised me, have you? You really haven't.'

I see the confusion on their faces. They're wondering if I was someone in their class. Or maybe they're wondering if Christopher Bray had a long-lost sister.

'Tell us what's going on,' Gemma demands again.

Where do I start? How do I begin to explain how Gemma's recklessness ruined so many lives? She killed a teenage boy, cut his life short when he had so much potential. His parents were shattered by the loss; their lives were never the same again; years were spent going to counselling, swallowing medication, sitting by his grave. His wider family – aunties, uncles, cousins – felt the pain too, and in an effort to achieve some element of justice began a campaign against me, a tirade of false accusations and smears that I'd allowed this tragedy to happen in my house by not doing enough to save him. My own family were harassed, and even though grief had devastated me I also felt guilty that my parents were getting their car vandalised, that eggs were being thrown at the windows.

I felt so guilty about it that I tried to take my own life.

The domino effect rippled through the years, through wrong decisions and bad choices for so many people. It all began when Gemma selfishly, senselessly, deliberately acted in a way that would cause the death of someone else. And although I hadn't intended to track Gemma down and get revenge, when the opportunity presented itself I knew that I shouldn't waste it.

So, OK. It's time for the moment of truth. I've spun them out for long enough.

'You two were the popular girls at the time, weren't you? I saw how everyone followed you around. Weird, isn't it, that people used to want to be just like you?' A gush of laughter spills out of me and sounds almost manic. It's not, though. I'm simply happy that we've finally reached this moment. 'But now *you* follow *me*! It's bizarre when you think about it. I suppose I was very different then. I didn't look anything like this and I was much thinner. School wasn't great and I hated being there. I didn't really make any friends. Christopher was the only person who understood me.'

'I don't remember you at all,' Gemma says weakly.

Sophy chips into the conversation. 'I don't remember anyone at school called Addie.'

'Well, I wasn't called Addie then.' I punch my own chest. 'My proper name is actually Adina, but when I was at school I was called Dina. Obviously, when I became an influencer I wanted to reinvent myself.'

I watch their faces as some vague memory scratches at the layers of their brains.

'Dina. You're the "D" that Reuben sent texts to,' Gemma states flatly. 'You were having an affair with him while he was with me.'

I hold up my arms. 'I've never denied that. But as I've said before, I didn't know that he was with *you* at the time. When I found out, though, it did feel like things had come full circle.'

'Dina.' Sophy's face drains of colour. She clasps her fingers around Gemma's arm. 'Dina Peacock.'

Realisation strikes. Gemma's mouth falls open. 'No. No, it can't be. It's not possible.'

'Peacock Girl,' says Sophy. 'You look completely different without all the goth make-up. No wonder we didn't recognise you.'

Gemma stares into my eyes. 'We thought you were dead. Everyone said that you'd killed yourself.'

'Oh yes, I know.' I nod vigorously. 'The rumours were rife, weren't they? I did attempt an overdose a few weeks after Christopher's death. Luckily, I was taken to hospital in time for them to save me. So I'm very much alive, as you can see. I just never returned to school after that episode where I attacked you. Basically, I was removed for *your* safety as much as my own. You see, people kept making accusations. They thought that I'd killed Christopher. You know, all the thing about Goths being obsessed with death and tragedy... They really thought it might have been some kind of pact like Romeo and Juliet.' I rest a hand over my face for a few moments. 'It wasn't a pact, though. It wasn't me who killed him. *We* know that, don't we, girls?'

Gemma is gasping for breath. I see how worried and woozy she looks in this heat, in the midst of this reminder of the thing that she's been trying to forget, trying to hide for these past twenty years. 'It wasn't me. It was a prank, an accident.'

Searing hatred rears up in me at her words. 'Do you know how utterly petrifying it is to watch someone have an anaphylactic reaction? To try and help them, grappling around for an EpiPen, to jab it in and find that it doesn't save them, and then the panic properly sets in as you have to call an ambulance, while you see the person you love fade away in front of you? Do you know how that feels? No? Or when you're pumping someone's chest and screaming at them not to die and telling yourself and telling them that it will be OK, the ambulance will be there soon and even if I can't save him then they will? And then have you ever experienced even a fraction of the horror of witnessing paramedics shocking someone with a defibrillator over and over again to try and restart their heart, to no avail? No? And I won't bore you with all the rest... all the grief that I got from Christopher's family afterwards with everyone assuming that his death was *my* fault.'

I notice, on the edge of my vision, that Tom has turned round and is making his way zealously towards us. His advancing presence makes me braver; it coaxes more of the truth out of me.

'So yes, I was taken away. I disappeared. It was probably a good thing, really. Because if I hadn't been, then who knows who else might have died?'

Sophy speaks up. 'What do you mean, *who knows who else might have died?* What, you had plans to kill someone?'

'I was so angry. Knowing that Christopher's death was preventable. I wanted to lash out, to get revenge. I would have done *anything*. At the time, I would literally have killed you both.'

'It wasn't us,' says Gemma pathetically.

'The thing is... I know otherwise. I worked it out. Someone saw you in the changing rooms. Someone told me they'd seen you swapping my container for yours. And you knew that Christopher was allergic to nuts, didn't you? And you wanted to split us up, didn't you? Because you were obsessed with him. Just like you were obsessed with Reuben. And it also makes me think... how obsessed were you with Matt? How far would you go to stop him finding out about your past and what you did?'

Gemma lets out a howl and lunges towards me, grabbing at my hair. I try to dodge out of her way, try to fend her off using the shoe that is in my right hand, whacking her arms and shoulders.

'Gemma!' Sophy shrieks. 'Gemma, stop it!'

But Gemma has me in a headlock; she's stamping on my shoeless foot; she's jostling me, ramming me into the rock...

'HEY!'

Suddenly Tom is here, slicing between us, splitting her away from me. I stand breathless, wordless, watching as he takes her arms and marches her away from us.

'Oh God,' says Sophy, who is stunned, motionless beside me.

I smooth my hair down and tackle the knot again on my shoelaces. Miraculously, it's freed within seconds.

'Oh God,' Sophy says again. 'I can't believe all this.'

I put my shoe back on and begin to walk, with Sophy following.

'Addie,' she says. 'Can I talk to you about something?'

'Go on. Let me guess what the subject will be.'

'So, yes. It's about Gemma. But I want you to know that what happened with Christopher... It's not what you think. And... oh God, I hope you don't think that *I* was involved, too?'

'Sophy, I know you've covered for her all this time. You were actually with her in the changing rooms when the containers were swapped. There was a witness. It makes you an accessory.'

'But if a witness came and told you what they apparently saw, then why didn't either you or her say something at the time?'

'OK, I'll level with you. It's a good question.' It's something I have regretted bitterly over the years. Justice could have been done ages ago, through the legal route, leaving me to get on with my life. 'The witness was a nervous girl who didn't want to speak to the police. And I know that I could have said something at the time, but my mental health was so far down the pan that no one would have believed me anyway. I was constantly on the boil, simmering with rage, unable to be around people. My schooling had ended and I had no qualifications: did you know that? But when I was healed enough to think logically about what had happened and what should be done about it, I'd lost touch with everyone. Gosh, I hadn't even known the girl's surname to be able to contact her again.'

'So, you have nothing that can be proven, then?'

'Just because I can't prove it doesn't mean that Gemma isn't guilty. And it doesn't mean that you weren't involved, too.'

Sophy grabs my arm, and I flinch. 'Addie, I want you to know that I did everything I could to prevent what happened. Everything. I was devastated to hear about Christopher's death because it should have been impossible...'

I pull my arm away. 'Whatever you did, Sophy, it wasn't enough, was it? And now, look at everything else that's happened. Matt is dead, too.'

Sophy shakes her head. 'What happened to Christopher, and what happened to Matt: they were just horrible accidents. That's all. There's no point trying to assume otherwise. There's no point in trying to get revenge...'

I step up my pace so that the rest of the group doesn't get too far in front. 'What? You think we should quietly go home and say nothing more about it all?'

'But Gemma's husband is dead. Surely to see her grieving is revenge enough for you?'

'It's about justice.' I stop and turn to face Sophy head-on. 'Gemma is dangerous and will do anything to hide the truth of what she did. She even tried to kill *me* last night. So, what I'm going to do when we get out of here is make a statement to the police, about her assault on me, and about what she did to Christopher. He deserves *proper* justice. And maybe you need to have a think about where *your* loyalties lie, and who you're going to cover for this time.'

Sophy stares at me, her mouth dropping open.

'I mean it.' I walk away purposefully, leaving her to consider my words.

Five seconds, ten seconds, fifteen...

There's a thud of footsteps behind me and a hand on my arm.

'OK,' says Sophy. 'I'll go to the police with you. I'll tell them everything.'

FIFTY-SEVEN

GEMMA

I lurch over each stone, each tuft of grass, as Tom drags me along. My lungs are burning; my skin is drenched. Surely the temperature will drop soon; it can't possibly get any hotter.

'Whatever has happened between you and Addie needs to stop. We're a group, and we're trying to get to safety, all of us.' He berates me like I am a child.

'Please, you're hurting my arm. I was just... she was saying about Matt...' I plead and whine until he relaxes his grip on me. 'Sorry, Tom. I'm OK now. I'm calm.'

Sophy is still some way behind us with Addie.

I force myself into step alongside Tom, grateful for his quiet, unquestioning company. I stop myself from looking behind me, to where Addie and Sophy are deep in conversation. We slog onwards, keeping Jozef's group in our sights as we wind this way and that, taking a chance on each turn, on each thin rut that has the potential to be an established path. Insects chant and chitter around us: our ears ring with their uproar. The air clears with each step, yet my mind becomes more frantic.

We stumble on, and somehow people adjust their walking speeds so that we are almost one big group again. Addie is back beside Reuben; Sophy is between Jozef and Eloise, and Tom keeps me closely by his side.

Suddenly, a helicopter trails high up across the sky, and, with a rush of hope and exhilaration everyone wears themselves out yelling and thrashing their arms in the expectation that it is going to land.

Then, nothing.

Ten minutes go by. Then another ten. And before we realise, it's been forty.

There is no further helicopter, no sign of a rescue operation. We walk on and on, exhausted, bereft of food, having drunk the last drops of our water rations. As the afternoon stretches out, we realise that we can no longer see the fire.

'Perhaps it's stopped burning,' says Eloise. 'Or perhaps water has been dropped on it.'

'Maybe it's not moving as quickly as we are. I think we should still carry on.' Jozef ushers us to continue.

Sophy pleads with everyone to stop walking. 'Let's rest up. I'm knackered. Please, just for a couple of hours. It can't be good for us when we're not thinking properly. Someone is going to break an ankle or fall down a gorge. We need to stop because really, I could do with a sleep, or a power nap to reset my energy levels.'

Reluctantly, everyone comes to the same conclusion. We seek out a grassy area to slump down on, removing our footwear to let our blistered feet recover. Addie ensures that she sits on the far side of the group, well away from me, and snuggles into the nook of Reuben's arm, smugly letting him kiss her hair. She cups a hand over her belly to remind me that she's pregnant, blessed with Reuben's baby, and I know that she's only doing this to torment me, to torture me until I can bear no more.

I look away, pursing my sun-cracked lips.

My mind is too busy, too overwrought to relax. All that has happened. All the secrets that have been spilled out. I turn them over and try to piece everything together as I fester on Addie's words and what she knows about me – what will she *do* with that knowledge? – Reuben's deception, and the crushing knowledge that my husband, my gorgeous Matt, is dead and won't be going home with me.

I jump at every scuttle, every click in the grass. I imagine that I can still hear crackling, smell burning, feel the hot air spilling over us again. Sophy is snoring gently; someone else is restlessly grinding their teeth.

Should I go to the police and tell them about everything? It's the only way I can clear my conscience and be free of Addie's hold over me. If they realise that everything – *everything* – has been merely a series of accidents then perhaps it will be all right. Because didn't I do everything in my power to ensure the safety of Christopher Bray?

The thing is, in those days, it was only ever about banter with Sophy, wasn't it? Impressing her and looking cool. Showing off to her and shocking her with my bravado. But I didn't *really* do the dirty deed. Even though I put peanut butter in *my* curry, my sleight of hand with the tubs meant that I took Sophy's curry to swap into Peacock Girl's bag. And hers was fine, totally free from any microscopic trace of peanut butter. Whatever went wrong afterwards at Peacock Girl's house with Christopher's allergy was nothing to do with *my* curry, which ended up being innocently taken home by Sophy.

For all I knew, Peacock Girl might have picked up the wrong spoon or something. For years I googled the hell out of nut allergies, finding that even a miniscule amount can have a lethal effect. Just a tiny smear on a kitchen utensil...

It wasn't us; it wasn't me.

I'd tried to tell Sophy afterwards. As soon as we'd heard about his death, I'd tried to explain that the tub on the right had been mine and the tub on the left had been hers and I'd deliberately picked up the one on the left so that there would be no risk to Christopher.

Maybe she didn't really understand what I'd done. Maybe she didn't even believe me.

'But, Soph, it was *your* curry that I picked up. And you took mine home instead. That's what happened. So it couldn't have been me who killed him.' I'd pulled pleadingly at her sleeve. 'Don't stare at me like that, Soph. I didn't do it.'

She'd given me a pinched expression and looked away. She shook her head and thrust her thumb into her mouth to gnaw at the nail. I hadn't been able to convince her. And then afterwards, over the years it was as if I struggled to convince myself, too.

Obviously, neither I nor Sophy could mention to anyone at the time about my so-called intended joke, because it would have looked so wrong. Fingers would definitely have been pointed at me. No, I realised early on that we'd have to keep it quiet and not say a word about swapping any tubs either, otherwise people could easily jump to conclusions.

But now, with these changed circumstances...

I construct the conversation that I will have with the police when I get home: a passionate torrent of statements that will end with me sobbing with remorse and begging them to show leniency. I picture everything vividly, including the courtroom and the judge, and then the force with which I am thrown into a cell with a barred window.

Oh God, I can't do it. I can't possibly risk getting locked up. I have to fight for my freedom, otherwise my body will be too old to have a baby by the time I'm released and I will never get the opportunity to become a mother.

Sophy stirs and sighs beside me.

'What time it is?' I croak. My smoky throat prickles with thirst.

She checks her watch. 'Ten past six.'

'OK. Soph?'

'What?'

'Everything will be fine, won't it? Like, we won't get into trouble for this, will we?'

'Well, me and Tom haven't done anything wrong, have we?' There's a sneery edge to her voice that is worrying.

Then an image of Matt's body flashes into my mind again, helpless, lifeless on the ground.

'Will you still be my friend, Soph? After all this is over, when we get home?' I need her even more now, particularly as I won't have Matt any more. I sneak my hand over to snuggle into hers, but she turns away to face Tom.

'Who knows what will happen when we get home,' she mumbles. Her expression is cold. She's rejecting me, I know she is. After all these years of being my best friend it feels like a rift has opened up between us.

A hot tear slips down my cheek. This retreat, with its promise of such hope and expectation, has instead been the start of my demise. I'll be friendless, a widow, returning to an empty home with an empty womb.

FIFTY-EIGHT

GEMMA

Reuben wasn't the last person to see Matt before he died. It's possible that it could have been someone else, and maybe it wasn't me, but yes, I did see him after he left Reuben.

I'd challenged Reuben. What had they been talking about? Was it anything about me? Had lilies or poetry been mentioned? Of course, he'd laughed and ridiculed me. He'd left me still wondering, still panicking.

I knew I had to find Matt. Whatever Reuben had told him about Christopher Bray... I had to put him right. I had to give him my version of events. How could I go through life, potentially through parenthood, with Matt thinking that I'd kept a dark secret for years about someone I'd killed? It wasn't me, though. It wasn't like that. It wasn't like that at all.

So, despite the failing light, I'd trailed along the path expecting to encounter Matt somewhere around the side of the mountain, maybe sitting in the night air and considering his options, planning his extrication from our marriage.

He wasn't around the side of the mountain. But Addie was. She was doing yoga, stretching herself into a Cobra position, completely unaware of my approach.

The sight of her provoked an outburst of blistering resentment, and I crept up on her silently, to find myself standing over that repulsively pliable body with harmful thoughts in my head.

The rest is a blur. I can't remember our conversation. A brief image comes to mind of my hands around her throat.

And, I suppose when it comes down to it, that was the last time I felt the tender hands of Matt on *my* body...

'What the fuck, Gemma! What the actual fuck have you done?' I remember Matt screaming in my face as he pulled me away from Addie; I remember landing hard on my hip as he threw me to the floor.

He was kneeling over her, shaking her shoulder, slapping her cheek. 'Addie! Addie, come on, come on, talk to me now.'

Fuck, what had I *done*?

Then I saw how gently he slid his right arm under her back as he tried to lift her like a kitten.

Oh God, he was taking *her* side; he was rejecting *me*! Just as it happened with Christopher; just as it happened with Reuben. I was going to be shunned in favour of *her*. And then what would she do? She would poison his mind against me! Whatever it was that Reuben and Addie thought they knew about me with all the taunting clues placed around the site, they would give a version of it to Matt and then he would despise me. I just knew it.

'It's not what you think!' I yelled at him. 'You don't realise what she was going to do to *me*! I had to stop her.'

I lurched towards him to tug at his arm, because... I didn't know. I didn't know what was happening any more. I didn't want him touching her.

'What are you doing? Have you gone mad?' He swiped my hands away.

'Don't! Please, it's not what it looks like. You've got it all wrong. You're helping *her* when you should be helping *me*! She's the dangerous one.' I was crying, big sobbing mouthfuls of breath that hurt my chest. 'She was going to destroy me. She was taunting me, provoking me.'

There was a sudden inhalation from Addie as she turned her head.

I lunged at Matt and knocked him away from her and we wrestled on the ground, grunting, grappling, not knowing whether to push or grab or try to crawl away, panting, as we inched closer and closer to the edge of the cliff.

'You bitch!' he yelled as I flung out my arm and scraped my fingernails down his face.

He shoved the top of my head and forced his foot against my hip, and I felt a gap opening up between us.

'Get the fuck away from me, Gemma!'

In a flush of exhaustion, I was inert for a few seconds before I flipped myself over and scrambled up from the ground. My arms hung uselessly and I felt like a shell. Matt held his injured face, writhing on the grass.

'Please, Matt, just hear me out. Let me explain everything because you can't trust her...' I looked over at Addie's motionless body. Was she still breathing? I took a couple of steps towards her and then behind me there was a shout, and the sound of gravel and loose rocks and then another shout and then a thud and then...

Nothing.

When I turned around Matt was gone.

Oh shit. I gasped as my chest crushed inwards. Oh God, he was gone.

But it wasn't me.

FIFTY-NINE

GEMMA

Dusk begins to drag its silver shadows over us.

'Come on,' says Jozef, stretching his arms out. 'We've been here long enough now.'

Everyone rouses their stiff, aching bodies to sit up, groaning. Everyone apart from me. I just want to stay here and die.

Tom kicks my foot. 'Come on, get up.'

Eloise looks over at me. Even *her* face has a stony expression. What has everyone been saying about me? What do they know?

Reluctantly, I push myself up and brush the dust out of my hair. Jozef coughs and clears his throat; we're all desperate for water. I feel too sick to eat, but my belly argues angrily with everyone else's as we stuff clothing back into our rucksacks. Addie and Reuben are having a motivational discussion. Eloise is telling Tom and Sophy about a time that she trekked in the Alps. No one speaks to me. I am utterly alone without Matt.

We loosen straps and laces on our footwear so that they will fit our inflamed feet, and set off at a benign pace, feeling the cricks in our knees and hips. I slip meekly in the space between Tom and Sophy. I need them now more than ever.

'Hey guys,' I say in a small voice. 'Are you two OK with me?'

Sophy mutters a non-committal response. Tom glances over his shoulder but says nothing. I'm sweltering despite their iciness, trudging along as if my feet don't belong to me. Why are they being like this with me? They're supposed to be my friends. Don't they care about the wretched turn my life has taken; don't they care about my anguish? Aren't they grieving for Matt, too?

Suddenly, Jozef points up into the sky again. 'Something might be happening.'

The drone is back over us, dipping and darting like a skylark. Then there's a swelling thrum, a noise that doesn't come from nature but from a helicopter in the distance.

'Whoa, here we are!' Addie jumps up and down, and then the others are joining in, shouting and waving.

'Looks like we might be getting rescued this time,' says Tom as the chopper circles and drops lower. 'He just needs to find a flat surface to land.'

But the helicopter continues to hover as we watch and wait expectantly.

'What's it doing?' says Eloise.

The door slides open a slit for a man to hang out with a megaphone. He has instructions for us. 'OK. So we have a team ready to pick you up. You'll need to make your way along the path to them,' the robot-voice says. 'It's about another mile. Are you able to do that?'

'Yes, thank God!' Addie and Eloise are almost crying with relief, holding their thumbs up to the helicopter.

My stomach flips.

What will this mean for me? What will happen now?

The others set off, a newfound buoyancy in their step. I'm frozen to the spot, unable to move, unable to know how to get my story straight. Won't it be better if I wait here for the fire to catch up with me, to put me out of my misery?

'Gemma!' Jozef turns to reproach my indecision. 'Come on.'

I put my hands over my face, unable to confront reality. 'I can't.'

Footsteps march towards me, then he's grabbing my arm, pulling me, forcing me to stride beside him as we make our way behind the rest of the group. Reuben and Addie are out in front again, her head nudging his shoulder as his arm spans her, keeping her safe, his beautiful successful wife carrying his unborn child.

It's too late for me to stop them now. I can't do anything about it. They'll have their baby and their fabulous life, and it will be just what they deserve because they are good, law-abiding people who have never caused the death of anyone else.

Unlike me.

Whatever is going to happen, I deserve it. I know that now.

* * *

The moon is already out and the sky is blue-black as we edge towards twilight, as we edge along a line of trees, winding up and around an incline where the grass has turned to gravel.

'Oh wow!' Sophy declares. 'Look down there!'

A bubbling stream. A wooden fence that holds a clutch of sheep in a small paddock. A little stone cottage with a muddy truck parked in front of the door.

And along the lane: two mountain rescue Land Rovers and a police car with a flashing blue light. There are holdalls unzipped on the ground, stainless steel flasks and a first aid kit. A volunteer in a high-vis vest shakes out a foil blanket; a police officer speaks into his walkie-talkie.

I feel my insides turn to jelly. My heart is fluttering, racing, tripping over itself. My knees are unable to hold me up.

AFTER THE RETREAT

SIXTY

ADDIE

Sometimes justice takes time. You have to be patient. During all those years when I'd been grieving for Christopher, I'd felt helpless and angry, wondering why some people seemed to get away with everything to live a life they didn't deserve.

But I'd seized my chance as soon as it presented itself. I'd let Gemma follow me, quietly reeling her in, luring her closer and closer until the time was right to pounce. Obviously, it was regrettable that Matt got caught up in such a devastating way, but his death was the crunch point that highlighted Gemma's depravity.

Good things have come out of this experience, though. Like my friendship with Sophy and Tom. They are such lovely, genuine people. If only I could have had Sophy as a friend at school, then who knows how everything might have turned out? Maybe Christopher would still be alive.

But there's no point dwelling on *what ifs*. I have a new project to plan. Although being a wife to Reuben and mother to Ezra is absolutely the best thing to happen to me, I don't feel able to give up my career. Challenges are what keep me going even though Addie's Five-a-Day needed to come to a conclusion. Maintenance of the account had become overwhelming, particularly after all the publicity from the fertility retreat.

I met up often with Sophy during the daytime and we took our children to cafés, play centres and baby yoga together. We compared notes on feeding, sleeping and cracked nipples, and provided each other with a shoulder to cry on when the hormones were down.

But then, the balance of my life didn't quite seem right. Despite my family and friendships being perfect, despite my satisfaction at the thought that justice had been done for Christopher, there was a sense that something was missing.

'Why don't you start a *new* account?' Reuben suggested.

It set me thinking.

My escapades with Sophy could be put to good use and having her as a business partner would seal our friendship further. I had incredible admiration for her bravery in turning her best friend of twenty years in to the police. That must have been difficult even though it was the right thing to do.

So now, my efforts will be wholly focused on my family and my – correction, mine and Sophy's – new Instagram account. Mums and Crumbs. I love the name!

I'm so pleased that Sophy has agreed to get involved. I think I've finally found the best friend that I've craved for the past twenty years.

Funny how things turn out, isn't it?

SIXTY-ONE

GEMMA

It's my worst nightmare come true. Maybe I'd been too complacent for the past twenty years, thinking that I was safe, thinking that it was all over.

Now look at me. I'm here, in prison.

Having to share a space smaller than my tiny kitchen at home with a woman convicted of armed robbery who will be released years before me if I get to be found guilty. Having to listen to her snoring on the bunk above me through the night and emptying her bowels first thing in the morning.

Having to survive on stodgy, bland food that often has a taint of disinfectant. Having to live without social media, not knowing what's happening in the outside world. Having to avoid the hard nuts, the tricksters, the unpredictable wild-eyed chancers off their faces on whatever illicit substance they can get hold of and who might stab you in the kidney with a sharpened pencil if the warden is looking the other way.

How did I deserve *this*?

It was self-defence, that's all. Accidental. I wasn't *really* going to kill Addie: I was just trying to keep a lid on all the Christopher Bray stuff. Matt didn't need to know about *that*.

When you're planning on having a baby together you need to trust each other, don't you? That sort of information might have caused him to have second thoughts.

And the way Addie went about it all was despicable. No wonder I was angry. And I know that Matt shouldn't have borne the brunt of my wrath, but he was all over Addie, trying to help her, not caring about how she'd hurt *me*. OK, I got physical with him. But at the time it seemed like it was the only way to show him how upset I was. And neither of us knew how close we were to the edge of that cliff, but...

It wasn't me.

He was there one minute, then gone the next. Perhaps he just rolled over the wrong way, I don't know. But it wasn't me.

My head is a mess, trying to work out what happened at the retreat, trying to work out what happened to my life. There are all these pictures and memories rumbling around and I can't seem to get my story straight.

The regrets come to me with every sleepless night. They come to me every morning when I wake up, expecting to be in my own bed, by someone's side, and find that I'm not.

It isn't fair, yet it *is* fair. Ultimately, a reckless idea, an obsession that went too far, that I'd had twenty years ago set me on the road that has led to me being deprived of my freedom.

My worst nightmare is that – bizarrely – my best dream has come true. Maybe I'd been too complacent, too willing to accept my inability to have children, too blinkered to see that a visit to a remote fertility retreat really could coax my womb into life.

On my admission into prison to await my trial, I was checked over and given a pregnancy test. It was the biggest surprise of my life to find that the two blue lines I'd craved for the last two years had turned up just when I least expected them.

There I was, after all that had happened, pregnant with Matt's child.

Everything was thrown into confusion. What would happen to me and my baby, because everything and everyone was telling me that I would be looking at a long custodial sentence? How did motherhood fit into that?

I press my hands against my huge, hard belly. At thirty-seven weeks I am full of love for my unborn child, feeling movement and kicks every day. The baby that I've been desperate for will be in my arms soon, and the thought of us being separated is shredding my heart into pieces.

There was talk of making an application for a place in a mother and baby unit, but a long waiting list is making that option look unlikely, and the placement only lasts until the child is eighteen months old. After that, they will need to be fostered, ideally with the father or other family. In the event of no one being able to raise the child, then social services will have to look towards securing long-term care or adoption.

But Matt is dead. My parents passed away years ago, and I have no siblings.

So, what will happen to my baby?

My head is in turmoil trying to deal with what might transpire, because I can't bear the thought of my child being brought up by a stranger.

Maybe, just maybe...

Sophy has been my best friend for so long. She's stuck loyally by my side for twenty years. Yes, I know that it seemed like she'd turned her back on me when Matt died, but surely that shared friendship in the bank must count for something.

She's a good mother, I know that. She'll have her own baby now – it will be about a month old, won't it? – so maybe she could bring up the two babies together. I remember she always said that she'd love to have twins.

I trust her implicitly. Despite the fact that she gave a statement to the police against me – and I'm certain that had more to do with Addie poisoning her mind than anything else – I forgive her because she's always been the best friend that I've ever had.

My memories of Sophy are firmly cemented in my brain, never to be forgotten. Maybe she still thinks of me. Maybe she will even come to visit me in the future, because it's looking like I might have a lot of years stretching out in front of me here. God, when I think about it and add it up it's like... Well, I could even die in this hideous place.

I kick the blanket off and carefully ease myself out of the bunk to stand in front of the cork noticeboard, the half that belongs to me.

'Soph, I need you. Just do me one more favour. Please. One more.'

There she is. I look at the photograph of us together. The picture of when it was my thirtieth birthday and we were clinking glasses of bubbly, and beaming our sunburnt faces into the camera like we deserved to have fun and weren't hiding the secret that I'd thought about for every day of my life since it happened. Christopher never got to have champagne; he never got to have his thirtieth birthday.

I kiss my finger and plant it on the picture of Sophy's face.

'Please, Soph. I'm believing in you. Remember, best friends forever.'

The baby kicks then. I feel its heel jolt against the palm of my hand, and a sudden burst of joy invigorates me because surely this means something, it means something good and I have to have hope, don't I? I will write to her and explain my predicament. She will understand; she'll come through for me, she won't desert me in my time of desperation. Surely, she'll be loyal, just like she always has been.

Yes, I know that I've written to her at least four times since I've been here without receiving a reply, but she has a busy life and... Well, these are different circumstances.

I take a pen and a piece of paper.

'Dear Sophy...'

SIXTY-TWO

SOPHY

After the catastrophic events of the fertility retreat, I'd had a long talk with Tom about what we wanted from life. We'd both been shaken by Matt's death, astounded to think that Gemma could be so callous, so violent, so unpredictable. Her denials, as usual, had been vehement.

'There were signs though,' I told Tom. 'Even at school, she had a nasty streak. She actually plotted to murder someone.'

He laughed in disbelief.

'No, really.' I told him then about Christopher Bray. Everything that I'd held inside for so long spilled out. I cried and Tom held me and said that I wasn't to blame when I fixated on the fact that I shouldn't have been so loyal to Gemma, that I should have done the right thing and told someone.

We moved house and relocated to the other side of the city, just two streets away from Addie and Reuben. Obviously, because of all our shared experiences, we met accidentally and then we met intentionally, and then our lives gradually wound tighter and tighter together.

The twenty-year episode of Gemma had ended, and our friendship was over the moment we'd arrived home from the retreat. During the weeks afterwards we were questioned by the police, and I gave a full and frank statement as the secrets frothed out of me like champagne. Addie's brutal words about me covering for Gemma had penetrated my conscience.

Christ, how had it gone on for so long? Addie was right. I'd been protecting Gemma, a killer, for all these years. It was shameful. I couldn't continue with my enduring loyalty. I had a husband and family: we had to be solid together; they needed to be safe; Gemma couldn't be part of my life any more.

Daunted, I sat down in that interview room knowing that Gemma's freedom was at stake. But then again, I'd always known it was hanging by a thread and I was the one that had the power to snap it.

This time though...

Yes, it was the right thing to do. I told them everything.

Well, my version of it anyway.

My life has gone in a new direction, and one that I never would have expected. It was Addie's idea. She suggested that I join her in producing a brand new Instagram account called Mums and Crumbs. It would be a fun venture encompassing baking and motherhood.

Addie hardly took a breath during our phone call. 'We could do mums baking food suitable for different ages of children. Or we could do baking that children can get involved in. Or we could review cafés and cake shops that are suitable for families. Or we could do quirky birthday cake recipes. All that sort of thing.'

I laughed. 'Why do you need me to be involved?'

'Well, for a start, Mum and Crumb doesn't have the same ring, does it? Hahaha! But, no, I'd love to have a work colleague, an equal partner, a project where we can incorporate our kids because – let's face it – who doesn't enjoy a cute baby video? It will be a laugh, doing stuff together. A double act. It's what I've always dreamed about, but I never had any proper friends that I could trust to do it with.'

'Oh, wow, I'm so flattered that you're asking me.' A smile tickled my lips, and I shifted baby Noah into my other arm. He was a bundle of chubby squidginess, almost as heavy as Addie's son Ezra, even though he was nearly two months younger.

'Well, it's great that you're flattered, but I just want you to say *yes*! Come on, Soph. What about it?'

I looked around at my life: my two beautiful children, my devoted husband Tom, a nice house. And here I was, with a successful influencer begging me to work with her! A cherry on the icing on the cake.

'Oh God, yes! Yes, of course I will.' It was a dream come true, wasn't it?

It was weird. The indescribable relief I felt after giving my statement to the police. I put my conscience into a box in my mind along with all the memories of my friendship with Gemma, and bolted it shut.

Hadn't I done everything I could to help her along through life? Hadn't I been the model best friend?

But sometimes there comes a point when you realise that, however much you've supported someone, nothing more can be done. The relationship has to end.

I should never have put myself in the position where I had to cover up for her. At fifteen years old, when a classmate dies it's enough to have to deal with, but when you're involved and having to tell lies and having to pre-empt what might happen... God, the stress of it all. It literally fucked me up for years.

I can still remember it like it was yesterday. I felt like a hero at the time, having had the foresight to step in and prevent some awful tragedy from playing out at Peacock Girl's date night.

You see, we'd finished our Food Technology class and put

our containers of cooled curry into our bags. Gemma had told me that she planned to swap her food for Peacock Girl's, and that she would do this in the changing room before netball. We'd already bickered enough about this mad intention that she'd described as only a prank, so I knew that it would be fruitless to argue about it again. Instead, I'd thought of a secret solution that would render her actions harmless.

So, on the way to our netball session, when we went to use the toilets, I offered to look after Gemma's bag while she was in the cubicle. I ran the water tap and kept talking to her as I carefully unzipped both our bags. She never suspected a thing. Within seconds, I had swapped her container for mine, knowing that if she put it into Peacock Girl's bag it would be safe for Christopher to eat. All would be well; disaster would be averted.

But then when we heard the next day...

I didn't know how it had all gone wrong. I honestly didn't. Could Christopher's death have been *my* fault? Could I have used the wrong spoon for my cooking and somehow contaminated my own dish?

It all came to light later in the day when Gemma, fraught with distress, tried to explain. She hadn't picked up her own modified curry from the Food Technology room; instead she had taken my harmless one. She had wimped out on her practical joke. So she couldn't have killed Christopher, could she?

Horrified, the realisation dawned on me that my solution to render Gemma's prank harmless had gone totally wrong. In the toilets, unaware of the earlier swap, I had planted the killer curry into Gemma's bag ready to pass onto Peacock Girl.

My interference had caused Christopher's death.

Oh God, I couldn't believe it. And I couldn't tell Gemma what I'd done because then it would become *my* fault.

The following week, when the police arrived in school there was no way I could try to explain how or why I'd swapped containers with Gemma. *Yes Mr. Officer, I swapped my curry because I was expecting Gemma to swap hers so that she could give someone an anaphylactic shock?* My account hardly made sense: who would believe that I'd done it in good faith? And surely, if I'd known what Gemma planned to do, I should have told a teacher, or Peacock Girl, or Christopher. I shouldn't have kept it secret.

The horrendous situation dragged out, and the longer I didn't tell anyone what had happened, the more unable I was to own up. And why should *I* have owned up? This was all Gemma's fault. All we could do was stick together and say nothing. All *I* could do was continue to let her believe that she had killed him.

It had worked for twenty years. It could work for the rest of my life.

* * *

I pick up the bundle of post. Some of it is a few weeks old because we're still getting letters redirected from our old address, although that is due to end very soon as we've been here for six months now. I shuffle through the flyers, circulars, an appeal from a water aid charity that Tom once made a donation to. And then...

Oh God, not another one. The brown envelope. The distinctive postmark. The familiar writing. I thought that Gemma had given up with her correspondence, but it seems I am wrong.

Shall I open it?

I've had three or four previous communications begging me to forgive her, imploring me to visit. Will this be yet another revisitation of those pleas?

I toss the letter onto the kitchen table unopened, while I sort through the rest of the post. Suddenly, on the baby monitor there's a cry, an aggrieved mewl from Noah that indicates he's finished his nap and is now hungry. Discarding all the junk mail onto the top of Gemma's letter, I go upstairs to attend to Noah.

'Oh, my gorgeous boy,' I croon as I pick him up out of his crib and kiss away his tears. My nipples are tingling as I sit in the nursery chair and settle him ready for a feed.

There is a sudden commotion downstairs: a crash and a smash and a curse. Tom has obviously come in from the garden and broken something.

'It's OK,' he shouts up to me. 'Don't come in the kitchen. I've knocked over a glass but I'll sweep it all up.'

Despite being the love of my life, he can be so clumsy sometimes. I listen as he clatters around, dropping the shattered pieces into the bin.

I hear his footsteps on the stairs, and then he pops his head around the door as I sit attached to Noah. 'Erm, that pile of stuff on the table? It all looks like junk mail, but did you want any of it? Because it's all covered in smoothie now.'

I grimace, imagining the green gunk everywhere. Since discovering smoothies at the fertility retreat, Tom has been addicted, particularly to the spinach and banana ones.

Noah gazes up at me then, pausing his suckling, to give me the biggest, most adorable smile. My heart melts.

'Ahh, look at him. Did you just see that smile?' I kiss his soft, downy head...

'Soph? Did you want any of that stuff? Is there anything important in it?'

I just want my baby. To nuzzle my face against, and breathe in his special scent and his warmth, holding the weight of him safe from the worries of the world. Isn't that the thing that every mother wants?

'No, it's all junk,' I reply, finally, to Tom. 'You can put it all in the bin.'

A LETTER FROM HAYLEY

Dear Reader,

THANK YOU SO MUCH for choosing to read *I Want What You Have*. I really can't believe that this is my fourth psychological thriller!

If you enjoyed reading this or any of my previous books and have a spare moment to leave a review, I would appreciate it hugely. I love to hear what my readers think about my stories, and it makes such a difference helping new people to discover my writing.

To keep up to date with all my latest book news, just sign up at the following link. Your email address will never be shared and you can unsubscribe at any time.

www.bookouture.com/hayley-smith

You can also connect with me through my Facebook profile, X or Instagram. I chat about all sorts of things – particularly books and music – and would love to hear from you.

Thanks again for reading.

Love,

Hayley

KEEP IN TOUCH WITH HAYLEY

facebook.com/Hayley.Smith.Writer

x.com/WriterHayley77

instagram.com/HayleySmithWriter

ACKNOWLEDGEMENTS

Firstly, I want to acknowledge my mother, Janet Smith, who inspired in me a passion for reading from an early age. Sadly, she died while I was writing this book, but she'd loved my other novels, and was hugely proud that I got to achieve my dream of being an author. For some strange reason, she always hoped to see my books on the shelves in Tesco (random, I know!) – maybe one day, Mum!! 😊

Next, masses of appreciation must go to the wonderful team at Bookouture – winners of 'Imprint of the Year' at the British Book Awards – and in particular my fantastic new editor, Nina Winters, whose creative magic gave me the boost I needed through some difficult times. THANK YOU!

I'm grateful to my family and friends who have supported me in all sorts of ways: character names, snippets of research, and recommending my books to others. And times at the pub to laugh and moan about stuff.

A special mention to Nicola Dudek – thanks for continuing to be my social media advisor and having the patience to explain how it works over and over again. I love all our book talks and I'm so jealous that you got to go to Hay Festival this year (take me next time!).

Cheers to my writing buddies, Lizzie and Sophie. Not as much wine was imbibed during the writing of this book, but your motivation helped me achieve my deadlines, and our conversations resulted in some fabulously creepy ideas. Mwa ha ha ha...

Finally, as always, love and thanks to Michael for encouragement and understanding, and knowing when to leave me alone and when not to. x

PUBLISHING TEAM

Turning a manuscript into a book requires the efforts of many people. The publishing team at Bookouture would like to acknowledge everyone who contributed to this publication.

Audio
Alba Proko
Sinead O'Connor
Melissa Tran

Commercial
Lauren Morrissette
Hannah Richmond
Imogen Allport

Cover design
The Brewster Project

Data and analysis
Mark Alder
Mohamed Bussuri

Editorial
Nina Winters
Sinead O'Connor

RAISING READERS
Books Build Bright Futures

Dear Reader,

We'd love your attention for one more page to tell you about the crisis in children's reading, and what we can all do.

Studies have shown that reading for fun is the **single biggest predictor of a child's future life chances** – more than family circumstance, parents' educational background or income. It improves academic results, mental health, wealth, communication skills, ambition and happiness.

The number of children reading for fun is in rapid decline. Young people have a lot of competition for their time, and a worryingly high number do not have a single book at home.

Hachette works extensively with schools, libraries and literacy charities, but here are some ways we can all raise more readers:

- Reading to children for just 10 minutes a day makes a difference
- Don't give up if children aren't regular readers – there will be books for them!

- Visit bookshops and libraries to get recommendations
- Encourage them to listen to audiobooks
- Support school libraries
- Give books as gifts

There's a lot more information about how to encourage children to read on our websites: **www.RaisingReaders.co.uk** and **www.JoinRaisingReaders.com**.

Thank you for reading.

Printed in Dunstable, United Kingdom